Peter Watt has spent time as a soldier, articled clerk, prawn trawler deckhand, builder's labourer, pipe layer, real estate salesman, private investigator, police sergeant and adviser to the Royal Papua New Guinea Constabulary. He speaks, reads and writes Vietnamese and Pidgin. He now lives at Maclean, on the Clarence River in northern New South Wales. Fishing and the vast open spaces of outback Queensland are his main interests in life.

Peter Watt can be contacted at www.peterwatt.com

Also by Peter Watt

Excerpts from emails sent to Peter Watt since his first novel was published:

'I recently read and thoroughly enjoyed *The Frozen Circle*. This much-loved copy was passed on to me and I am now interested in reading more Peter Watt.' Reader from Canada

'My husband and I recently read *The Silent Frontier* and were enthralled. It is unusual that we both enjoy the same book.' Reader from New Zealand

'I have read *Cry of the Curlew*, *Shadow of the Osprey*, *Flight of the Eagle*, *To Chase the Storm*, *To Touch the Clouds*, *Eden*, *The Silent Frontier*, *The Stone Dragon*, *The Frozen Circle* and have just finished reading *To Ride the Wind*. Absolutely fantastic – everything else has to wait once I start to read your books, Peter. I am so looking forward to the next instalment of this saga – please bring Matthew home!'

'I have just finished *To Ride the Wind* and am left holding my breath – when can we expect the sequel?? Please say there is one!!!'

'Your books are the best read ever.'

'Thank you for providing me with many hours of enjoyable reading. I have read all your books. I served with the RAAMC for twenty years so have particularly found the stories set around military conflicts interesting and enjoyable. Your descriptions of early Australia are great and the thread about Wallarie is very touching.'

'I greatly enjoyed your novel *To Ride the Wind*. However I am now looking forward to the completion of the overall story. Can you please advise when you will be publishing the next novel in the series? To put me out of my misery?'

'Have just finished reading *To Ride the Wind*. Absolutely brilliant. The story just keeps getting better and better. I have read all eleven books and I believe anyone who has not, has missed out on something magic.'

'Just thought I'd let you know how much I enjoyed *To Ride the Wind*. Thank you for bringing to life part of Australia's history.'

'I have to say I am now a big fan of yours. I have fallen in love with these characters.' Reader from Vietnam

'I must say you have completely got me hooked on the Duffy–Macintosh saga. From the first book, *Cry of the Curlew*, it's apparent that I can't stop now.' Reader from the UK

'I've done it again. Every year I buy myself an early Christmas present – your latest novel – so I can have a good read over the holiday period. Once again the temptation to have a sneak look at your latest *To Ride the Wind* got the better of me and once started I couldn't put it down. Write faster. Your novels are rather addictive.'

'May I commend you on your writing style, for writing a bloody good yarn and either your knowledge of NQ or your research on NQ.'

'I have just finished reading your latest offering *To Ride the Wind* and felt compelled to contact you. Although I can hardly compete with the eloquence of other emails sent to you on your wonderful books, I wanted to share how special your books have been in the life of my family and understanding its history. I can assure you that your goal of putting a human face on Australian history has certainly been achieved in my case.'

'I am so totally enthralled by your books.'

'I just want to say thank you for a great read. I have read every one from *Cry of the Curlew* to *Ride the Wind*. I have enjoyed each one immensely.'

'Thank you sooooo much for *To Ride the Wind*. I wanted to write long before I finished reading the book but persuaded myself to wait, not an easy thing to do. You have given me such pleasure! The last few chapters were read with a lump in my throat, and that lump goes right back to Sean Duffy thinking "If hell had a French name it must be Fromelles!".'

'I'm sure hundreds of folk contact you to say how much they have enjoyed your books and I am happy to join them. I always loved Wilbur Smith but it's wonderful to read about the birth of our own nation.'

'I enjoy these books so much that I can lose myself in them.'

'I haven't read a novel in twelve years but I just read *Papua* and *Eden* and I could not put them down. The stories were brilliant and I think I'm hooked.'

'I just wanted to tell you that I just finished *The Frozen Circle*. I could not put it down!!!' Reader from the USA

PETER WATT

THE PACIFIC

PAN
Pan Macmillan Australia

First published 2011 in Macmillan by Pan Macmillan Australia Pty Ltd
This Pan edition published in 2012 by Pan Macmillan Australia Pty Ltd
1 Market Street, Sydney

National Library of Australia
Cataloguing-in-Publication data:

Watt, Peter, 1949–

The Pacific / Peter Watt

ISBN 9781742611167 (pbk.).

Subjects: World War, 1939–1945—Pacific Area—Fiction

A823.3

Typeset in 13/17 pt Bembo by Post Pre-press Group
Printed by IVE

For Geoffrey Radford,
great friend and agent

PROLOGUE

Paris, France
Early Winter, 1944

Ilsa Stahl sat on the edge of the bed in the tiny but comfortable hotel room. She was dressed in her thick airman's leather jacket and tan combat trousers, both still muddied from the battle lines. Her fingers shook as she read the telegram. Forgotten beside her was the mug of strong sweet coffee she'd made from the army ration pack she carried with her everywhere.

She'd seen more than her share of death and destruction during the last five years she'd spent as a war correspondent, but this death was too close. She started to weep. Months of pent-up tension mixed with the overwhelming grief of her loss. She had been following the Allied crusade across the Normandy beaches and into the open fields of France in pursuit of the retreating German

Army, and her life had been in danger more times than she cared to admit.

Despite her German origins, Ilsa Stahl was an American citizen covering the war for an internationally acclaimed New York newspaper. Her father had been a high-ranking Nazi official who had defected to the USA before the war. Ilsa had grown up in America; a highly intelligent child, she had known from an early age that she wanted to be a journalist, and her parents, both dead now, had encouraged her in this. Her first overseas posting had been to the Pacific after the outbreak of war in Europe when the USA was still neutral. She'd been writing for a Lutheran journal and had been given the task of investigating the conditions of German missionaries in the territories controlled by the Australian government.

Later she'd been recruited by the New York newspaper and had begun covering the campaign in the Pacific; in the last few years she'd been based in England, attached to the brilliant but ruthless General George Patton. Her dispatches had been sent home to be read by New Yorkers over their morning coffee, safe from the horrors of this war.

Twelve hours ago she had suddenly been recalled from the front lines, with no explanation other than that she was to take leave until a certain matter could be sorted out.

She looked up from the telegram, her vision blurred with tears. How ironic it was that she was sitting in a hotel room overlooking the River Seine as it snaked its way through a city famous for its romance.

There was a gentle knock at the door and Ilsa quickly

used the thick sleeve of her jacket to wipe away the tears. She couldn't believe Clark was missing.

'Who is it?' she called, trying to sound composed.

'It's me. Randy,' came a familiar voice.

Ilsa unlocked the hotel door to a short, solid man wearing a similar uniform to her own. Between his lips was a thick unlit cigar. He put his arms around her and held her tight as the tears came again. Randolph Herbst was her photographer and their friendship had been forged through difficult and dangerous times.

'I'm sorry,' he said. 'I heard from head office that you'd got bad news. I know how much you loved Clark.'

Ilsa stared at the peeling wallpaper. 'MIA,' she said bitterly. 'Which, as we both know, usually means injured so badly that no identification can be made.'

Ilsa began to tremble and Randy took her hand and led her to the bed.

'Sit down,' he said. 'There's something I have to tell you.'

Ilsa could tell from the look on his face that it was bad news. Surely things couldn't get any worse.

'You have orders to report back to the New York office,' Randy said slowly. 'You're to catch an army flight back to London tomorrow morning and then fly on to New York. Your bookings have already been made.'

Ilsa jumped to her feet. 'Goddamned Patton and his staff are behind this, I know it.' She felt a surge of anger and, somehow, that was easier to bear than the grief.

Randy shrugged as if he suspected that she was right. He walked to the door.

'Thought you might like to join me later to toast your

illustrious career,' he said, then added gently, 'I know you're in pain, kiddo, but just for tonight you can drown your memories in good red wine.' He clenched his cigar between his teeth and shut the door behind him.

*

Ilsa left the next day for London, with a bad hangover. At least her pounding headache distracted her from her disappointment at being recalled at such a crucial time in the Allied offensive. She had the awful suspicion that she would be expected to see out the rest of the war covering social events in New York. She'd be damned if she was going to do that.

Her German blood made her determined but it was the touch of Irish in her that made her impulsive. For that, Ilsa could thank the biological father she barely knew on the other side of the world. It had come as quite a shock to learn that the man she'd grown up thinking of as her father was in fact her stepfather, and she had been conceived during a love affair her mother had had before her marriage. Now it seemed that her natural father, Jack Kelly, and his son, her half-brother, were the only family she had left in the world, although they were virtual strangers. She had met them once but lost contact in the turmoil of war. With her fiancé missing in action, Ilsa found herself strangely in need of a father's reassurance. She didn't know how she was going to manage it, but she was determined to find a way to travel to the Pacific and find Jack Kelly again.

*

Imperial Japanese Navy Headquarters
Rabaul Harbour, New Guinea

All hell broke loose as Petty Officer First Class Fuji Komine marched smartly across the parade ground in front of the Japanese Imperial Naval Headquarters.

The air around him was suddenly filled with the explosive crash of anti-aircraft fire. Fuji broke into a run to clear the open space as five shapes in the sky turned from dots to the distinctive American P-38 Lightning fighters, with their twin booms and short fuselage. Large .50 calibre bullets from the M2 Browning machine guns mounted in the aircrafts' noses poured with deadly effect onto the targets below. Fuji heard the thud of the heavy bullets tearing into the stone headquarters.

As he sprinted for the shelter of the building, a soldier in front of him raised his rifle to counter the surprise attack by the low-flying American fighter planes. Geysers of earth sprayed up around the soldier and he was thrown backwards, a bloody, mutilated corpse. Fuji looked up; the fighter was so low overhead that he could see the goggled face of the pilot and hear the spent cartridge cases hitting the ground.

Fuji had hardly reached the steps of the grand building when the departing drone of the enemy aircraft signalled the end of the attack. The five Lightning fighters roared upwards into the clear skies, leaving behind ripped and mangled human flesh and drums of fuel burning down on the docks.

Fuji's heart was thumping with fear and exertion. The attack had only lasted seconds but it had felt like hours. He became aware of a hand patting him on the shoulder, and looked up to see his fellow petty officer and friend Oshiro.

'They must have had ammunition left over,' said Oshiro. 'Decided to use it up on us on their way back to base.'

Fuji nodded his agreement. Most aerial attacks had ceased on Rabaul Harbour, but now the Australian Army had cut off the strategically vital naval base at the narrowest section of the island just south of Japanese naval headquarters. The American fighters had not dropped bombs, so Fuji concurred that they had simply detoured over the harbour to use up their ammunition.

So far the Australians had not attempted to take the Japanese base at Rabaul; they knew better than to engage in a pitched battle with over 90,000 garrison troops determined to die to the last man. But the enemy had effectively disabled the Japanese by first setting up bases all around them and cutting off resupply, and then besieging the harbour town. How times had changed since those heady days of 1942 when the Japanese had overrun the Asian and Pacific lands to the north and west. Now the Allies, chiefly the Americans, were pushing the Japanese back home and the only relatively safe way to enter or exit Rabaul Harbour was by submarine.

'Are you to attend the meeting?' asked Oshiro.

Fuji nodded. He and Oshiro were outsiders amongst the senior noncommissioned naval officers. Oshiro had been born in Okinawa, one of Japan's most southern prefectures, and Fuji had been born in Papua. Although they considered themselves unstintingly loyal to the Emperor, their comrades still looked down on them.

The two of them reported to a clerk, who consulted

some papers and then indicated they should make their way to a room at the end of the corridor. There they were ushered inside by a smartly dressed Japanese soldier. The room was spacious and an overhead ceiling fan circulated the musty air. There were twelve Special Naval Landing Forces marine troops sitting in chairs facing a lectern. Fuji knew that these men, who considered themselves an elite fighting force, were survivors of the mauling handed out by the Australians at the Battle of Milne Bay.

One of the marines called attention and everyone in the room jumped to their feet to stand rigidly staring straight ahead. From the corner of his eye Fuji could see two commissioned naval officers enter the room, swords at their sides.

His blood ran cold and he began to tremble. The junior of the two officers was the man who had executed Fuji's Motuan lover, Keela, a couple of years earlier. He remembered a beach in southern New Guinea and the beautiful girl kneeling as the curved sword blade flashed in the bright sunlight. Then her head rolled across the blood-soaked sand as Fuji watched helplessly. Now the same man stood arrogantly beside the lectern and commanded the men to sit.

'On behalf of the Emperor's Imperial Navy, I welcome you men to this briefing,' said the senior officer, a grey-haired *kaigun daisa*. 'You have been selected because of your unique skills and proven courage. We have a mission of great importance to the progress of the war against our enemy. It will require the utmost test of your bravery, but you have been chosen as true warriors willing to sacrifice everything for your Emperor.'

Fuji was so mesmerised by the sword hanging in the

scabbard worn by the junior officer that he hardly heard his name being called. He could feel himself filling with a murderous rage. Oshiro nudged him sharply in the ribs and Fuji stood bolt upright with his hands stiffly by his side. 'Sir,' he answered dutifully.

'Petty Officer First Class Fuji Komine has previously carried out dangerous operations behind enemy lines and is able to speak the local native language,' the senior officer said. 'He also has a good knowledge of our enemy, as he was born amongst the barbarians and speaks English. He will be your liaison officer with the native population on this mission.'

Another name was called and a marine stood to attention as his credentials were read out. Each member of the team proved to be tough and experienced in jungle warfare.

'The Americans are attempting a two-pronged attack against us,' the senior officer continued. 'General Mac-Arthur has led his army through New Guinea and landed in the Philippines, whilst Admiral Nimitz is crossing the Pacific with his fleet to attack the chain of islands to the south of our homeland. The Allies are weak people who do not like to suffer casualties and they will not be able to withstand our forces when they encounter them closer to our homeland. They will be driven back into the sea and forced to concede to a treaty with us. Your mission is to disrupt their lines of communication in their rear echelons, which will help our forces defeat the coming battles for the homeland islands. You will be under the command of Kaigin dai Yoshi, who will brief you on the tactics to be used in disrupting the enemy. Because of the unfortunate circumstances of our situation at the moment, I should inform you that I cannot guarantee that you will receive a lot of support from our imperial forces in your mission. You will be outnumbered and in time your presence will no doubt be known to the enemy. Other than naval contact by submarine and radio, you will be alone. Your deaths will be those of heroes to the Emperor.'

With these words he turned to the man beside him and acknowledged his smart salute before leaving the room. Despite his hatred for Lieutenant Yoshi, Fuji found that he was eager to hear how they would contribute to the war against the barbarian enemy. Lieutenant Yoshi took his position behind the lectern and, using a long cane, began pointing out geographic locations on the large-scale map behind him.

That evening Oshiro drank more sake than usual and burst into the sad folksongs of his beloved Okinawa, his arm around Fuji's shoulders.

'I will never see my family again,' he said in a moment of melancholy. 'But my family will remember that I was a hero for Japan.' He raised his cup in a bitter salute.

Fuji raised his cup in silent reply. It seemed inevitable that he would die in the service of the Emperor but he would be damned if Lieutenant Yoshi didn't die with him.

ONE

The sun was rising over a tropical sea of glass. To the port side of the forty-foot wooden motorboat, the *Riverside*, lay the New Guinea coast. Lukas Kelly gripped the handles of the American machine gun, sweat rolling down his naked chest.

'Take her in, Mel,' he quietly commanded his helmsman.

Melvin Jones was a heavily built American in his sixties, a former merchant seaman now employed by the American Army in their Pacific campaign. He and Lukas, who had recently been discharged from the New Guinea Volunteer Rifles, crewed the civilian vessel for resupply duties, as well as to move small forces along the coast. The boats were under the control of the United States Army

Transportation Corps. It seemed strange to Lukas to steam under the American flag and, to all intents and purposes, be a private in the American Army.

Before the war Lukas had been employed flying Hollywood stars, such as Errol Flynn, around the region. Now he was part of a service that employed those between the ages of fifteen and seventy who were medically unfit to serve. Lukas had comrades who were missing a limb but still served in the small-boats flotilla. He himself had lost an eye in an air crash in America but had managed, in the early days of the war, to bluff his way into active service with the militia unit formed by the expatriate men of the Papua and New Guinea territories. Now, because of his experience navigating his father's plantation supply schooner, he was the skipper of one of the converted civilian boats that ran the gauntlet of enemy naval and air forces along the coast of New Guinea.

Like Lukas, Mel was stripped to the waist. His big belly hung over his waistband and sweat trickled down his hairy chest. He was under a canvas awning that stretched the length of the boat, and behind him stood three Papuans wearing their traditional lap-laps.

Mel opened up the throttle. They were late for the rendezvous and should have been on post before first light deep in waters patrolled by Japanese warships. Other than the .50 calibre machine gun, they had only a collection of small arms, but that did include a couple of Bren guns as back-up, with a good supply of ammunition, as well as Owen submachine gun for use ashore in the dense jungle.

The *Riverside* cruised in the placid waters until it was close to the coconut-covered stretch of sand where the supplies for the resident coastwatcher were to be landed. Lukas knew these waters well, as he had sailed them with his father before the war.

Lukas Kelly was in his late twenties, with broad shoulders and a hard, muscled body. He wore a short beard and his hair had not seen barber's clippers for some time. His skin was bronzed by the tropical sun, and his black leather eye patch made him look like an old-time pirate.

'Thought I saw movement off the starboard bow,' Mel said, squinting against the glare of the rising sun.

Lukas swivelled the machine gun to the right, hoping that it would be a welcome party from the Australian coastwatcher, but the little fountains of water stitching their way across the flat sea soon dispelled that hope.

Lukas immediately opened fire and Mel swung the *Riverside* out to sea. Suddenly a large spout of water erupted less than fifty feet from the boat.

'Bloody mortar,' Lukas swore as water fell onto the deck. 'The bastards must have been waiting for us. Don't like the coastwatcher's chances.'

Mel opened up the throttle to its full power and began steering a zigzag course to make the *Riverside* a more difficult target. Three more bombs exploded dangerously close to the boat, sending small columns of water into the air.

On the stern, one of the Papuan crew had set up a Bren gun and was firing back at the shore. The gun was hopelessly out of range, but it was better than doing nothing. After a few heart-stopping minutes the *Riverside* made its way far enough from shore to be safe from the land guns, but Lukas knew their problems were not over. No doubt the Japanese would have radioed either their air force or navy to inform them of the boat's escape and to give its estimated position at sea.

'Steer south for a couple of miles and take her back to shore,' Lukas said to Mel, who looked at him with surprise. 'If the Japs follow us they'll be expecting us to continue south to Moresby or Milne Bay. I know a small inlet along this stretch of the coast where we might be able to hide. It's a long shot, but it's the only chance we have.'

Mel reached for a large cigar, lighting it. The thick smoke whisked away on the breeze. He nodded and kept the throttle open while Lukas organised the second Bren gun to be mounted astern against a possible air attack. Lukas had calculated how long it would take for a fighter aircraft to be dispatched from the nearest Japanese-held airfield. If he was right they should be under cover before the pilot realised they had not continued south.

The journey seemed to stretch into eternity as the crew anxiously scanned the horizon for any sign of an aircraft or warship.

Around midmorning Lukas spotted the landmarks that indicated the approach to the small inlet where he planned to hide the boat. He was fully aware that it was in enemy-held territory and could be currently in use by the Imperial Japanese Navy. But he had kept this piece of information to himself, knowing that Mel would never have agreed to the plan if he'd known. He could only hope and pray that the enemy had withdrawn from this part of the coast.

*

Sergeant Jack Kelly lay on his back attempting to snatch a few minutes' sleep. He was under a canopy of tall rainforest trees only a couple of hundred feet from a sandy beach adjoining a lagoon. Beside him lay his Owen submachine gun, primed and ready. He swatted irritably at a mosquito buzzing around his head.

Jack was a noncommissioned officer in a unit the Japanese had nicknamed 'the green shadows'. The Papua Infantry Battalion was composed of Papuans and New Guineans who had volunteered to fight the Japanese and operated under the command of Australian officers and NCOs. This was Jack's second war. He was in his mid-fifties and under normal circumstances would be considered too old for active military service, but he'd been transferred from the New Guinea Volunteer Rifles to the Papua Infantry Battalion, which had given him the opportunity to continue soldiering.

For almost two years he had fought the Japanese Army alongside the Papuan troops. The Papuans had proved to be first-class soldiers on their home ground, and to the Japanese they were dreaded savage fighters who emerged silently from the dark shadows of the jungle, inflicted disproportionate casualties on them and then melted away again.

Jack had been given a patrol of seven PIB soldiers to conduct a reconnaissance along the coast for any elements of Japanese troops still remaining. His corporal, Joseph Gari, was forward with two men, covering the beach while the rest of the patrol rested and cleaned their weapons.

Jack closed his eyes. The extreme heat was something he was acclimatised to – this was his adopted homeland, after all – but the strain on his body was not something he could ever get used to. Bouts of malaria and dysentery had stripped his muscular body to lean flesh, and while he still retained some of the toughness of his youth, he sometimes felt like a very old man.

A hand shook him out of his doze.

Jack opened his eyes with a start and found himself looking up into the glistening face of Corporal Gari. The soldier's eyes revealed his excitement. Jack did not have to ask what had brought the corporal back from his post, as he could hear the steady putt-putt of a boat's engine making its way to the beach.

Jack sat up, snatching his weapon. 'Japs?' he asked and Corporal Gari nodded.

'How many?'

'Eight Jap men in a canoe with two white men.'

Jack indicated for Corporal Gari to follow him and then made his way to the hidden observation post off the beach. They were about evenly matched in number, and he and his men had the element of surprise on their side. He had been instructed to avoid any contact with the enemy unless absolutely necessary – they were patrolling for information, not for engagement – but mention of the two white men had changed matters.

Jack could see the approaching dugout canoe, powered by a small outboard engine, heading straight for them. The Japanese appeared to be wary; they had their light machine gun, mounted in the bow, directed at the shoreline. Jack pulled out a small set of binoculars and focused on the crew. Sure enough, Corporal Gari's keen eyesight had differentiated correctly between the white men and the Japanese soldiers. Jack could see that they were two dishevelled men dressed in ragged United States Air Force flying suits and, from the growth of their beards, they had obviously been shot down some time ago. They appeared to have their hands tied behind their backs and when Jack shifted his binoculars, he could see a young Japanese officer standing at the stern with his hand on the scabbard of an evil-looking samurai sword.

A cold chill swept through Jack.

'Bring in your two men and order the others to make their way here too, and quickly,' he growled to Corporal Gari.

Within minutes all his men were assembled around him, their eyes burning bright. They were true warriors who relished the prospect of engaging with an enemy that had burned their villagers, raped their women and killed their clansmen during their retreat north.

'We let the Japs land on the beach,' Jack instructed. 'We take up positions around them and take all care not to reveal ourselves until I give the order to open fire. The white men are Americans. We must be careful not to shoot them, so I want you to fire your rifles high and immediately charge the Japs with your bayonets fixed. Corporal Gari, take three men through the bush to the opposite side of the lagoon. The rest of you come with me.'

Without hesitation the patrol broke into two parties; Gari disappearing into the bush while Jack remained in the cleverly concealed OP. As the canoe slid up onto the beach, Jack was pleased to see that the Japanese officer had selected his approach a mere thirty yards from the OP.

The Japanese soldiers leaped warily from the canoe,

clutching their rifles. One remained behind in the boat to man the light machine gun. The two prisoners were hauled without any ceremony from the canoe and into the shallow water, then battered with rifle butts until they were on the beach. They fell to their knees on the sand.

Jack had a very bad feeling about this. He prayed that Gari was in position because the Japanese were not wasting any time in what was shaping up to be a summary execution.

The officer slid his sword from its scabbard and held the hilt in both hands with the tip of the blade pointing downwards. Jack grabbed the .303 rifle from the man nearest to him and thrust his own SMG into the hands of the startled soldier. Jack took aim at the officer just as he was bringing up his sword to slice down on the neck of the terrified young American airman. The other prisoner had turned his head to avoid witnessing the death of his compatriot.

Jack squeezed the trigger and the Japanese officer's head flew back as the high-velocity bullet ripped through his skull. At the sound of the shot the soldiers on the beach froze in shock. This bought precious seconds for Jack and his men. Almost immediately the rattle of gunfire from Gari's section took out the light machine-gun support in the canoe.

Jack slipped the bayonet on the end of his rifle and then his men were on their feet, charging the Japanese. A couple of Jack's men were waving machete-like jungle knives and were on the Japanese soldiers before they could organise a defence. A short, vicious hand-to-hand struggle ensued. Bayonets plunged into bellies and chests; machetes slashed and hacked; it was all over very quickly. Only two Japanese soldiers were left alive, and they turned and fled into the jungle rather than face the fury of the green shadows.

When the fighting was over, Jack realised that in the heat of fear and adrenaline he had bayoneted one of the Japanese soldiers to death. Already his men were going through the clothes of the dead men to see what they could find, and Corporal Gari was hauling the machine gun from the Japanese canoe.

The two Americans were on their knees in the sand, looking at Jack as though they could not believe they were still alive when only minutes earlier they had resigned themselves to death.

Jack slipped the bayonet from his rifle and began cutting the bindings around the men's wrists.

'Sergeant Jack Kelly, Papua Infantry Battalion,' he said, freeing the airman, who was barely out of his teens. The young flyer simply gaped up at him with a mix of confusion, fear and shock. The second prisoner was older, perhaps in his late twenties.

'Sergeant Kelly, thank you,' the man said, rising unsteadily to his feet. 'I'm Lieutenant Nixon. My Lib went down three weeks ago and only myself and my gunner here were able to bail out. I can't believe you guys saved us.'

'I guess we just happened to be in the wrong place at the wrong time for these Japs,' Jack said. He reached inside his webbing pouch for the tin that contained his cigarettes. Placing the rifle between his knees he lit a cigarette, passing it to the American officer, who in turn passed it to the young gunner, who was now shivering uncontrollably.

Jack lit another cigarette and this one Nixon accepted, drawing the smoke deep into his lungs.

'Goddamn, that feels good,' Lieutenant Nixon sighed.

'Well, my old China,' Jack said, 'we have to get out of here – I'm willing to bet these Japs will be missed before too long. I'll radio our boys that you are alive. And I'll organise with our HQ to get you two back to civilisation for a shave and cold beer.'

★

The troop train steamed into Sydney's Central Station just after sunrise. It was summer in the Southern Hemisphere and when the newly promoted Major Karl Mann stepped onto the railway platform he felt the promise of a hot, humid day. He was still getting used to the change in climate. German-born, he had been raised on a plantation in Papua, and for the last two years had been serving in the tropics; by comparison Australia's climate was very pleasant indeed. After a short stint with Sparrow Force in Japanese-occupied Timor, he had served as a commando in Papua and New Guinea.

Karl Mann was a born soldier. His courage, leadership and initiative had been recognised by senior officers, as had his role with British Special Operations Executive in Palestine, which had earned him a decoration. He had been summoned from Cairns to attend a special briefing, although, in typical military style, he had not been informed as to the nature of the meeting.

Karl hefted his kitbag over his shoulder and walked through the swirling cloud of steam from the train. Even at this early hour the grand railway terminus was filled with men and women in various uniforms, and their voices echoed in the cavernous interior of the great hall. Pigeons fluttered into the high ceilings. Karl stopped to glance at his watch. He was a bear of a man, in his late twenties, with a ruggedly handsome face, although his skin had the telltale yellow pallor of the anti-malarial drugs used by all the forces serving in the tropics.

Knowing he had the rest of the day before he was to check in to his allocated quarters at the officers' mess in the Victoria Barracks, Karl was in no hurry. He stopped at the Salvation Army kiosk and asked for a cup of tea. He needed something to steady his nerves. All he could think of was Marie. He had attempted to contact her from Brisbane, on his way down from Cairns, but had had no luck. The letters she'd once written to him so regularly had mysteriously dried up, but he had put this down to his being in such far-flung places, fighting the Japanese. He had decided to surprise her at her little cottage at Point Piper – it was Sunday and there was no reason for her to be at work.

Karl finished his tea and made his way outside to hail a taxi cab. Sydney had the air of someone sleeping off a heavy night of partying and booze. The few military men Karl saw around the railway station looked dishevelled and the worse for wear. There was no longer the threat of occupation by the Japanese, and the city Karl remembered from 1942 seemed to have returned to its pre-war decadence.

'You blokes have finally got the Japs on the run,' the cab driver said to Karl as they drove off. 'You're doing a bloody good job, although most of the bloody ungrateful civvies would rather know who won the last race at Rand-wick than how you boys are doing out in the islands. It's a bloody crying shame.'

Karl nodded. He had noticed the same sort of indiffer-ence to the soldiers' suffering in Brisbane. It was as if the war were over already; most people seemed oblivious to the terrible slog of the fighting that was still going on in the battlefields of Europe and the Pacific.

'Been away long?' the driver asked cheerfully, swerving to avoid a drunken American soldier with his arm around an equally drunken Aussie girl.

'Too long,' Karl answered.

'Bloody Yanks have taken over,' the taxi driver growled. 'Think they own the place.'

Karl did not comment and the drive continued in silence. Eventually the taxi pulled up in front of a neat white cottage in a row of equally neat houses.

'Well, digger, this is the address,' the driver said and Karl reached in his coat pocket for the fare. He looked up and saw the door of the cottage open. Marie stepped out-side and bent down to retrieve a rolled-up newspaper on the doorstep. Karl's heart felt as if it had stopped beating. This was the woman he had dreamed of returning to, the thought of whom had kept him going through some of the worst days in the jungles of New Guinea and hills of Timor.

'Wrong address,' Karl uttered quietly. 'Please take me to the Victoria Barracks now.'

'Right you are, cobber,' the driver said quietly.

Karl leaned back against the seat and stared ahead in a bitter daze. He should have known why Marie had stopped writing to him. He should have read the signs. Karl did not need to be a doctor to see that she was well into the final weeks of pregnancy. As he had not seen her in more than two years, the child she carried was obviously another man's.

TWO

Lukas and his crew had spent the day steaming under the palm fronds and jungle undergrowth they'd cut to conceal the *Riverside*. It had been uncomfortable, but preferable to being found by the Japanese. As soon as it was dark, Lukas had given the order to start the engine and head out to sea.

'You know the Japs aren't going to let us off lightly,' Mel had said. 'Their destroyers have that radar equipment now.'

'We'll hug the shore,' Lukas had explained. 'Maybe they're more worried about looking after their own skins than going looking for a boat as small as the *Riverside*.'

The American had searched his pocket for a cigar. 'The Japs were waitin' for us as sure as hell and they must have known we were resupplying the coastwatchers. I reckon that in itself is enough to give them cause to hunt us down. We were goddamned lucky they got itchy trigger fingers and fired on us too early.'

Lukas had not replied, although he had agreed with the big American. It was well known that some of the New Guineans were working with their Japanese occupiers; it was possible that one of them had betrayed them. That meant bad news for the coastwatcher too.

Lukas wondered now just how long this war would last. Despite the fact that the Japanese were being rolled up along all fronts of the Pacific theatre, they still remained in small pockets, fighting to the last man. He knew that the Allies considered the war all but over in Europe, with Hitler's forces being pushed back into Germany, but in the Pacific the Japanese were another matter. They were not afraid to die, whereas the Germans had some common sense and would surrender rather than throw away their lives for a lost cause.

At least Port Moresby was now safe from the Japanese since they had been turned back along the vital Kokoda Track and defeated at Gona and Buna on the north coast. That meant nursing sister Megan Cain would be safe, and she was Lukas's main reason to try to keep surviving out here.

Lukas was fortunate that he knew these waters very well and could navigate them even in the dark. Very cautiously they crept along the coast, all guns manned. Beneath his feet he could feel the regular throb of the engine and he felt the cooling sea breeze turn chilly as fine mists of spray washed over the bow. They were making good time and

Lukas handed over the helm to the American. Lukas lay down on the deck to sleep, slipping quickly into a state of restless dreams.

It was the silence that woke Lukas.

He struggled to his feet. It was still dark. The myriad of stars shone with a brilliance that Lukas thought was beautiful even in these dangerous circumstances.

'What is it?' he asked, shaking off the vestiges of sleep.

'I dunno,' Mel grunted, crouched over the opening to the engine well and peering inside using a small torch. 'The goddamned engine just stopped running.'

Lukas gazed around at the dark sea. To his starboard he could just make out the silhouette of the New Guinean coast. They were dead in the water in an area patrolled by Japanese submarines and soon the sun would be rising. Lukas uttered a curse.

'Masta Lukas!' one of the New Guinean crew gasped, stretching out his arm towards their port side.

Lukas looked in the direction he pointed and caught the shimmering phosphorous wake of what had to be a submarine's periscope. It was as though thinking about the enemy threat had conjured it.

'Man the guns!' he commanded quietly, knowing full well that they had little or no chance against an enemy sub. He doubted that the Japanese commander would use a precious torpedo on them; he would probably prefer to surface a safe distance away and use his deck gun.

Mel immediately uncovered their radio to send off a signal reporting the encounter. Lukas swung the heavy machine gun in the direction of the periscope and calculated that it was a good four hundred yards away. He pulled back the cocking handle to chamber a round and slid his hand down the belt to ensure that it was not entangled. Meanwhile, Jones turned knobs and spoke urgently into the radio mike, identifying the call sign of the *Riverside*.

Lukas could see the submarine surfacing nose on, to provide a smaller target for his own guns. He glanced around at the rest of his crew and was grimly satisfied to see they were in position. For a brief moment Lukas thought of Megan and wanted to cry. Not for his own death but for the fact that he would never see her beautiful face again, or experience the warmth of her arms around him.

'Wait until the Japs are on deck before you fire,' Lukas called to his men. He doubted that he would be able to sweep the decks clear. The gun on the Jap sub had the power to turn his little craft into splinters, whereas his could only put a few holes in the enemy vessel.

The dark shape of the underwater craft finally surfaced and Lukas swung his sights to where he calculated the gun crew would emerge.

'Get ready!' he called, and for a moment sent out a prayer that Megan Cain would never forget him.

*

Karl Mann had spent the night in the bar of the officers' mess, sitting alone drinking in a comfortable cane chair, once the property of the Chinese government before being looted as a prize of war during the Boxer Rebellion. He had not invited company but had brooded in silence, growing steadily drunker, although no amount of alcohol could ease the pain of losing Marie.

This morning, feeling the worse for wear, Karl had skipped breakfast and instead found a seat in the corner of the mess to read the newspaper. At 0800 hours he found himself reporting to an orderly who directed him to an office further down the corridor. The door was simply stencilled *Operations Room* and Karl knocked.

'Come in,' a familiar voice commanded.

Karl stepped into the operations room, with its walls covered in maps, and a table laid out with black and white aerial photos. He smiled grimly when the uniformed British naval officer stepped forward to extend his hand.

'Congratulations on your promotion, Major Mann,' Captain Featherstone said, shaking Karl's hand. 'I see that you got that gong you so deserved for your work with us in Palestine.'

Karl smiled grimly; it was ironic that the same operation had also brought Marie into his life and his consolation prize was the medal for conspicuous service. Karl had been a platoon commander serving against the Vichy French in Syria when he had been summoned to Jerusalem. It had been the Englishman, Featherstone, working for the SOE who had gone through the files and nominated Karl for an undercover mission in an attempt to root out a German spy ring operating in the Middle East. Posing as a downed German airman, Karl had infiltrated the enemy spy ring and, in the process, met Marie. He was struck by her exotic and beautiful Eurasian charms, and despite the fact she was working for the Germans he fell in love with her. Marie switched sides for the sake of her attraction to Karl, and he was able to make a deal with Featherstone to bring her back to Australia. She set up a profitable perfume business in a world starved of the luxuries desired by women. For a time she had expressed love for the tough soldier. But that was only for a time.

'I see that you have gone up in the ranks, too, sir,' Karl said, observing that the tall but slightly built man was now the naval equivalent of a full army colonel.

'Ah, yes, we both seem to have benefited from the Palestine operation,' Captain Featherstone replied.

Featherstone reminded Karl of the English actor Leslie Howard. He had the manners of a British aristocrat, which was exactly what he was. Karl knew he had been educated at Eton and Oxford, then had volunteered to serve his country and had proved himself during the evacuation of British and French forces from Dunkirk in 1940. Karl was also aware that this almost effeminate man was as dangerous as any enemy Karl had faced on the battlefield. Featherstone belonged to the shadowy world of the British Special Operations Executive and much of his work was shrouded in secrecy.

'No doubt you are curious as to why you have been transferred from active service back to Sydney,' Featherstone said, taking a cigarette from a gold case and placing it in a slender holder. 'Fag, old chap?' the British officer asked politely, holding open the case.

'No, thank you, sir,' Karl answered.

Featherstone closed the case and slipped it into his trouser pocket.

Karl sensed that the man was slightly uneasy.

'I've been keeping an eye on your career, Major Mann, and have decided that you're the ideal man for a vital operation we have in mind . . . Take a seat and make yourself comfortable.' Featherstone sat down on a chair at the edge of the photo-strewn table.

Karl took this as an ominous sign – the British officer obviously wanted him relaxed. He would have to be on his guard, he thought as he took a seat opposite.

'The British government feels strongly that we will win the war against Hitler before Christmas, and that Japan will capitulate when it loses its main ally,' Featherstone said. 'That will leave a vacuum in this part of the world – even now we are facing home-grown independence movements springing up in the face of Japanese occupation, which could cause major problems when we return to Burma, Malaya and Singapore. At the moment the communists are doing a good job harrying the Japs in Malaya, but we also know that they march to the drum of Uncle Joe Stalin, who Winnie feels is just as much a threat to world balance as Herr Hitler. Unfortunately, Churchill is unable to convince the Yanks that this war is only a curtain-raiser to the next if the communists take advantage of the Jap capitulation in Asia and seize power.

'And that brings us to the matter of why you are here,' Featherstone said. 'You may be aware that you Aussies have an organisation based in Melbourne called the Inter Allied Services Department.'

'I know about it,' Karl replied. 'As you know, I have been working with our Z Special Unit.'

'Of course,' Featherstone said. 'Well, the IASD has been working with the British to insert teams into Malaya to work with the communist guerrillas.'

'So you want me to be inserted into Malaya, sir?' Karl said.

'Not exactly,' Featherstone said, clearing his throat and stubbing out the cigarette in an ashtray. 'I want you to volunteer for a very special and very secret mission even further north. You will have only one man to assist you on this operation, a chap we have borrowed from our Free French allies.'

Karl frowned. This had the whiff of an extremely dangerous mission.

Featherstone stood up and pointed to a large map of the Asian theatre of operations. 'We want you to go to Saigon in Indochina,' he said, pointing with his slender cigarette holder to a place on the southern end of the former French colony, now under Japanese control. 'We need you to make contact with a German citizen living there who our Free French allies have identified as having information vital to our cause.'

Karl raised his eyebrows at the task. He would be a long way from any home bases in the former French colony.

'Off the record, Major Mann, I did not agree with the plan proposed by de Gaulle for the former French colonies, but Winnie has backed the arrogant bastard for some years now, despite the fact Roosevelt despises de Gaulle. Like us, the French are planning to get their old colonies back after the war. But that's all politics, of no consequence to men like you and me. Your job will be to assume the guise of a German national, and make contact with our person of interest in Saigon and ensure that she gets out of Indochina.' Featherstone obviously noticed the look of surprise on Karl's face. 'Oh, I forgot to tell you that our contact in Saigon is a rather beautiful German fräulein, Herlinde Kroth.' He walked back to the desk and picked up a large photograph, which he passed to Karl. 'Her father is a high-ranking officer in German intelligence. He was fortunate to escape Hitler's purge of those he saw as conspiring against him after the July bomb blast.'

Karl looked into the large, luminous eyes of a truly beautiful woman in her mid-twenties. 'Why can't the French resistance get her out of the country?' he asked.

'Because we cannot afford to have her fall into the hands of our Yankee cousins in the OSS, and they have a strong influence with the French resistance. I know that they are our brothers in arms but this is a very sensitive matter they would not fully understand. If she became their property they would make a dog's dinner of her.'

Karl glanced up at Featherstone. 'What is the contingency if it appears she will be captured by the Japs during the escape attempt?'

'In that eventuality you kill her, and I would strongly suggest you keep the second bullet for yourself. You do not want to be taken alive by the Japanese secret police. You will be given a detailed briefing when you are joined by your French colleague,' Featherstone said, taking the photo from Karl and locking it in a drawer. 'Morning tea should be served in the mess very soon, and I, like you, missed breakfast this morning. I suggest we adjourn to the mess and forget that this meeting ever happened.'

★

Ilsa Stahl could turn the head of any red-blooded male, whether dressed in her army dungarees while covering the landings at Normandy or walking into her newspaper's

New York office, wearing a tight skirt, high heels and nylon stockings. Ilsa had received recognition for her work as a war correspondent on two fronts and being recalled to New York felt like an attack on her professionalism. For a moment she reflected on whether her recall had been the work of American intelligence services. Did they doubt her patriotism? Surely not.

At least her position on the staff of the paper had its benefits. The lists of killed, wounded and MIA were channelled through her paper for public release. Amongst the announcements on last night's wire, Lieutenant Clark Nixon had been reported as being found. Ilsa could hardly believe it, even now. Her return to America had been a grim one; she had felt utterly alone in the world – her parents dead, Clark almost certainly dead; who was to care whether she herself lived or died? She had tried to hold her grief inside, but it had come flooding out when she'd read the wire. She'd been deliriously happy, which was why she hadn't been able to understand why she'd started crying so hard. Later, when she'd calmed down, she'd realised how much emotion she'd been suppressing, not only about Clark but also about all the terrible things she had witnessed in Europe.

Now Ilsa barely knocked on her editor's door before pushing her way in to confront the bespectacled middle-aged man behind his desk.

'Don't tell me, let me guess,' Aaron Weisenberg said, hardly glancing up. 'You want a transfer to the Pacific to cover the war.'

Ilsa was taken aback by his response. That was exactly what she wanted. 'You know about Clark being found?'

'I saw it on the news wire last night,' he replied, looking up. 'You must be thrilled.'

'To put it mildly,' Ilsa replied.

Weisenberg leaned back in his chair. 'You'll have to temper some of your reports,' he said. 'Getting a couple of my old army pals in Washington to accredit you will not be easy after that report you filed on General Patton.'

'The man is a bloody glory-seeker who—'

Weisenberg held up his hand to still his angry reporter. 'I have relatives in Europe and every day Patton advances means a day closer to their liberation. You may not agree with the way he puts his task before lives, but that is the nature of war.'

Ilsa felt a twinge of guilt. She might not like the way Patton operated, but she couldn't deny he was getting results. 'If you let me cover the war in the Pacific, I'll even promise to tone down my reports on MacArthur.'

Weisenberg smiled at her. 'I doubt that. You've got too good a nose for conflict and scandal. Get your kit together and, with any luck and a couple of bottles of good rye, I should have you cleared within forty-eight hours.'

Ilsa loved this man. He had been tough but fair with her in a world dominated by men. She stepped forward to shake his hand, although she would have preferred to kiss him. Aaron accepted the gesture with a sigh.

'Now get out. I have a lot of work to do,' he said gruffly.

Jubilant, Ilsa left the room before he could change her mind.

THREE

Sergeant Jack Kelly's patrol had not suffered any casualties but the young American gunner had a severe case of malaria. Jack had dosed him as best as he could with anti-malarial tablets but during the night the young American flyer died, calling for his mother.

Lieutenant Clark Nixon and Jack kneeled over his wasted body under a canopy of tropical rainforest giants. Jack was acutely aware that they were still deep in enemy territory with their own lines a good ten miles away, beyond a ridge and a swiftly flowing creek.

'We should bury him,' Lieutenant Nixon said quietly. 'He was one of my crew.'

'No time for that,' Jack replied, scanning the dim forest undergrowth. 'Corporal Gari says he can smell the Japs around here, and I trust his nose.'

'Sergeant, if we do not bury him, then we carry his body out,' the American said. 'We do not leave our fallen behind.'

Jack pulled a pained face. 'With all due respect, Lieutenant,' he said, 'this is my command and what I decide goes.'

'With respect, Sergeant,' the American officer replied icily, 'I am an officer in the American Army Air Force and I outrank you under the laws and regulations of our two allied forces. That means I have the last say in any decisions to be made.'

Jack understood the protocols of authority and knew that, strictly speaking, the Yank was right, but Jack was a practical man who also understood his mission, which was to keep all of them alive. The American was allowing emotion to guide his decisions. 'Tell you what, Lieutenant Nixon, we'll record the location of his body, and when it's safe to transmit I'll send details of the location and your blokes can come and get him later.'

Nixon seemed to accept the compromise and nodded. Jack immediately ordered two of his men to mark trees around the body for future reference, then the patrol resumed their march east to link up with the PIB HQ along the track.

They had not gone far when all hell broke loose.

★

Lukas Kelly levelled his heavy machine gun on the conning tower and thought bitterly that they would go down fighting. Before he could fire, a distant American voice called from the sub, 'Are you the *Riverside*?'

Lukas could hardly believe his ears. He felt as though they had just been given a reprieve from the firing squad.

'We're the *Riverside*, all right,' Lukas shouted back.

'We intercepted a message from your coastwatcher that you had been ambushed by the Japs,' the voice replied. 'We were in the area and thought we might look for your wreckage.'

'Hard to sink this old tub,' Lukas replied with a broad smile. 'But we could do with a bit of help. Our engine is out of action – do you have an engineer who could help out?'

There was a pause and finally the voice shouted, 'We'll send our engineer to see what he can do, but we can't hang around for long.'

'Thanks, cobber,' Lukas called back and soon a dinghy with two sailors aboard splashed alongside. One was a senior noncommissioned officer Mel Jones recognised from his days with the American navy.

'You old son of a bitch,' Mel said, slapping his former colleague on the shoulder as he hoisted him over the side. 'I thought you would be home on retirement, you dumb Polak.'

'I could say the same about you, Taffy,' the grizzled sailor said, taking Mel's hand in a strong grip of friendship.

Melvin Jones might be a second-generation American, but Lukas knew he would never forget his Welsh roots.

'This is Chief Petty Officer Polaski,' Mel said, turning to introduce his former shipmate to Lukas. 'I taught him everything he knows when we shipped together on the China station.'

'So how come you need my help with your engine, you overfed, underworked Welshman?' Polaski asked with a wry smile and both men launched into a diagnosis of what had gone wrong with the marine engine, disappearing into the cramped engine room as they talked.

The second sailor to come aboard introduced himself to Lukas as Ensign Jack Mitchell. From him Lukas was able to ascertain that the coastwatcher had been forced to retreat from the rendezvous point because a Jap patrol had stumbled into the area, seen the *Riverside* approaching and, in their haste to get into position, opened up too soon with their mortar and small arms. However, the coastwatcher was able to get off a message to Allied HQ, giving the route the supply boat had taken and requesting that its welfare be ascertained.

After an hour and a trip back to the American sub to find a replacement part, the engine was repaired. The rumbling cough of the boat coming back to life was one of the sweetest sounds Lukas had ever heard. The ensign and the engineer departed to the sub and were clambering aboard when Lukas's relieved smile disappeared.

'Jap plane!' Mel Jones shouted, and Lukas looked over his shoulder to be blinded by the sun rising over the sea. In that split second he saw the outline of a Japanese float plane coming in low. Even as the Japanese pilot lined up the vulnerable sub, the hatches were slammed shut and water began flooding the ballast tanks.

Lukas immediately flung himself across the deck to his .50 calibre machine gun. The Yanks had risked everything to help them and now they were under threat. The aircraft released two small bombs, then headed straight at the

Riverside. Jack was pleased to see that his crew were already firing at it with their Bren guns, but the Japanese pilot was using his machine guns to take them on. Splinters of wood were ripped up from the deck by the enemy bullets. Lukas felt something hit his chest but he was too busy squeezing off a volley at the aircraft's nose to see what it was. After the strafing pass over the *Riverside* the Japanese pilot rose into the sky, circled and made a second pass on the sub, which was disappearing beneath the calm sea.

Lukas could feel something warm running in rivulets down his chest but he ignored it and instead swung around on his target. This time it presented a side-on view to him and he levelled the sights a few yards in front of the aircraft, squeezed again, and saw the smoky trail of tracer bullets hose into the sky, curving and ripping down the full length of the fuselage of the Japanese seaplane. The enemy aircraft seemed to pause for a moment before a thin stream of smoke began trailing behind it. The pilot banked and turned away.

Lukas continued firing at the retreating float plane until the last round was expended from the belt. His crew cheered when they saw the distant shape suddenly dip and disappear into the sea with a great splash.

'You got the goddamned son of a bitch!' Mel whooped, slapping Lukas on the back. Lukas glanced out over the water; there was no sign of the sub. He hoped it would surface somewhere safe.

'You need a bit of patching up, Kelly,' Mel said, suddenly sounding subdued.

Lukas looked down at the blood dripping around his feet and realised that a couple of wooden splinters had torn deep cuts in his chest. One was still sticking out of his flesh and he pulled it out with a grimace. Now the adrenaline was wearing off, the wounds were beginning to hurt. He would have to clean them carefully to avoid infection and bandage them up as best he could until he could get medical attention.

'Let's get out of here, Mel,' he said. 'I happen to know a nurse at Moresby who can look after me.'

The American opened up the throttle, and the supply boat, battered by the short, sharp attack, growled into life. Lukas sat down on the deck and stared at the New Guinea coastline. He felt as though he had been fighting this war all his life; he was growing weary of it and was beginning to think he would not live to see peace again.

*

The explosion was almost lost in the chatter of a Nambu machine gun and the crack of rifles, but Jack felt the impact of the grenade at first hand. Wicked metal fragments shredded the left side of his back and arm, throwing him on his face in the mud of the forest floor. He gripped his Owen and could hear Corporal Gari screaming orders to counter the ambush.

Jack rose unsteadily to his knees and glanced around to ascertain their deployment. Nixon was on the ground a few feet away and Jack could see Gari bounding into the scrub in the direction of the Japanese machine gun.

Jack crawled forward to find one of his men stretched out, dead, blood oozing from a bullet hole in his head. There was no time for emotion. He stripped the dead soldier of his weapon and ammunition and tossed them to the American pilot.

'Here, get useful with these,' he shouted above the noise of the gunfire.

Suddenly the gunfire tapered away, and in the distance Jack could hear a man screaming. At the same time he looked around for any of the section who were still alive. The Japs were good, he thought grudgingly. They had let them walk into the ambush before springing it. These were no frightened conscripts but battle-hardened enemy.

Pain wracked his body; every movement was agony, and Jack gritted his teeth in an effort to stop from swooning. He thought he saw one of his men in the thick under-growth a few yards ahead of him but was stunned to see a Japanese soldier suddenly emerge with a bayonet-tipped rifle pointed directly at him. Jack attempted to bring up his gun but the Japanese soldier lunged with the long bay-onet, and Jack staggered backwards and fell. Just as Jack thought he was done for, the Japanese soldier was suddenly jerked backwards by the impact of a high-velocity bullet.

Jack looked up to see the American pilot crouching with the rifle at his shoulder, already chambering another round.

'Stay down, Sergeant Kelly,' Nixon shouted. 'I'll get you help.'

What help? Jack thought with a twisted grimace of pain. He was the only real help the patrol had.

Nixon made his way cautiously to Jack. The firing had tapered away and only the distant shouts of his men could be heard as they called to each other. After what seemed forever, Corporal Gari returned to Jack's side, covered

PETER WATT

from head to foot in blood. He was a fearsome sight but reassuring at the same time. Gradually the rest of the patrol made their way to Jack.

'How many have we lost?' Jack said through gritted teeth.

'Two, Masta Jack,' Gari answered. 'One fella wounded.'

'Can we get our wounded man out?' Jack asked and Gari nodded.

'Got a wound in the arm but he can still fight,' Gari said.

'Okay, we continue on to HQ,' Jack said, getting to his feet, trying not to cry out as the pain surged through him.

Nixon put his arm around Jack's waist to support him but Jack shook off the gesture. 'I'll be able to keep up.' Jack hoisted his Owen gun to his waist to prove that he was armed and ready to march.

'According to the Jap order of battle, their MG section is around a platoon size,' Jack whispered to Nixon as they made their way through the thick undergrowth. 'That makes me think there'll be others out there looking for us. Those two bloody Japs we didn't kill back at the lagoon must have bumped into one of their own patrols and tipped them off that we're working behind their lines.'

Nixon nodded, and then they trudged on in silence. Eventually they made their way down a very steep slope, slippery and treacherous, to a narrow but rapidly flowing creek. Entering the icy water, guns aloft, they struggled to the other side, where they proceeded to climb an equally steep slope.

Jack issued an order to his men to make the passage obvious to any enemy tracking them. Halfway up the slope he stopped and issued orders to take up an ambush site covering the route they had just taken. His men quickly prepared their cover and settled in to wait.

Nixon took up position beside Jack.

'You expect the Japs to be following us?' he whispered.

'One thing we have learned about the little yellow bastards is that they are persistent, and from the uniform on the dead Jap back on the other side of the creek, we are being hunted by some of their best. They'll be close behind us, you can be sure of that, and when they come I intend to reduce their enthusiasm as much as possible,' Jack said, wincing with pain. He was losing blood as it oozed from the numerous small punctures caused by shrapnel from the grenade. It must have gone off only a few feet away, he reflected, and cursed himself for allowing himself to be ambushed in the first place.

Jack realised that when the Japanese did come into contact with them, they would automatically go into their military drill of attempting to outflank his position. He knew that he did not have enough men to fight off a concerted attack, but he hoped that if they tried to carry out an outflanking movement, the creek would slow them down. By then he and his men would be on top of the ridge and not far from the PIB base.

They waited for a good half-hour in silence, although the sound of the creek below, with its almost comforting babble, would mask any noises they made.

'Are you married, Sergeant Kelly?' Nixon whispered eventually, catching Jack off guard.

'I was,' he answered. 'Twice. My second wife was American. She was killed at the beginning of the war.'

'I'm sorry to hear that,' Nixon replied with genuine sympathy.

'I've got a son who should be back in Australia rather than risking his life out here,' Jack continued, pleased to have something to take his mind off the pain sweeping through his body in agonising waves. 'He used to fly Hollywood big shots around before the war – until he lost his eye in a prang. He began serving with our Volunteer Rifles a couple of years ago and has ended up working with the small ships supplying the coast. The stupid galah is not fit to be on active service. He should just go home.' Jack paused and continued. 'I also have a daughter, somewhere in Europe, I think.' But he didn't want to talk about Ilsa.

'I'm putting Corporal Gari in for a decoration for his work back at the ambush,' Jack said, changing the subject. 'I'd appreciate it if you supported the recommendation. As an officer your support would go a long way.'

'It will be a pleasure,' Clark answered. 'From what I observed, he single-handedly took out the machine-gun crew with his machete.'

'How about you, Lieutenant Nixon?' Jack asked. 'Do you have someone waiting for you?'

'I do, Sergeant,' he replied. 'My fiancée is a war correspondent, and I worry about her.'

'She must be an extraordinary woman,' Jack replied, then suddenly fell silent. He could see a Japanese soldier on the opposite bank of the creek, cautiously observing the signs of their crossing. The soldier was crouching and his eyes swept the hillside, scanning for any sign of trouble. The men of Jack's ambush watched him, tense with anticipation. Rifles were cocked, primed grenades close at hand.

The soldier rose, signalled and commenced to cross the creek. Behind him a patrol of twenty soldiers emerged from the thick foliage and followed him across the icy cold water. Jack waited until the first enemy reached the shore. They had been forced to assume a single file for the crossing and Jack had calculated that the range was around seventy-five yards. He had selected their site because it gave a good field of fire.

Jack eased his Owen into a firing position, took a bead on the last men in the file and opened fire. His weapon signalled the opening of the attack and the rest of the patrol joined in. The Bren gun ripped into the ranks of the Japanese caught in the open. Spouts of water erupted in the creek and when Jack had emptied the magazine of his submachine gun he reached for a grenade, hurling it into the jungle this side of the creek where a couple of the enemy had struggled ashore to take refuge. His grenade was followed by others, one even reaching the water's edge to explode amongst the soldiers milling in frightened confusion. The water was quickly taking away the streams of blood as the enemy fell in the deadly ambush.

'Time to get out of here before the little yellow bastards reorganise for a flanking assault,' Jack said to Nixon, rising to his feet and glancing around to ensure the rest of his patrol knew what was expected of them. They were good soldiers and quickly formed into a disciplined patrol to climb the ridge. Beyond which lay a hot meal and a chance to sleep without one eye open.

Off to their left the crump of an exploding mortar

bomb shook the leaves. The Japanese were well armed but Jack hoped that the enemy was firing in blind anger, without much idea of where their target was. A second bomb landed a little closer but Jack led on without stopping. His men followed, and after a gut-wrenching, lung-tearing time they reached the apex of the ridge. Utterly exhausted, all the patrol wanted was to simply collapse and suck in air, but Jack, despite his agony, forced them over the other side. He knew that the Japanese would not give up in their pursuit. They were tough, dedicated soldiers who only expected death for their service. Jack wanted to live.

*

Captain Hung van Pham's face reflected his French mother more than his Indochinese father. His French education in Paris had moulded him into a Francophile. His service in the French Foreign Legion before the war had marked him as a professional soldier of the highest order. In his late twenties, he was handsome in any language and Captain Featherstone found him attractive, with his enigmatic aura of a Eurasian aristocrat.

'Please, Captain Hung, take a seat,' he said when the Vietnamese officer entered the office in a nondescript house in a leafy Sydney suburb. 'You may smoke, if you wish.'

Pham nodded his thanks, sat down in a comfortable leather chair and removed a packet of English cigarettes from the top pocket of his Free French Forces uniform jacket, displaying the ribbons of his considerable service and bravery.

'This will be our last briefing alone before you meet your colleague on the mission,' Featherstone said, standing in the centre of the gloomy room now filling with smoke. 'You will be nominally under the command of Major Karl Mann from an Aussie commando company.'

'Mann – that's a Boche name,' Pham said, speaking English with a distinctive French accent.

'Ah, yes it is,' Featherstone answered. 'However, his loyalty is beyond question.'

Pham gave a slight nod of acknowledgement, and Featherstone continued. 'Major Mann speaks German fluently and has experience working in covert operations. He will be the commander of the mission but you have the authority of the British and French governments to act as you see fit.'

'Major Mann does not know of this?' the French officer asked.

'Alas, I was not able to brief the major on the true purpose of the mission. He has been told that he is to extract a German national from Saigon because her father, a high-ranking German intelligence officer, has asked us to do so. In return he will furnish us with vital information on the location of sensitive records currently being held in Germany – if we get his daughter out of Saigon.'

'But, as you and I know, my mission has nothing to do with saving some Boche woman,' Pham said. 'My mission is to ensure the future of my country.'

'We are very well aware of the importance of your making contact with the Indochinese national resistance movement but I think you will discover that our missions are mutually beneficial.' Featherstone gave a strained expression. 'Major Mann gets our woman out, and you can carry on with your own agenda,' he added with a touch of sarcasm.

'Which of our joint objectives has priority?' Pham asked quietly.

Featherstone thrust his hands behind his back, clasping his hands tightly.

'I have demurred to our government's wish that, if push comes to shove, your mission takes priority,' he replied, attempting to conceal his anger. Featherstone did not like the way his superiors in London had insisted on putting the French interests first, in the name of Allied goodwill and cooperation.

'And if I feel that Major Mann is compromising my mission in Saigon?' Pham asked, taking a puff on his cigarette and blowing smoke towards the ceiling.

'Then you have the permission of my government to terminate his role, and that of the German woman.'

Featherstone sighed. As always in his work, individuals were sacrificed for the greater good of winning the war. Fortunately, he had great faith in Major Mann's ability to stay alive.

The French Indochinese colonies were of little interest to Featherstone, but he knew the French would have to take on the nationalist leader Ho Chi Minh when they returned after the war. There would be a vacuum created by any victory in the Pacific, and the French needed time to build an army of occupation before Ho Chi Minh and his Viet Minh movement could fill the vacuum with a government of their choosing.

When the meeting was finished, Featherstone accepted

a salute from the Free French officer and watched him walk out the door. How strange, he thought, withdrawing a cigarette from his gold case, that in his opinion an Aussie officer born in Germany was preferable to a Frenchman born in Indochina.

FOUR

They were swimming in a beautiful lagoon, small fish darting around them, and his beloved Victoria was laughing and splashing him. Jack smiled and reached out to grasp her but she suddenly snarled and turned into a Japanese soldier aiming a bayonet at his belly.

'Shh,' came a sound in his ear. For a terrible moment he did not know where he was. Was he back in Moresby, sharing an evening drink with his wife, Victoria?

Jack opened his eyes and the pain swept over him. Lieutenant Nixon kneeled over him in the dark of the tropical night, holding his hand on Jack's mouth.

'You were having bad dreams,' he whispered. 'I had to shut you up.'

Jack could smell the fetid, rotting undergrowth and

realised that a light rain was falling through the tree canopy and dripping heavily down on them.

A second voice came out of the dark and Jack momentarily forgot his pain. He recognised the language as Japanese although he did not understand what the man had said. Jack felt for his weapon, reassured to find it close by. He could hear the slight rustle of undergrowth and feel the tension of the American flyer leaning over him.

The sound slowly faded until only the night sounds of the forest remained.

'How long?' Jack croaked his question.

'Since midafternoon, when I gave you a morphine shot. You almost passed out with the pain,' Clark replied. 'I took command. The Japs have been hot on our heels, so I ordered that we lay up and place the men in an ambush position. I think they've missed us.'

Jack was impressed by the American's initiative. 'How did you know to do that?'

'Corporal Gari has been giving me advice,' Nixon answered. 'Your boys are goddamned good.'

'We'll have to reroute around the Jap patrol,' Jack said, sitting up with great difficulty. He knew there was a danger of his wounds becoming infected and he also knew that he would soon get to the stage where he would compromise the safety of his men.

'You're going to have to lead the men out,' Jack said. 'I'll stay behind and cover your rear as best I can.'

'Sorry, Sergeant Kelly,' Nixon said. 'You're coming with us. I'm not leaving a wounded man behind for the Japs – I know how they treat prisoners.'

Jack wanted to protest but could hear the determination

in the American officer's voice. 'Only if I'm capable of walking out,' Jack said. 'Otherwise, you leave me to cope with any Japs coming my way. I promise you they won't take me alive.'

For a moment Nixon was silent in the dark. 'A deal,' he finally replied. 'Do you think it is safe to radio your boys?'

Jack considered the question. 'Yeah, better send them a sitrep.'

Contact was made with PIB HQ and the message relayed. After a short period of time a message was returned, with the coordinates of what was considered the safest leg back to camp. Being an aviator, Nixon was a brilliant navigator – even in the jungle, in the dark. With map and compass he plotted the track home.

Jack was able to get to his feet and walk with the aid of a crutch made from a sapling. Slowly the patrol made its way through the pitch darkness of the jungle, ever alert to a possible ambush. But Jack's men were born to this country and their skills ensured that when the sun eventually rose, they were already at the base of the tall ridges and on the kunai-covered plains between the rugged rainforest-covered hills.

As they trudged on their course, hacking their way through the long grass, they were surprised by a section of PIB soldiers rising up to greet them. They were home, and within hours Jack was on a medical evacuation flight to Port Moresby, on the other side of the Owen Stanley Ranges.

Lieutenant Nixon was also on the flight and his stretcher was below Jack's on the Douglas. They shared the sturdy aircraft with PIB soldiers suffering from scrub typhus, malaria, dengue fever and war wounds. Jack's body was covered in bandages and he felt like an Egyptian mummy.

The aircraft dropped down onto the coast and into the busy Port Moresby airfield, coming to a halt at the end of the strip, next to a row of Kittyhawk fighters displaying Australian markings. The door was flung open and the hot tropical air filled the interior of the transport plane. RAAF nurses wearing trousers and shirts were waiting as each litter was brought out onto the tarmac.

When Jack's litter was manhandled onto the back of a modified jeep he looked up into a beautiful familiar face staring at him with wide-eyed concern.

'Hello, Sister Cain,' he said, half-grinning and half-grimacing with pain. 'Has my lady seen my son lately?'

Megan Cain turned her head to issue orders for a drip to be inserted into Jack's arm and then took his hand. 'I haven't seen Lukas in five months,' she said. 'But I certainly hope he's in better condition than his father right now. You should both be out of this bloody war.'

Jack saw that Megan was forcing back tears and he regretted his cavalier question.

Soon he was inside a Nissan hut in the military hospital, with slowly sweeping ceiling fans stirring the hot air to a slightly more comfortable temperature. Megan was still by his side, administering a shot of morphine to him. Lukas was a bloody lucky man to have the love of such a woman, Jack thought as he drifted off into oblivion.

★

Megan visited Jack every day and together they reassured each other that Lukas would return soon. Many times Megan chided Jack for remaining on the front lines when he was far too old to be a soldier. But Jack would remind her that he was fighting for his homeland – Papua and New Guinea. Megan would sigh and pat his hand before moving on to her next patient.

On the fifth day Jack's wounds were healing well enough to allow him to get out of bed and sit in the garden cordoned by bright bougainvillea bushes. He could feel the stiffness in his left side from the drying wounds but was otherwise feeling much better.

'Hello, Sergeant Kelly,' a voice said and Jack turned with a wince to see the American pilot resplendent in a crisp, clean uniform affixed with his shiny pilot's wings.

'Mr Nixon,' Jack said, holding out his hand 'What are you doing here?'

'I came to say goodbye,' Nixon said, shaking Jack's hand. 'I'll be rejoining my outfit tomorrow.'

'I know, you can't tell me where,' Jack said.

'It's crazy, but General MacArthur doesn't seem to trust our Aussie allies,' Nixon said, taking off his peaked cap and wiping sweat from his face with the back of his hand. 'I can tell you that it won't be far from here. Maybe no further than Moresby airfield,' he said with a knowing smile.

Jack nodded and for a while the two men gazed out at the garden filled with butterflies and tiny birds. It was so peaceful that the war could have been over, but both men carried the memories of deadly jungles and hostile blue skies.

'What are you going to do when they let you out?' Nixon asked, breaking the silence.

'First thing I'm going to do is head for the nearest pub, and if you bloody Yanks haven't drunk the place dry, I will.'

Nixon chuckled. 'Not enough of us left to do that,' he said. 'Most of the boys are up north, liberating the Philippines. I expect I'll be posted that way soon enough myself. Are you going to return to your PIB boys?'

Jack stared at a butterfly flitting between the big, colourful flowers of a hibiscus shrub. 'I promised myself that I would see out this war until the last Jap was either dead or gone from my country.'

'Australia?' Nixon asked in surprise.

'No, this place here – New Guinea,' Jack responded. 'This is where I've lived since I was a young man prospecting for gold. This is where I brought up my son. My wife is buried here.'

Nixon shifted awkwardly in his chair and Jack wondered what the American's home was like. Probably a far cry from this land of swamps, jungles and impassable mountains, all crawling with every tropical disease known to man.

'Well, I'll have to say goodbye for the moment, Sergeant Kelly,' Nixon said, rising and replacing his cap. 'The good news is that my fiancée has cabled to say that she will be flying out to cover the backwash of the war over here. Kind of pleased she has opted to remain away from the European front.'

'I'm pleased to hear that too, Lieutenant Nixon,' Jack said. 'I hope it all goes well for you both.'

'When she arrives you'll have to meet her,' Nixon said, taking a pair of dark sunglasses from his shirt pocket and slipping them over his eyes. 'I'm sure you'll like her.'

'I'm sure I will,' Jack said politely as Nixon shook his hand goodbye.

'So long,' Nixon said. 'Until next time.'

Jack watched the tall American stride away with the jaunty walk that seemed a characteristic of these easygoing American allies. He hoped the war would be over soon, and Nixon and that girl of his could settle down and raise children in peace.

★

Petty Officer First Class Fuji Komine watched the execution impassively. It was not the first time he had seen Lieutenant Yoshi behead a helpless civilian with his samurai sword.

'Tell the villagers that this is the treatment they can expect if they betray us,' Lieutenant Yoshi called to Fuji as the head of the village leader rolled away from his lifeless body. Women wailed and children cried, while the men stood in silence.

Fuji obeyed his order and addressed the inhabitants of this small village deep in the rainforest of northern New Guinea. He accepted that terror was an effective means of keeping control over the village where they had established a base of operations, but it was the fact that the commanding officer was the man who had murdered Fuji's own woman years earlier that left the bitter taste in his mouth.

Fuji could see the frightened acceptance in the villagers' eyes, but from his experience growing up in Papua he also knew that they would turn on them at the first opportunity. This was a temporary reign of terror.

'Now, tell them what we have for those who help the Emperor,' Lieutenant Yoshi said, cleaning the blood-spattered blade on the shirt of the headless body at his feet.

Petty Officer Oshiro stepped forward with a metal ammunition case containing silver coins. He marched to the centre of the clearing between the palm frond and timber huts adjoining plots of vegetables. Pigs rooted amongst rubbish, and skinny, scabby dogs began to sniff around the body, lapping at the blood seeping from the exposed neck.

Oshiro stepped back to allow his commanding officer to scoop out a handful of Australian shillings. Fuji thought that the coinage was surely an admission that they were losing the war. The Japanese currency of occupation no longer seemed to appeal to the native people, as word spread from valley to valley that the Japanese were slowly being forced back home and that the Europeans were returning to once again assume control. Very soon the *kiaps* – patrol officers – would be back to dispense justice, and the Japanese occupiers would be gone.

Oshiro joined Fuji and behind them stood the other twelve tough marine troops sent on this mission; with their bayonet-tipped rifles they were a formidable presence.

'I hated travelling here in that submarine,' Oshiro whispered to Fuji. 'But this cursed place is worse than being stuck inside the sub.'

Fuji was about to say something when he caught Lieutenant Yoshi's eye. With chilling certainty he knew he was going to be singled out for punishment. Lieutenant Yoshi strode towards him, trailing his sword.

'Petty Officer Fuji,' he screamed into Fuji's face. 'Did I give permission to speak?'

'No, sir,' Fuji answered dutifully, averting his eyes. The vicious back-handed slap across his face almost sent him reeling but he stood his ground, blood trickling from his nose.

'You are not a true Japanese warrior!' Lieutenant Yoshi shouted. 'You are a product of the decadent west and not to be trusted. As punishment for your insolence, you will remain standing to attention here until I give you permission to return to your billet.'

'Yes, sir.' Fuji replied, tasting the blood in his mouth from where his teeth had cut through his lip. He accepted that Lieutenant Yoshi was enforcing the iron discipline of the Japanese armed forces, but he could not accept the insult of his lack of loyalty to the Emperor. Fuji knew, however, that there was nothing he could do to redress this slur on his character and so he stood to attention as the villagers looked on, watching curiously until they were sent back to their duties in the gardens and huts.

Fuji remained standing to attention under the hot sun until it grew dark and Oshiro came to him with a canteen of water and sympathetic words, saying that their commanding officer had given permission for Fuji to stand down.

As Fuji greedily gulped the water he recalled happier times working alongside his father, a boat builder, and living near Port Moresby, in the Central Province of Papua. It was true he had suffered the discrimination of the Europeans, but they had left his family alone to prosper.

Imperial headquarters constantly informed them all that it was impossible for the Japanese to lose the war. But lately, rumours had started to spread that they might have to sacrifice their lives to force the Allies into a position to concede a treaty. This was not considered defeat but simply a means of keeping the barbarians off the sacred soil of Japan and retaining the Sun God Emperor.

Maybe it was true that Fuji had been too exposed to the decadent western ways, because he could see his country really was beaten and that the Europeans would not rest until they had achieved a crushing victory over Japan. He knew that there would be no armistice or treaty – just total defeat and humiliation.

'Here, drink this,' Oshiro said, producing a flask.

Fuji took a swig and felt the fiery rice wine start to ease away his hurt. 'How did you get the sake?' he asked.

'The commander will not miss a bit out of the barrel,' Oshiro chuckled. 'I think this whole mission is a pile of buffalo manure. Our navy has dumped us in the middle of nowhere with the idea that Lieutenant Yoshi knows what he is doing. We have been sent along to make it look good, when we all know this war is lost.'

Fuji gripped Oshiro's wrist. 'Be silent,' he hissed. 'If you are overheard, you will be executed as defeatist.'

'Do you truly think that we will win?' Oshiro asked sadly. 'I keep dreaming that I am back in my village, watching my wife and children in the fields. I hear the chatter of the gossip by the old people and wish I was home with them. I beg of you, if I die and you do not, go back to my home and tell my family how much I loved them.'

Fuji saw that his friend had tears running down his

cheeks. As tough as he was, Oshiro yearned for peace. Fuji knew the only peace they would experience would be the long sleep of death.

★

Bing Crosby's 'White Christmas' drifted to Ilsa from a radio in the bar on the beach. For days now she had been stuck in Honolulu in the Hawaiian Islands. Her flight to Australia had been cancelled for no apparent reason, and here she was in limbo in a place most people would give their right arm to be.

Ilsa lifted her martini and silently toasted those old friends and colleagues who would not see Christmas this year, white or otherwise.

She had idled away her time in Honolulu, between island bars filled with rowdy servicemen and her hotel overlooking the beach. Several men had attempted to woo her but she was only interested in one man.

She and Clark had first met early in the war when she had been sent to an airfield outside New York to file a story about bomber crews training for service overseas. She had been assigned a handsome young bomber pilot whose easy smile caught her attention immediately. When he removed his sunglasses she was mesmerised by his sparkling eyes and, from then on, she had been smitten with Lieutenant Clark Nixon. Over drinks in the officers' club she learned that he was the son of a cattle rancher, but he had been smart enough to draw out her story too. Up until then, Ilsa had found that most men simply wanted to impress her with their achievements and wealth, yet this man seemed interested in her as a person. Later she learned that he came from a very wealthy family and would one day inherit a cattle empire. Before he was shipped out, she was able to obtain leave to travel to Clark's family home in Montana, where she was seduced by the rugged beauty of the vast plains and mountains. She had been treated with great warmth by Clark's parents and for the first time in her life had a sense of belonging to the US.

Ilsa had had no letters from Clark since well before he went missing. She knew that her moving from one place to another did not help the mail system, but she still felt frustrated and disappointed.

Each day she would enquire with the armed forces movements section as to whether she had a berth on one of the many aircraft flying in and out of Hickham Field. With each no she would return to her hotel room, pick up her copy of John Steinbeck's *The Grapes of Wrath* and head to the beach, and then, when the sun went down, she would drink and talk with the men returning from the bloody battle fronts of the Pacific.

On Christmas Eve a parcel of letters was delivered to her room, redirected from the New York office. Her heart lifted at the sight of Clark's familiar handwriting. Her fingers trembled as she attempted to shuffle the letters into chronological order according to the postmarks. Then she sat down by the window, a balmy breeze blowing in off the water, and opened the first letter. Tears flowed as she read and reread each word of endearment. Clark described his rescue, adding the name of the Aussie PIB sergeant who had saved him from certain death.

Ilsa froze. Surely not! Jack Kelly! It was possible there

was more than one Jack Kelly in New Guinea, but Clark's description of this tough old soldier sounded just like her father.

Ilsa stared out at the ocean. How was it possible that her own father had saved the life of the man she loved most in the world?

She put down the letter and poured herself a glass of bourbon, then sat down to continue reading.

Ilsa had never mentioned Jack Kelly to Clark; it hadn't seemed important even when she had lost both her mother and her wonderful stepfather. Both had died of natural causes and, on her deathbed, Ilsa's mother had confessed that Gerhardt Stahl was not Ilsa's biological father.

But now she felt a growing need to seek out and connect with her biological father and half-brother as they were all the blood family she had left.

Ilsa continued reading the letters until the sun went down and the town came alive with the noise of servicemen seeking a good time on this night of peace and goodwill to all men. So many people had assured her the war would be over by Christmas; how wrong they'd all been.

The Germans had mounted a massive counteroffensive through the Ardennes Forest in Belgium, and the Allies, particularly the Americans, were reeling from the massive onslaught of armour, artillery and infantry that had rallied against them. Ilsa cursed not being with the troops to cover their stand against the German Army. She had warned the American public in her articles that the Germans would fight on and for that she had been chastised by an overconfident military. Ilsa's predictions had proven correct when a massive German Army burst out of the supposedly impassable Ardennes Forest, and pushed back the American Army almost to the point of defeat. It had only been the courageous resistance of small pockets of American soldiers and the fortification of the town of Bastogne that had held the onslaught to a standstill. But being proven right had not saved Ilsa from being discredited by the arrogant higher military headquarters that had stated the war would be over by Christmas 1944.

Ilsa heard a knock at her door. Goodness, was it that late? She had lost track of time and forgotten all about the arrangement she'd made to go out with Ed Self, the pilot who had been Clark's best friend back in Montana.

Captain Ed Self held a bouquet of tropical flowers in his hand and greeted her with a broad smile. 'Are you ready?' he asked, eyeing Ilsa still attired in a light sundress. He was as tall as Clark and handsome too; in fact, the two men could have passed for brothers.

'Just give me a moment,' Ilsa answered, opening the door for him.

'I thought these might bring a little colour to your world,' he said cheerfully, looking around for something to place the flowers in. 'I also brought them as a bribe to get you to come to our Christmas party at the club.'

'I would be delighted, Ed,' Ilsa called from the bathroom. 'I have a damned good reason to celebrate Christmas this year.'

'You sound happy,' Ed said. 'What's happened?'

'I've finally received letters from Clark,' Ilsa said, popping her head around the bathroom door. 'He's back flying and has been promoted to captain.'

'You know, old Clark has always been a lucky son of

a gun,' Ed said with a warm smile. 'He got you when I, the better man, missed out, and now he gets to come back from the dead. I suppose he will even be posted Stateside so that you two can get married, and me, I'll have to settle for the best man's job.'

Ilsa liked Ed and under different circumstances he might have had a chance. 'He's not being posted Stateside so it's up to me to go to him. Which is where you come in,' she grinned. 'I'm going to beg you to find a flight over to New Guinea so I can continue reporting the war.' She gave him a coy little smile and pretended to bat her eyelashes at him.

Ed laughed. 'You've got me wrapped around your little finger. Give me a week and I'll get you a seat on one of our bombers, but you'll have to have clearance from the command to be on the flight.'

'I can manage that,' Ilsa replied with a warm smile. 'And now, let's get to your club and celebrate another year of being alive.'

FIVE

The day Jack Kelly was discharged he headed straight to his favourite hotel for a cold beer. The bar was crowded with soldiers, sailors and airmen. All so young, Jack thought sadly. A handful of Australian soldiers were raucously singing along to Bing Crosby. 'I'm dreaming of a white mistress, just like the one I had before . . .' Jack could not see a single familiar face amongst the rowdy patrons, and why should he, he thought – most of his mates were either buried somewhere out in the jungle or serving on the other side of the world.

He bribed the publican to sell him a few more bottles of beer than the ration allowed and decided that it was time to go home to the family plantation to spend Christmas with his Papuan workers.

He borrowed an old T-model Ford from one of the few planters he knew who still hung around the town, and drove the rutted, ill-kept coastal track out of Moresby until he reached the copra plantation at sunset.

As he stepped out of the car he could see that the place had fallen into disrepair but he was soon distracted by a group of happy workers and their families welcoming him back. He knew the property could easily be cleaned up once the war was over and production began again, but he still felt regret and sadness that his once beautiful home was now so dilapidated. Blame it on the war, like everything else.

Jack took bottles of beer up to the house and sat down on the verandah to gaze out at the now tranquil sea. So many wonderful evenings had been spent on this same verandah with his old friend Paul Mann, and it had been a place to talk with Victoria when the day was done. Now chickens pecked away at the timber flooring of the verandah and pigs rooted amongst the shrubs of what had once been a neatly kept garden.

Jack took one of the bottles and knocked off the top. The beer was warm but he didn't care; he just wanted to get drunk and forget all the things he had lost in his life.

The Papuan supervisor, a man in his forties, brought Jack a meal of rice and fish at some point in the evening but Jack did not eat it. Instead, he kept drinking until the bottle slipped from his fingers and he fell into a deep, troubled sleep.

When morning came, he awoke with a throbbing head and a dry, coppery taste in his mouth. The sun shone in his eyes and he considered going for a swim down at the beach, to clear his head. It was Christmas Day, he realised with a pang.

Just then the sound of an engine disturbed his thoughts.

'Car come long road, masta,' the supervisor yelled from the garden.

Jack rose to his feet to see a Dodge WC driving into the yard. It bore the insignia of the RAAF and Jack wondered who on earth would be visiting from the air force on Christmas Day.

The car stopped and both driver and passenger doors opened at the same time. Jack's hangover was instantly forgotten when he saw his son Lukas alight from the driver's side, a broad grin on his handsome, rugged face. Megan appeared on the other side of the vehicle, wearing her air force nurses' uniform. Her grin was almost as big as Lukas's.

'Merry Christmas, Dad,' Lukas yelled, holding up a small wicker basket. 'Thought you might like some company.'

Jack fought back the tears as his son walked towards him. In moments, Lukas was on the verandah, hugging his father in an embrace guaranteed to crush a lesser man. Behind him Megan beamed.

'Happy Christmas, Jack,' she said. 'I found this pirate son of yours wandering around the streets of Moresby. My boss kindly lent me the staff car to bring him home to you.'

Jack extended his embrace to enfold Megan and held them both tightly. When they finally broke away, Jack found two more old cane chairs to sit on.

'How did you know I'd be here?' he asked.

'Where else would you be today?' Lukas shrugged,

digging through the wicker basket. 'My first stop when we got back to Moresby was the hospital to find Megan, and she told me you'd been wounded and brought in for treatment. You're looking better than I expected. How are you feeling?'

'I'm fine,' Jack replied with a dismissive wave of his hand. 'Even better now you're home safely.'

Lukas brandished a couple of cans of American spam. 'As you can see, Dad, we have a ham for Christmas lunch, followed by fresh fruit salad.' Lukas produced a can of mixed fruit. 'All this washed down by what is left of your stock of fine beers. But first, the traditional morning swim to commence the day.'

After a swim the three sat on the verandah, eating the meal and sipping on the warm beer. There was so much news to exchange that the day passed in a flash. Late in the afternoon Megan excused herself to go inside and change back into her uniform.

'I have to be back before 1800 hours,' she said. 'I'm on duty tonight but Lukas can stay. I can see that you have your own transport.'

Both men escorted her to the Dodge and watched her drive away. Jack had the funny feeling that something had changed between Lukas and Megan, although Lukas had not mentioned anything. Jack knew Megan had miscarried when Lukas had been away fighting as an infantryman along the Kokoda Track. It seemed to Jack as though Megan were struggling to mask her complex feelings of loss, whereas his son only wanted to close that tragic part of their lives and move on. Megan needed Lukas's support, his love and his strength but instead he had closed himself off from her, leaving her isolated in her sadness. Jack tried to dismiss his concerns; it was Christmas Day, after all, and he'd just received the best present any parent could have – his only son returned to him safe and well.

That evening he and Lukas walked around the grounds, greeting the families of the workers and discussing how the plantation could be brought back into operation when the war was over. Jack was pleased to see how eager his son was to take over managing the property.

'Have you seen Karl?' Lukas asked when they returned to the house.

'Not since '43,' Jack replied. 'I heard that he was serving with a commando company, and God knows where they might be at any given time.'

'I ran into the bugger last year when we were supplying our blokes up around the north of Milne Bay,' Lukas said. 'He was a captain then and we had a brief moment to swap stories. He looked older. I suppose we all do.'

Jack glanced at his son in the half-dark of the veran-dah. He did look older, thanks to the war; his skin was still golden but his eyes – the good one, anyway – looked weary, as though he'd seen too much in his young lifetime.

Father and son sat talking long into the night. Jack had scrounged a kerosene lantern, which provided them with light, and they burned insect repellent to keep away the mosquitoes. The Papuan supervisor brought them slabs of barbecued pork pieces on banana leaves, along with cooked plantain and rice. The alcohol caused the two men to drift back to memories of life before the war. Lukas had only the vaguest memories of his mother, as she had died from the terrible influenza outbreak when he was a very young boy and while his father was still returning from the Western Front. Lukas was left in the care of his gruff father and, as the years had passed, the two became inseparable. Lukas found a mother's love in Karin Mann who raised him alongside her own son Karl in the absence of any female in Jack's life when Lukas was young. As the wife of Jack's best friend, Paul, Karin accepted her 'adopted son' as if he were her own.

Then Victoria had come into their lives. Beautiful and charming, Lukas had found a woman who also understood a young man's need of a woman's calming influence in his life. Both men adored Victoria, and when, early in the war, a Japanese submarine sank their company island trader off the Papuan coast, killing Victoria, a vacuum was left in their lives that could not be filled. At least now Lukas had found Megan, and Jack dreamed of the days ahead when she and Lukas would tie the knot and make him a grandfather.

The two men continued talking into the early hours of the morning, not wishing to break the precious connection between them.

Later they bid their plantation workers goodbye and drove into Port Moresby, where Lukas was to return to the *Riverside* and Jack to report to PIB HQ for the posting back to his unit. Before they parted ways they hugged each other fiercely, refusing to acknowledge what lay between them – that this might be the last time they saw each other alive.

★

Jack did not have to wait long in the orderly room before he was called into the office of Bill Travers, a PIB major he'd known before the war. They were the same age, but the major had long since lost his hair, and his bald head reflected the afternoon sunshine pouring through the open window.

'Hello, Jack,' he said, gesturing to his sergeant to take a seat. There was little formality between the two old friends. 'I got your report recommending Corporal Gari for a gong and I have sent it upstairs with my concurrence.'

'Thanks, Bill,' Jack said, making himself comfortable.

'I've already made enquiries into your medical status,' Travers said, flipping open a manila folder. 'You must have used that Irish charm on someone to get a clearance.'

'No, fit as a fiddle,' Jack replied with a straight face, knowing that Megan had had to convince the air force doctor to sign off on his fitness. 'So, do I get posted back north with the battalion?'

Bill Travers gave him a pained look. 'You ever thought that you might be better off going back to your plantation and getting that up and going again?'

'Yeah, Bill, when the war is over,' Jack drawled. 'Lukas is going to help me.'

'I suppose you know that he saved a Yank sub on his last mission?' Travers asked.

That was news to Jack. Bloody typical, he thought. Lukas hadn't told him because he did not want to alarm him.

Travers stood and walked to the window. 'Jack, you're not being sent back north – despite your medical clearance.

75

It has been recommended that you remain in Moresby on my staff. We need men with your experience to guide things from here.'

'Don't I have any bloody say in the matter?' Jack said, anger creeping into his voice. 'Bill, you know what it's like to be a part of the battalion. They can't do this to me.'

'Sorry, cobber, nothing I can do – the posting has already been confirmed by the colonel. You're to report to this office from now on. You've been assigned a room at the sergeants' mess and, frankly, you're lucky to have that, considering the brass felt you were getting a bit old for active service. Look at it this way,' Travers continued more gently. 'You'll be at the hub of everything that's happening, and you'll be in a position to see what young Lukas is up to whenever he returns to Moresby.'

Jack stared blankly at the major's desk, guessing that his old friend would have fought for him to be allowed to return to the battalion.

He rose, replaced his slouch hat and saluted his friend. 'Thanks for at least keeping me in, Bill,' he said, extending his hand. Bill Travers took it firmly and Jack could feel the strength of friendship in the clasp.

'I believe Lukas is courting the prettiest nurse in Moresby,' Bill said.

'No, the prettiest young lady in the Pacific,' Jack corrected with a cheeky smile. 'After the war I hope my son makes her a Papua New Guinean.'

'Well, I'm sure she'll be pleased to know that her possible future father-in-law is out of the jungle and in a position to look out for her possible future husband,' the Major said. 'Go and get your kit sorted and report back after lunch. I have a lot of aerial photos of Jap dispositions up north that I want you to go through.'

Jack nodded and left the office. He was bitterly disappointed at not returning to active service but this unhappiness was offset by the fact Major Travers coordinated Lukas's small ship's operations. Jack knew that he would be able to use his position at HQ to ensure that his son was kept away from the most dangerous waters around the island – whether Lukas liked it or not.

★

Major Karl Mann bumped into an old school friend, Charles Kensington, on Boxing Day and was invited to a New Year's Eve party at his house in Rose Bay. Charles was employed by the Commonwealth Government in a protected occupation of senior rank and, as such, worked closely with elected politicians.

On the evening of the party Karl found himself standing on Charles's porch with a cold beer in his hand, overlooking the harbour and reflecting again on how Sydney seemed almost oblivious to the war to the north of them. He was the only person in uniform and he was reluctant to enter into conversation about the war with men who had little idea of what it was like to lie out in the jungle waiting to kill or be killed, to live in the heat, mud and drenching tropical downpours, racked by illness, hunger and exhaustion. There were a few of his old schoolmates amongst the party, but he no longer seemed to have anything in common with them. Conversations, once started, petered out uncomfortably.

'I feel sorry for you,' a female voice said behind him.

Karl turned to find a beautiful young woman in her early twenties looking at him. She was wearing an expensive evening dress; her raven hair was cropped fashionably short and her eyes were a deep green. 'You must find it hard to fit in with Charles's friends and colleagues after you've have been in the thick of the fighting up north.'

'I'm just pleased to be in company this evening,' Karl said. 'Being here reminds me of why we are fighting.'

'You sound as though you're being facetious,' she said, moving closer to Karl. 'My name is Sarah, by the way, and I am Charles's sister.'

'Ah yes, I remember now. You're better looking than Charles,' Karl said with a broad grin, holding out his hand. She shook it and he could feel the soft, warm flesh of her fingers. 'I am Karl.'

'I know,' Sarah said. 'My brother has told me a few stories about you and your friend from New Guinea. He told me you were a couple of wild savages straight out of the jungle.'

'You must be referring to Lukas Kelly,' Karl said. 'I myself was brought up in a civilised manner by respectable parents.'

Sarah gave him a dubious look. 'Where is your friend now?' she asked.

'I last heard that he was skippering one of our supply boats out of Port Moresby,' Karl answered.

'I am sorry for what happened between you and Marie,' Sarah said suddenly.

'You know Marie?' he asked in surprise.

'Yes, I've known her since she set up her perfume business here in Sydney. I am afraid she came out with us one evening and my brother introduced her to his friend, James, and, well, things just happened from there. I had no idea she was spoken for.'

Karl took a long swallow of his beer, emptying the glass. 'These things happen in war,' he said, trying not to sound bitter. 'James wouldn't happen to be James Stanley, by any chance?'

Sarah looked up at him. 'Yes, that's him.'

'That doesn't surprise me,' Karl said softly. 'He always was a slimy bastard, even at school.'

'I hope you don't intend him any harm,' Sarah said. 'He and Marie are married now, they have a baby boy. And James is an important member of the government.'

'If Marie is happy with him, then I am pleased for her,' Karl lied. 'I have other matters to worry about right now.'

'Are you being posted back to active service?' Sarah asked.

'I leave tomorrow,' Karl replied.

It had been a long time since he had been in the company of a woman – let alone a very beautiful and intriguing young woman – and he decided he wanted to spend his last hours in this harbour city enjoying the company of this vibrant and charming woman, without talk of the war clouding their short time together.

'Can I get you a drink?' he asked, glancing down at his own empty glass.

'No, but I would like to get you one,' she said with a gentle smile. 'I'm sure you don't wish to return to a room full of stuffy public servants.'

'That would be nice,' Karl replied, passing her his glass.

Sarah slipped inside, leaving Karl to contemplate his feelings for Marie. The pain had not left him yet but he was a pragmatic person who had long learned to live for the moment rather than dwell on the past.

Sarah returned, passed Karl a full glass of beer and proceeded to light up a cigarette. She offered him one.

'I don't smoke,' he said.

'And I don't drink,' Sarah retorted with a wistful smile. 'So, what do we have in common then?'

'The solitude of this verandah,' Karl responded. 'And the peace of this night.'

Sarah tilted her head and gazed at him. 'I can see behind those eyes of yours, Major Mann, that you have experienced a lot of pain in this war.'

Karl was taken aback by her observation; he prided himself on hiding his feelings. 'No more than the average digger,' he shrugged.

'What do you intend to do when the war is over?' Sarah asked.

'Return to my home in Papua and my old job as a patrol officer,' Karl answered and didn't miss the look of disappointment on her face at his response.

'Surely you're sick of jungles and savages by now,' she said, taking a puff on her cigarette. 'I would think that you might seek a less dangerous profession.'

Karl fell into silence. 'Maybe you are right,' he said finally. 'What are your plans for the end of the war?'

'Oh, to go to a lot more parties and spend the family fortune as quickly as I can,' she sighed. 'I suppose I'll do the right thing by the family and meet an acceptable man, and look after the house and children while he goes off to work.'

'You don't strike me as the kind of woman who would settle for domestic bliss,' Karl said, taking a sip of his beer.

'How do you know?' Sarah retorted. 'You've only known me for a few minutes.'

'I would like to get to know you better,' Karl said quietly, and then cursed himself for being so blunt.

'Believe it or not, Karl,' Sarah said, 'the feeling is mutual. I have a flat not far from here. In fact, five minutes' walk away. Let's go there.'

Karl made his apologies to Charles for having to leave before the new year was ushered in and then slipped away to meet Sarah outside. She was standing under a dimmed streetlight and for a moment he thought about the popular German song 'Lili Marleen', and the soldier's girl waiting under the lamplight outside the barracks.

Sarah slipped her arm through Karl's and together they walked along the streets filled with people preparing to welcome in a new year they prayed would finally bring the end of the war. At least in Europe the Allies had regained the momentum towards victory. Only in the Pacific did the war drag on with no clear end in sight.

Once inside the flat, Sarah leaned up and kissed Karl passionately on the lips. Taking his hand she led him to the bedroom, unbuttoning her evening dress on the way.

They made love as if nothing else mattered in the world, the sounds of 'Auld Lang Syne' drifting to them from nearby parties as the year ticked over into 1945.

As the sun rose on the new year, Karl lay awake knowing that within hours he would be on a plane flying north to the Queensland township of Cairns. Beside him Sarah lay naked under a sheet, her head on his broad chest.

She murmured when he moved, and he remained still so as not to disturb her. He wished this moment would never end. He didn't know whether it was love but it was something precious snatched in a time when life was so precarious.

Karl glanced at the luminous dial of his watch and realised he would have to leave now to be on time for his flight. Very gently, he eased Sarah's head from his chest and slipped out of bed. He gathered up his uniform and quickly dressed. He rubbed his chin, knowing that he should shave as regulations dictated. This was one rule he would have to break today, he thought.

When he was dressed, Karl left the flat, quietly closing the door behind him, and stepped into the street. He only had to walk a short distance before he flagged down a passing taxi. Three hours later he was sitting inside a transport aircraft taking off from Sydney going north to the tropics. As he sat with his back to the fuselage he kept thinking about the hours since Charles's party. Karl had not said goodbye to Sarah but that was the way of war. Saying goodbye was too much of a reminder that it could be goodbye forever. Without knowing it, Sarah had helped ease the pain of his loss and prepare him to face an uncertain future.

SIX

That the pilot hardly looked old enough to shave, let alone command the Douglas transport, did not surprise Ilsa – servicemen seemed to be getting younger and younger as the war dragged on. He stood beside his aircraft, chewing gum and grinning broadly. He looked as though he had stepped off a tractor in Idaho to be given a pair of dark sunglasses and his very own aeroplane and he still couldn't quite believe his luck.

Ilsa had finally had her journalist credentials restored. She had not waited for the clearance, as seats on transport aircraft were hard to come by. Ilsa had counted on luck to stay alive and the desire to be reunited with her fiancé and find her father again overrode her willingness to remain in the States.

Ed had organised a flight out of Hawaii heading to

Port Moresby, where Clark, it seemed, was still based.

'Welcome aboard, ma'am,' the young pilot said from behind his sunglasses. 'I'm a big fan of your work.'

Ilsa returned his smile and wondered if he had read her columns in between reading comic books. 'Thanks, Lieutenant,' she said as he indicated for her to clamber aboard with her kit. She found a canvas seat between wooden crates of medical supplies and buckled herself in.

With the roar of its two powerful engines, the Douglas taxied out and sped down the concrete strip to rise into the tropical sky over the waters of the Hawaiian Islands. Ilsa had been briefed that their first stop would be Fiji, where she would be able to avail herself of a comfortable bed, hot shower and good meal before the transport aircraft continued its next leg to a strip in New Britain. Although still active further north, enemy aircraft no longer posed a threat to Allied aircraft in this part of the Pacific, so the flight should be relatively uneventful.

Ilsa settled into her seat, stared at the brown wax paper bag near her hand and hoped that she would not have to use it. Flying was not something she liked much and she forced herself to take her mind off the stuffiness of the aircraft's interior and the bumpy flight with thoughts of her reunion with Clark and meeting up once again with Jack Kelly. At least she could thank him for saving Clark and that would be a start.

*

Major Karl Mann crouched behind a large tropical tree and covered his ears with his hands. The roar of the nearby explosion swept over him with a concussive wave of heat.

'Very good, sir,' an English voice said, and Karl turned to look up at his assessor, Sergeant Major Robbins, a British warrant officer with a stiff moustache and swagger stick under his arm. Karl was amused to see that the normally immaculately turned-out Robbins was spattered in mud. Karl had handled demolition charges hundreds of times and had deliberately set his charge to produce this effect – it was childish perhaps, but he was finding the retraining very boring. Still, at least it gave him a chance to assess the Free French officer beside him. He and Karl had been introduced to each other in the secret training camp near Cairns, and had been singled out from the other trainees there to carry out special training on their own.

'Your turn, sir,' said Robbins, attempting to ignore the mud dripping from his face.

Karl watched as Captain Hung van Pham opened the canvas bag containing the plasticine-like explosive and placed it on a rainforest log. Karl prided himself on being able to get on with most men but he had found the Eurasian aloof to the point of rudeness. Perhaps the French officer did not like people of German origin, not that Karl like the French much himself. The Australian Army had fought the French Foreign Legion in Syria and had beaten them too.

Pham had only seemed animated when briefing Karl on his country, people and culture.

'Indochina is composed of three main regions,' he had told him, standing before a large map drawn by French surveyors before the war. 'Tonkin in the north – with its capital of Hanoi; Annam in the middle – the capital being Hue; and, finally, Cochin China in the south – with Saigon as the main centre. We refer to ourselves as Vietnamese and I have been told that we are the result of a mix of those from the south in the islands of Dutch East Indies and the Chinese from the north, who are also our traditional enemies. Many people have tried to invade and occupy us over the years but we have resisted. Even the great Mongol armies fought us in our jungles and were defeated. Only the French have been successful and it is to them that we owe much. Our style of writing script is European, and my people have acquired a taste for bread. My land is a country of rice paddies, jungles, wild mountains and monsoon rains. It is beautiful beyond your imagining, but the peasants need the stability of government that the French have imposed on us. Do you have any questions?'

Karl stared at the slim and neatly dressed young officer. 'Are you French or Vietnamese?' he asked bluntly.

'I am French,' Pham answered without hesitation. 'I am accepted by the French as one of them.'

Karl did not comment; he suspected that the French were as racist as the Germans, and that Pham was living in a bubble.

However, during the weeks of retraining in special warfare tactics, Karl had to concede that the French officer knew his stuff. Even now he moved with the litheness of a hunting cat as they retreated to their protected position. The explosion went off as planned, shattering the rainforest log, and this time Robbins retreated several yards to avoid being splattered again.

Karl stood and stretched. His uniform was wet with

sweat and stiff with mud. He noticed a movement in the trees and caught sight of a familiar face.

'Why does it not surprise me to see you here, sir?' he said to Captain Featherstone.

'Ah, Major Mann, it is good to see that the Zed people have not killed you off yet.' Featherstone said.

'How are you, Pham?' the British officer asked.

'I am well, sir,' Pham answered in French.

'You are to report to the orderly room for your movement papers,' Featherstone continued in French. 'Tomorrow, be prepared to fly out. Your transport will be provided courtesy of the American navy.'

Karl noticed Pham glance at him and then turn on his heel to walk away.

'What's happening?' Karl asked.

'Pham is being deployed tomorrow,' Featherstone replied. 'You will be following soon enough. We just have to ensure that if anything goes wrong, then we lose only one man on the insertion. I would rather that not be you, Karl.'

'I am touched,' Karl smiled. 'I didn't think you had any human feelings.'

'You would be surprised,' Featherstone said dryly. 'You are to report to HQ at 1900 hours to receive your briefing,' he said. 'I can tell you that you will be first going to join one of our teams on the Malay Peninsula, before entering Indochina. Pham should be in position by the time you arrive and have made contact with the resistance people in Saigon. But first you will stay over at Moresby.'

Inwardly Karl groaned. He felt as if he were a pawn in

a game he didn't really understand. 'When the mission is complete and I return,' Karl said, 'I want a guarantee that I will be reassigned to an infantry battalion as a company commander. I want to see out this war fighting alongside my fellow Australians, not be sent out to die in some bloody forgotten part of the planet.'

Featherstone looked Karl directly in the eyes. 'I promise that if you return, you will be given this guarantee.'

'Thank you, sir,' Karl replied dutifully, although he hadn't missed the fact that Featherstone had said 'if' not 'when'.

'If Sergeant Major Robbins has finished with you today, then I'm sure you would appreciate a drink in the mess, old boy.' Featherstone turned to the British warrant officer discreetly hovering out of hearing. 'Sergeant Major, permission to dismiss Major Mann from his training for the day?' he said loudly.

Robbins came to attention.

'Yes, sir,' he snapped. 'Major Mann has finished his training on the range.'

Karl picked up his pack and rifle, and walked with Featherstone away from the demolitions range.

'I may as well tell you now, old chap, that this mission was not my idea,' Featherstone said. 'But it is vital that when the war is won, the French return to Indochina and take possession before Ho Chi Minh seizes control. We know even now that the native peoples of Asia are stirring for freedom from their old colonial masters, and that includes our Chinese communist allies in Malaya.'

Featherstone stopped suddenly and turned to Karl with an anxious expression. 'I would caution you to keep an eye on Pham at all times. Try to stay out of his dealings with his fellow countrymen. Your task is to get Herlinde Kroth to safety so that we can debrief her.'

'I thought that we were helping her because of her father,' Karl said.

'Ah, yes, that is correct,' Featherstone answered uneasily as the two men walked into an open area of tents and Nissan huts around a small gravel parade ground. He stopped at the edge of the clearing. 'Miss Kroth is the mistress of a high-ranking Vichy official collaborating with the Japanese. She is in a position to reach members of the Japanese imperial staff in Saigon. After all, the Japanese and Germans are on the same side.'

The British officer wished that he could describe the bigger picture to his courageous and loyal agent, but the military protocols were strict in these matters. Karl was a mere, and expendable, pawn in an international game of deadly chess where the pieces would be moved around the board with one of the players blindfolded. In this case it was Major Mann. Featherstone's superiors continually and erratically changed their priorities in the strategic game of politics. The Allies were sure of victory and were even now plotting a new world order when the guns fell silent across the globe. One Australian Army major was of little or no consequence to their devious end game and Featherstone often found it hard to sleep when he knew that he had to lie to those who trusted him.

'What will my cover be in Saigon?' Karl asked.

'Your papers will say that you are a German civil engineer sent out by Albert Speer – the Nazi minister for industry and armaments – to liaise with Jap equivalents there. The role should get you close to Miss Kroth. Need-less to say, we have prepared all the documents you will need to carry the whole thing off. You did this in Palestine and I know you can do it again.'

Karl was not reassured – he had barely made it out of Palestine alive. Featherstone was right about one thing, though, he could do with a drink. He was going to drink a heck of a lot this evening, and put it all on the SOE officer's chit. It was the least Featherstone could do for him.

★

The flight from Hawaii was a series of island-hopping exercises south and then west from New Britain to Port Moresby. Despite his youth, the pilot was skilful enough to land on islands in the vast expanse of the Pacific, deliver-ing supplies and picking up mail. They were flying in the backwater of the war, but the islands fought over by the US marines and army still bore the fresh scars of battle: shattered coconut trees, shell craters full of stagnant water, and the lingering stench of decomposing flesh.

During the landing stops, Ilsa availed herself of any opportunity to bathe and freshen up at the rear echelon rest areas, where gaunt-faced young boys stared at her with the eyes of old men. She knew that these old eyes in young, emaciated bodies wracked by dysentery and tropi-cal disease had seen too much of the inhumanity of man. She also knew that their bodies might recover but didn't think their souls ever would.

At the appointed time Ilsa returned to the airstrip,

stepping carefully over great land crabs scavenging for the scraps of human flesh still fertilising the tropical earth. Her aeroplane was loaded and the young pilot beckoned cheerfully to her from the window of his flight cabin. Ilsa was helped aboard by a smartly dressed US Army colonel wearing his full uniform. He helped her to her canvas seat against the wall.

'You heading for Moresby?' he asked as Ilsa buckled herself in.

'Yes, Colonel,' she replied as the side door was slammed shut. 'You too?'

'Got a conference there,' he answered, strapping in beside Ilsa and being cast envious looks from two young soldiers opposite. Rank had its privileges. 'What's a pretty young thing like you doing in a war zone?' he asked condescendingly.

Ilsa took an immediate dislike to this middle-aged officer who was most probably in some staff appointment, safely tucked away from the fighting.

'I'm a correspondent for a New York newspaper and have just completed a posting with General Patton's armoured advance through France,' she replied and noticed the pompous colonel's expression change. The Allied press had given much coverage to the colourful American's victories in Europe and it was known that he led his men into the worst of the fighting.

The roar and shake of the aircraft throttling up for a take-off dampened any further conversation and Ilsa was glad. She tucked behind her head a dappled poncho rolled into a ball and dozed off as the plane ascended into the azure sky. She did not know how long she had been asleep when she was jolted awake by the aircraft being flung about.

Ilsa strained her neck to look out a porthole and was alarmed by what she saw. It was obvious that they had flown into a fierce tropical storm and all the pilot could do was fight to keep his aeroplane in the air. When she turned to glance at the colonel, she could see he was ashen with fear. 'These are tough birds,' she shouted over the crack of lightning outside. 'I am sure we'll be out of this soon.'

The colonel bent forward, reached for a brown wax paper bag and was instantly sick. Now the stench of vomit mixed with the smell of aviation fuel inside the stifling interior. The two young soldiers opposite attempted to look brave but Ilsa guessed they were as frightened as she was.

Suddenly the twin-engine aircraft dropped, causing the unseated loadmaster checking the strapping on the supplies to be flung upwards; he crashed back down onto the metal floor and did not move. Ilsa saw the pool of blood oozing from his head and knew that he was either dead or gravely injured. She unbuckled her restraint and went down on her knees to crawl towards him, and was joined by one of the young soldiers.

Ilsa could see from the expression on the loadmaster's face that he was dead. His eyes were open and staring up without seeing. She felt for a pulse and could not find one.

'Is he okay?' the young soldier asked over her shoulder and she shook her head. He gaped at the airman's dead body and Ilsa sensed that this young man had never seen death before.

'Are you a reinforcement?' she asked, to distract the soldier from his fear.

'Yes, ma'am,' he replied, backing away from the body.

The aircraft was flung sideways then and the soldier toppled onto Ilsa, staining them both with the blood of the dead man. When Ilsa disentangled herself from the soldier, she noticed that there was an eerie orange glow inside the aircraft. She glanced out through a starboard porthole. One of the engines was on fire and trailing a plume of flames.

'God in heaven,' she groaned. They were surely going to crash into the Solomon Sea.

*

Lukas Kelly had returned to Port Moresby just ahead of the tropical storm. His mission to supply Milne Bay had gone off without any trouble and the old boat had performed well in the increasingly stormy waters.

Cruising into the harbour through the warships and transports, Lukas strained to see whether he recognised anyone standing on the wharf amongst the bustle of sweating workers unloading ships. He could see no sign of Megan and felt a twinge of disappointment. Then he caught sight of a familiar figure – what was his father doing here?

Lukas found a spot vacated by an old cargo ship and expertly brought the *Riverside* into the wharf. The Papuan crew leaped nimbly to the wharf to secure the lines, and Lukas cut the engine while Mel Jones stood on the deck, eying the ships in the harbour.

'Hello, Dad,' Lukas said, smiling up at his father. 'I'm

surprised to see you here. I thought you would be up north with the boys.'

Jack held out his hand and helped his son onto the wharf. 'The army says I'm too old to go out with the boys, so I'm attached to our intelligence section here. Going cross-eyed staring at aerial photos and drinking too much grog. How have you been?'

'Good. Nothing much to report, although we just missed a bad storm near Milne Bay,' Lukas replied, walking with his father through the mass of half-naked bodies unloading the ships. Cranes lifted cargo nets from the ships' holds to the wharf, where native workers and servicemen worked side by side to sort and load waiting lorries. 'Have you seen Megan lately?'

An odd look crossed Jack's face. 'She didn't have a chance to tell you,' he replied, 'but yesterday Megan was posted up north with her RAAF nursing detachment. She was only able to give me a quick call to say where she was going and to ask me to pass on the news to you.'

'Bloody hell!' Lukas exclaimed. 'That'll put her closer to the front.'

'She'll be okay,' Jack reassured him. 'There are very few reports of the Nips being active where she's going. She'll be in a rear-echelon area.'

Lukas shook his head but trusted his father's assessment. After all, working with intelligence meant he had access to the latest news on the enemy.

Jack's face broke into a broad grin. 'I know Megan is not here to meet you but, by chance, I found some big bastard wandering around HQ yesterday, looking a bit lost. I left him at the pub and he said he thinks it's his turn to shout.'

Lukas looked at his father in bemusement. 'Who in bloody hell could that be?' he asked.

'Wait and see,' said Jack mischievously.

★

In the crowded bar of the hotel, Lukas found himself face to face with Major Karl Mann. The two men had to blink back the tears as they embraced each other in a great bear hug and then stood back to assess how the war years had changed them both.

'You old bastard, what in hell are you doing here?' Lukas asked, reaching for a bottle of beer.

'Just passing through,' Karl said, reaching for his own beer. 'I bumped into Uncle Jack yesterday at PIB HQ. It seems that someone has had enough sense to keep him away from the fighting.'

'Not my bloody decision,' Jack growled. 'Why should younger people have all the fun of dying for King and Country?'

'How long are you going to be with us?' Lukas asked.

'Not sure,' Karl replied. 'I'm supposed to be somewhere north of here but the army changed its mind at the last moment, and so I am here with you two reprobates to catch up on some drinking.'

As night descended, the rowdy patrons were evicted from the hotel and the three men staggered back to Lukas's boat, where he kept a small stash of alcohol. The boat was temporarily deserted, so the three men sat down on the deck under a star-filled night and passed the bottle between themselves.

'Got to show you something,' Lukas said, staggering to his feet and reeling off towards the cabin. Jack and Karl listened hazily as Lukas crashed around in the cabin, returning minutes later, gripping a tiny box. He flopped down awkwardly and passed the box to Karl, who opened it to see the tiny flash of a gemstone catching in the feeble moonlight.

'Giving this to Megan when I see her next,' Lukas said, reaching for the bottle passed to him by his father. 'I got it sent up from Sydney from a mate in the business. Reckon she'll like it?' The worst-kept secret amongst the tight-knit group of Papuan hands and old timers was Lukas Kelly and Megan's romance. There was simply a presumption that they were already engaged to be married, and many of Jack's friends would kid him that he was not far off becoming a grandfather.

'She'll like the ring – but I don't know about the bloke giving it to her,' Karl grinned.

'Yeah, you stupid galoot, what would a square-headed Hun know about romance?' Lukas slurred. 'You still seeing that French sheila?'

Karl ceased smiling and stared across the bay. 'She met another bloke and married him,' he answered finally, taking a long swig from the bottle Lukas handed to him. 'A bloody civil servant. He was a bloke we went to school with.'

Lukas reached over to put his arm around Karl's shoulders. 'Sorry, cobber. Her loss.'

The men passed the bottle around in silence.

'Are you going back to being a *kiap* when the war is over?' Jack asked eventually.

'I think so,' Karl answered. 'But I have to survive until then.'

'You going on a dangerous mission, son?' Jack said with concern.

'Yes. Wish I could tell you what it's about but I don't have much of an idea myself,' Karl answered sadly. 'All I know is this damned war is going to drag on as long as the Nips are prepared to die to the last man for their bloody emperor. Our kids will end up fighting this war, the rate things are going.'

The three men eventually fell asleep on the deck and, just before first light, awoke with the worst hangovers any of them could remember having had for a long time.

Karl staggered to his feet and looked for a supply of cool drinking water. The harbour was already alive with activity and when he glanced up at the wharf, he saw a smartly turned-out young naval lieutenant, dressed in the uniform of an intelligence officer, gazing down at him with some concern.

'Major Mann,' he called and Karl rubbed his face; he felt as though hundreds of tiny spiders were crawling across his skin.

'I'm Major Mann,' he answered, and the lieutenant saluted him.

'Captain Featherstone wishes to see you within the hour,' the young officer said. 'I have come to pick you up.'

Jack and Lukas, both looking as bad as Karl felt, wandered along the deck to see what was going on.

'Who's Featherstone?' Jack asked.

'A pommy bastard who spends most of his time trying to get me killed,' Karl answered, brushing down his

97

dishevelled uniform. 'I was rather hoping I'd left him behind in Cairns.'

Jack placed his hand on Karl's shoulder. 'You keep your bloody head down,' he said gently.

'Thanks, Uncle Jack,' Karl responded and looked away so Jack wouldn't see his eyes filling with tears. He was not so much afraid of dying as of being killed in some lonely place away from anyone who was important to him. If he died on this mission, these two men who were like family to him would never be told the details, never know where or how he spent his final hours. 'The same to you and this stupid galah you call a son.'

Grinning, Lukas lashed out playfully with a snap punch to Karl's arm. Despite his hangover, Karl was quick and dodged the punch, countering with a block. 'You're getting old and slow, Lukas,' he said as they hugged each other emotionally.

'How did this Featherstone bloke know where you were?' Jack asked as Karl clambered up onto the wharf.

'The bastard knows everything about me,' Karl answered. 'I can't even take a crap without him knowing what I ate the day before. Well, so long, boys, your shout when I get back.'

He gave a brief wave, then turned his back and was gone.

SEVEN

In the chilly clear blue skies over Berlin the trailing white streaks of the American bombers' contrails could still be seen. *Hauptsturmfuhrer* Konrad Herff barely looked up as he entered the shrapnel-scarred building that contained his office. He wore the smart uniform of a *Sicherheitsdienst* officer under a long black leather coat and carried his brief-case in his hand. His eyes were rheumy with lack of sleep from when the English bombers came in the dark of the night to unleash hell over the country's capital, and by day the Americans visited to do the same.

Herff was in his mid-thirties, lean and blond in the image desired by his organisation's leader, Heinrich Himmler. Herff reported directly to his section leader, Ernst Kaltenbrunner, commander of the *Sicherheitsdienst,* the security service of the *Schutzstaffel*, the secret state police known as the SS. Since the latest terrible attempt on the Führer's life, in July 1944, the *Abwehr*, the military intelligence department, had been put under the control of the SS, as it had proved to be a breeding ground of traitors. Many of them had died slowly, hanging from wire nooses in grim basements, for their treachery.

As a captain in Department C of the *Ausland* division of the SD, in charge of monitoring intelligence primarily from the Russian and Japanese fronts, Herff had read the latest report of Allied prisoners taken by their Japanese allies. One name had jumped out at him as he had sat at his desk, poring over the lists – Ilsa Stahl, American war correspondent. Herff knew that name well, as a predecessor of his in the fledgling SS had defected to the Americans and given away valuable information. Herff knew that the traitor Gerhard Stahl's daughter had become a journalist for the American press and been spouting anti-Nazi propaganda.

What had made Fräulein Ilsa Stahl more interesting was that her father had known the esteemed Führer in the early days of his rise through the beer halls and streets of Munich. It was known that Hitler had had a deep hatred for the traitor Stahl and would almost certainly be delighted if the man's daughter, with her vitriolic editorials against the Nazi party, were eliminated.

Herff smiled to himself. She was a prisoner of the Japanese, who would, most undoubtedly, hand her over to the SS if requested. A film of the woman twisting at the end of the thin wire would definitely please the Führer, who would see that his loyal SS people could still reach halfway around the world to snatch those who had betrayed the Fatherland. No doubt Herff would be mentioned as the man who had identified her and organised for her to face Nazi justice. Herff would simply inform the Japanese that Ilsa Stahl was wanted for questioning and then await their notification of her whereabouts. From there it was simply a matter of ending her life as slowly and painfully as possible.

★

The confines stunk of unwashed bodies, fish and diesel, and sweat glistened on Ilsa's skin like oil. Her hands were tied tightly behind her back and she kept her eyes lowered under the stare of her guard. There was no throbbing from the engine of the Japanese submarine as it glided beneath calm, tropical waters under power from its electric batteries.

It was two days since the young American pilot had ditched his cargo plane in the eye of the storm. They had drifted wildly off course and come down in the Bismark Sea. The Douglas had hit the water so violently that it had severed the spinal cord of the young soldier who had been so shocked by the loadmaster's death, and he had died before the others had even been able to get to him. The survivors had struggled from the disabled plane into a life raft. The raft had carried Ilsa, the colonel, the young pilot and his copilot, as well as the remaining soldier. The colonel had taken immediate command because of his superior rank, and the passengers had watched the black horizon as the storm threatened once again to engulf them.

Ilsa's body had ached so much from the impact that

she almost hadn't cared whether they survived the storm. She felt she had survived man's wrath on the battlefields of Europe only to be killed by nature. It seemed too bitterly ironic.

She had not been alone in her injuries. The young pilot sustained a severe head wound and the colonel had suffered a broken arm.

A few hours after being thrown about in the ever more furious seas, a submarine had surfaced nearby.

'It's a bloody Jap sub,' the colonel groaned, dashing all hope of rescue. 'Did you get a mayday off before we crashed?' he asked the pilot, who nodded. 'I think the Japs might have intercepted your signal.'

The terrified survivors watched as the armed Japanese sailors emerged on deck. The submarine closed the distance until it came alongside the raft. One of the Japanese, wearing the insignia of an officer, glared down at them.

'What rank?' he yelled.

'Colonel, United States Army,' the colonel answered through gritted teeth. 'There is also a lieutenant of the United States Air Force and a private first class soldier . . . and the lady is a war correspondent.'

The Japanese officer seemed satisfied at the answer. 'You, colonel and lady, come aboard.'

At his order a couple of submariners reached down to hoist Ilsa and the colonel onto the slippery wet deck of the sub. The colonel screamed as his broken arm was wrenched in the boarding, but his pain did not elicit any sympathy from his captors.

'What about the other three in the raft?' the colonel gasped, doubled over in agony.

'No use,' the officer said and then a machine gun broke into an ear-splitting roar. The survivors watched in horror as the bullets ripped into the bodies of the three men left behind in the raft.

That had been two days earlier, although it seemed a lifetime ago now to Ilsa. She did not moralise over the event – she had heard from soldiers returning from the Pacific fronts that no mercy was asked or given on either side.

The Japanese officer who had ordered the killing had a limited knowledge of English but his radioman, a young sailor with a kind face, was quite fluent and he conducted the questioning on behalf of the officer.

When Ilsa provided her full name the radioman said, 'You have German name.'

'How do you know that?' she asked, surprised, feeling that this man was not in the same brutal mould as the officer supervising the interrogation.

'I once work with German navy on secondment,' he answered. 'Are you German citizen?'

Ilsa was tempted to say she was, but knew her lie would be hopeless, since she wore the uniform of an American correspondent and carried identification.

'No, but I was born in Germany,' she replied.

The radioman turned to his superior and said something in Japanese, and the expression on the officer's face changed. He leaned forward and delivered a vicious backhanded blow to Ilsa's face, splitting her lip.

'You traitor,' he screamed and Ilsa could taste her own blood. 'I kill you, traitor.' He grabbed her by the hair but the radioman said something and he relaxed his grip.

She sensed that whatever the man had said had saved her life – for the moment, anyway.

Since then, Ilsa had been left in a stinking corner of the sub's tiny storeroom. She did not know where they were holding the colonel, or whether he was even still alive. The only time she was allowed out of her confinement was to go to the toilet, and she was fed only a small serving of dried fish and rice each day.

On the third day the kindly Japanese radioman came to her. He even brought her a supplementary meal of soya beans and rice.

'We know who you are, Miss Stahl,' he said, untying her hands so she could eat with her fingers. 'You are daughter of . . . what you say . . . high-ranking intelligence officer. German officer wants you to be taken to him for further questioning. I am sorry.'

'My father is dead and I know nothing of his work in Germany. What about the other man who came aboard with me?' Ilsa asked, shovelling the salty food into her mouth with her fingers.

'The American officer is being held forward,' the radioman answered. 'He has been treated for broken arm.'

Ilsa finished the meal, thinking how strange it was to be talking to a man who was her enemy but towards whom she could not help but feel warmth. He looked so young, and not unlike the many soldiers she had met in the course of her work covering the Allied armies.

She was about to ask him more questions when suddenly the tiny room reverberated with a concussive thump. The radioman leaped to his feet, his face ashen with fear. The thump was followed by another and the submarine heeled to port for a moment. The radioman ran out of the storeroom and disappeared. Clearly a depth charger had been dropped nearby, and the lighting flickered for a moment, then went out. It came on a moment later, more dimly now.

Fortunately Ilsa's hands were still untied and she was able to brace herself against the violent reverberations caused by deadly drums of high explosives drifting down on the Japanese vessel. She caught herself praying that they would survive and wondered that her instinct to live could outweigh the wish to see her enemy destroyed. The thought of dying in this enemy coffin filled her with dread.

Ilsa remained in the storeroom, tins clattering down around her, but the sub appeared to be weathering the underwater barrage. Eventually the barrage lifted and she could hear the muted voices of the crew talking to each other in urgent whispers. Ilsa was ignored for a good few hours until eventually the radioman returned.

'We will not be taking you to Singapore,' he said, gesturing for her to turn around so he could retie her hands. 'Submarine take bad damage and captain decide to put you off with our army on coast.'

'What does that mean?' she asked.

'I do not know,' the sailor replied, not looking her in the eye. 'I pray you safe.'

Ilsa shuddered. It sounded as though where she was being sent was even worse than the steel coffin she was in now.

Two more days passed and then the sub's brutal commander came for her. She was hoisted to her feet and dragged to the hatchway opening onto the deck. It was then that she saw the American colonel for the first time since their captivity, and noticed with horror that he had been severely beaten about the face and body. He was stripped to his pants and his pale chest was covered in livid bruises and burn marks.

Ilsa was forced up to the deck first and, despite her fear, she revelled in the sudden exposure to the fresh air of a tropical night. The sailors escorting her poked at her with rifles to climb aboard a native canoe and, even under the dim moonlight, she could see that it was manned by four soldiers wearing the uniform of Japanese Special Landing Forces. She had been schooled in recognising Japanese uniforms and insignia before leaving the USA and from what she knew of these men, they were as good as her own country's marines.

The colonel was lowered into the canoe and the Japanese marines pushed away from the hull of the sub. When Ilsa twisted around to look at the colonel, she saw that his head was slumped and he was almost unconscious. She could also see that the sub was already making its way back to the open sea. By now she could smell the fetid scent of rotting vegetation wafting from the shoreline. She felt a rush of terror for what lay ahead. Thoughts of escape did not enter her mind, as she did not know where on earth she was. Were they rowing to an island or to the mainland? Where in the hell of the Pacific were they?

The boat beached on a strip of sand lapped by tiny waves and Ilsa was forced to step into the shallows. Warmish water lapped around her knees as she waded ashore, to be confronted by two shadowy figures.

'You are Miss Ilsa Stahl?' one of the figures asked in fluent English.

'I am,' she replied as the American colonel was forced to his knees beside her.

'And you are Colonel Ira Hazelton?'

The colonel grunted and Ilsa realised that until now she had not known his name.

'I am Petty Officer First Class Fuji Komine and I will interpret on behalf of Lieutenant Yoshi of the Imperial Navy. Do not think of escape – you will be caught and severely punished. However, if you are obedient, you will be well looked after while you are a prisoner of the Emperor.'

Ilsa looked to the officer standing beside Fuji and, even in the dark, she sensed that this might not be so. She and the American colonel were marched off the beach into the jungle, along a winding track to a village. There, she was forced into a cage made from bamboo; Hazelton into another a few feet away, whilst a guard with a bayonet-tipped rifle stood by on watch. Ilsa wanted to cry in her despair but would not allow herself the luxury. It was obvious that her stepfather had been a man of importance to Hitler's regime. Ilsa had only been a very young girl when her family defected from Germany and the machinations of Nazi politics were beyond her. Her stepfather deliberately shielded her from his world of intelligence intrigue but after his death she was able to put some of the pieces together. When she asked a friend in the FBI why he was important to the Americans, she had been quickly informed that the information was classified – even from her. All that Ilsa could glean was that her stepfather had been in a position close to the German leader and knew much about the infrastructure of the Third Reich; she had a new life as an American citizen and had put all that behind her in her pursuit of her journalistic career. Ilsa expected that the Japanese would eventually hand her over to the Gestapo for interrogation. She was aware of what interrogation meant in the hands of the dreaded German security police and knew that the best she could hope for was a quick death before they got their hands on her. She considered suicide but a tiny flame of hope still flickered. She was alive at least, and in far better condition than the colonel in the cage next to her.

So far she had not seen any of the local villagers from the surrounding huts and wondered if they were still alive, but when the morning dawned she woke from a fitful sleep to look up into the face of a cluster of curious wide-eyed children watching her. The youngest of them stood naked with thumbs in mouths, just staring, and Ilsa guessed that they had never seen a white woman before. She felt suddenly self-conscious, as she knew she must look terrible in her torn and frayed trousers and shirt. She had not bathed since leaving the last American air base and was losing track of time – had it been a week, a month?

The Japanese man who had identified himself as the interpreter appeared and spoke to the guard, who opened the cage. Fuji had a bowl containing a gruel of rice and fatty pork pieces. It stank, but Ilsa took it gratefully.

'You may come out and stretch your legs, Miss Stahl,' he said. 'No doubt you will wish to avail yourself of some privacy.'

Ilsa nodded her head, biting into the cold, greasy pork

pieces. Like the radioman on the enemy submarine, this man seemed sympathetic to her condition. She had always been told that the Japanese were devils incapable of humane treatment of prisoners; but, in her short time incarcerated, two of them had proven otherwise.

When she glanced over, she could see that a guard was furnishing the colonel with a similar meal. He was propped against the back of his makeshift prison, eating with feeble motions, and did not look at her.

The Japanese interpreter – Fuji, that was his name, Ilsa remembered now – sat on a log, pistol on his hip, watching her eat in silence. When she had finished, she wiped her fingers on her trousers and he took her to a bush latrine; when she had finished, he returned her to the cage and left her without a word.

Later in the day, two armed guards dragged the colonel from his cage and into a building at the end of the open space in the centre of the village, now alive with people, pigs and mangy dogs. None of the villagers dared come close, although they stared at her from a distance. However, it was not only the villagers who watched her.

From the edges of the jungle, a patrol of PIB soldiers lay in the scrub, watching the village. They had noted the captives and duly scrawled down the sighting. There were only three soldiers in the patrol, so they were not in any position to attempt an attack on the enemy, and they moved on at nightfall.

Ilsa huddled with her knees under her chin and tried to blot out the screams coming from the far end of the village. She knew that the enemy were torturing the American officer and wondered if she would be next.

Ilsa broke down then and sobbed quietly – lest her guard hear her despair.

★

Captain Clark Nixon bridled at waiting for a new bomber and replacement crew. While waiting he had been assigned to the operations room at the Moresby airfield, used mostly by the RAAF but also as a transit base for American crews. At least his temporary posting put him in a position to see the bigger picture of air operations in the region.

Armed with a mug of coffee and a cigarette, Clark slumped into a deckchair in the operations hut and began to skim through the daily situational reports of air ops. His mug froze an inch from his mouth when he saw a name on a search and rescue report for a downed transport Douglas: Ilsa Stahl, war correspondent.

Clark felt sick. The report referred to a search carried out a week earlier. She had mentioned that she was attempting to catch a flight to Port Moresby to meet him.

'Captain Nixon, you all right?' the clerk asked, entering the office with a mug of coffee and observing his superior officer's ashen expression and trembling hands. Clark did not respond. 'You got a touch of fever?' the clerk persisted.

'No, Corporal,' Clark finally answered, dragging his eyes from the terrible words that had burned their message into his brain – *Missing In Action*. 'I'm okay.'

A jumble of thoughts filled his head. MIA – not confirmed dead. There was hope in that, wasn't there? After all, he had been listed MIA and was now safe. He tried to order his thoughts, to think through this logically. Where had the aircraft last been sighted? The coordinates of the search area took in a large region, and Clark stood up and walked over to a large map on the wall, tracing the latitudes and longitudes he had lifted from the report. He knew this was a region still considered hostile and he hoped that they had made it to an island or even to the mainland. But he felt his hopes crash when he recalled that the search mission had not spotted any rafts in the now calm seas.

He returned to his chair and buried his face in his hands. His tears were silent but his broad shoulders heaved with his weeping, and the corporal, seeing the captain's distress, quietly backed from the room and left him to his grief.

EIGHT

Stunned, Jack Kelly sat at his desk, scattered with reports and aerial photos.

The overhead fan turned slowly, barely moving the air in the tiny room, as Captain Clark Nixon waited for the Australian to respond.

'Ilsa,' Jack said finally. The American pilot had explained how Ilsa had told him in her letters that Jack was her father and that she hoped to meet him again soon. Jack had hardly been able to take in what Nixon was telling him. 'And her flight went down off the northern coast?'

'I only found out this morning myself,' Clark said. 'I felt you had a right to know.'

Jack shook his head, still reeling from the news. How ironic that he had unknowingly saved his daughter's boyfriend from the Japanese, and now she herself was missing.

'Bloody hell!' Jack suddenly said, leaping to his feet and reaching for a clipboard of field reports. 'There was a report from one of our PIB recon patrols yesterday of a European woman and unidentified male taken prisoner by the Japs up on the northern coast. They reported that the woman they'd seen was relatively well nourished – what are the chances of that if she'd been a prisoner for long?'

'Where did the patrol position the prisoners?' Clark asked, walking over to a large-scale map of New Guinea and the surrounding islands.

Jack scanned the typed report and read off the coordinates. Clark traced the latitude and longitude with his finger, to settle on a spot on the coast. He shook his head.

'It is a long way from where her plane was reported missing,' he said in a dejected tone. 'Maybe there's some other European woman the Japs have as a captive. The bastards could have taken her from some POW camp for their own amusement. Why didn't your boys attempt a rescue?'

'They didn't have the numbers, so they fell back and made the report. Our boys will put together a fighting patrol and go in some time soon.'

'If the woman is Ilsa, isn't there anything more we can do?' Clark asked, sounding desperate. 'That part of the coast is under Aussie control.'

'Regardless of who the woman is, our boys will attempt a rescue,' Jack answered calmly. 'But your MacArthur has a policy of detouring past small detachments of Japs. So we'll have to make do with the meagre forces we have, and it could take a while to muster enough men to go after the Nips.'

'If you were certain it was Ilsa,' Clark said quietly, 'would you pull out every stop to rescue her?'

'Of course,' he replied. 'I'm her father. But I'll do the very best I can, whoever this woman is.'

The two men looked at each other. 'You know,' Clark said, 'you could be my father-in-law. A goddamned Aussie.'

Jack smiled at the thought. 'Don't worry, Yank,' he said, mustering all his bravado, 'I don't believe Ilsa is dead – she has Kelly blood, and it takes more than the Japanese navy and army to kill a Kelly. If she's out there I will personally get her back for the wedding.'

The American officer thrust out his hand. 'Thanks . . . Jack,' he said, dropping all military formality of rank. 'You give me hope – because I have seen you in action.'

Jack gripped the American's hand. 'I have friends in sig-int,' he said. 'Maybe they have something we can work from.'

Clark frowned. 'Those signal intelligence people are a secretive lot, but if anyone can get information out of them, Jack Kelly can. Now,' he said, replacing his cap, 'I have to return to base. I am due for a new crate tomorrow and new crew. It is back to the war for me but I will make sure I am in regular contact in case anything develops. Keep me posted.'

'I promise I will,' Jack said, returning to his desk to find his little black book of names and military positions. 'I promise you that we'll get her back.' Despite all logical arguments about the odds of his estranged daughter still being alive, Jack dismissed any doubts, with the paternal and unshakeable logic that no harm could come to his daughter. He, after all, was her father and the powers above gave him the right to live in confident hope that he would find her.

When Captain Clark Nixon had left the office, Jack sat staring at the wall. He slid open a drawer and pulled out a cherished photograph. It had been taken by Ilsa's photographer the one time they had met. Ilsa looked so much like her mother that it could have been Jack and Erika in the photo; even so, there was a stiff formality in the poses of both father and daughter that indicated they were virtual strangers.

Jack remembered how wild and unpredictable Erika had been. The young and beautiful sister of his best friend, Paul Mann, she had been obsessed with a former German army corporal she had met in his early days of street oratory – Adolf Hitler. He had dined with the Mann family and his passion to restore Germany's greatness had inflamed Erika's own vision of her country's future. Erika had deserted Jack when she was pregnant by him with Ilsa.

Jack stared at the photograph for some time, then put it back in the drawer and walked out of the office.

*

'Bloody hell, Jack,' the signals corps sergeant moaned. 'You know I can't tell you what we decode.'

Jack had found an old gold-prospecting colleague who had been enlisted into the signals corp. Since his posting to the Port Moresby HQ, Jack had swapped stories and beers with the signals corps sergeant in their mess and had never once pried into his old friend's work – until now. The two men were drinking beer in the mess, an old building set up not far from where they both worked. It was virtually empty, which was what Jack wanted.

'What if you suspected that your daughter was being held a prisoner by the Japs up north?' Jack asked, sipping his beer. 'Wouldn't you tell someone who might be in a position to do something?'

'Okay, Jack, I get your point,' the signals sergeant sighed. 'We did happen to decode some transmissions from a Jap post up north, but I doubt that any Yank woman called Ilsa Stahl could be related to you.'

At the mention of his daughter's name, Jack almost dropped his glass. He reached out and gripped his friend's arm. 'You're sure the name you had was Ilsa Stahl?' he asked, startling the other man.

'I'm sure,' the sergeant answered, staring at Jack with some surprise at the intensity in his friend's eyes. 'I was on duty when the sig was decoded. It seems the Japs want her to be transported to Singapore. That's all we know – except that earlier we intercepted a message from a Jap sub saying it was bringing her and a Yank colonel to the post for safekeeping until the woman was picked up. She must be of some importance for the Japs because they're sending a sub to fetch her, and we hope to provide a RAAF welcoming party when the sub arrives.'

Jack swallowed the rest of his beer and slammed some coins on the bar to pay for the next round of drinks. 'Thanks, cobber, I owe you one,' he said. 'Matter of fact, I'll make sure you get a case of the best Scotch I can find, if what you tell me pans out.'

Jack hurried back to his office. There was a lot of work

to be done, and most of it would not be strictly in compliance with the regulations of the Australian Army and Navy. Jack was acutely aware that he would have to rely on the loyalty of a lot of people if he were going to ask them to risk their careers and, in some cases, even their lives to help him rescue his daughter.

Jack rubbed his face and sighed. He would need transport, a force of soldiers and a plan to extract Ilsa and the other prisoner without them all being executed in the process. Jack doubted that he would receive official help in his mission; the Allied forces had already moved north of New Guinea in the quest to conquer the Japanese and this operation would be considered little more than a waste of resources. No, if he were to make an attempt, it would have to be with the help of friends, and one or two sympathetic officers in the PIB.

Jack stood up and walked to a safe that held the names and locations of the coastwatchers. It was an extremely sensitive system of files, due to the covert nature of the courageous men serving behind enemy lines and reporting on their movements at sea.

He dialled the combination he had committed to memory and removed a file covering the region where Ilsa had been sighted. He found a name of a coastwatcher working fifty miles from the location the PIB patrol had given. The coastwatcher should be able to provide a safe landing place for an amphibious assault, Jack mused. As for a craft to take a force in for a landing, he knew who would provide that. Lukas had already left Moresby for a supply run to the northern coast and, with any luck, could be contacted when the *Riverside* broadcast a sitrep.

Now all he needed was a force of tough, experienced soldiers to assist him. Corporal Gari and his section came immediately to mind. The last he had heard was the PIB NCO was still in the north and that his recommendation for the Distinguished Conduct Medal had been approved.

With the help of the coastwatcher, Lukas and Corporal Gari, Jack was sure he could pull off a rescue. All he needed now was to get permission to go north and join them.

Jack knocked on the door of Major Bill Travers's office, gave his smartest salute and walked in without waiting for permission.

'Sit down, Jack, and tell me what you want,' the major said wearily, placing his fountain pen on the desk.

'What makes you think I want anything, Bill?' Jack frowned.

'I know you, Jack,' the Australian major retorted. 'And I also know about this Yank sheila you seem to have a peculiar interest in.'

Jack was momentarily taken aback at his superior's knowledge, but then guessed that the signals sergeant must have said something; he couldn't really blame him, he was only covering his back. 'She's not just any Yank sheila, Bill,' he said, leaning forward slightly. 'She's my daughter.'

Travers stiffened in surprise. 'I thought you only had young Lukas.'

'It's a long story,' Jack replied. 'But she's definitely my daughter. I only met her briefly, back in '42, and I am afraid we lost contact – until now.'

'Jesus, Jack!' Travers exclaimed. 'Our intelligence chaps tell me she's the daughter of a high-ranking German intelligence officer who defected before the war. Apparently he gave away a lot of their secrets, and now, it seems, the Huns want their revenge.'

'He's her stepfather,' Jack said in a tired voice. 'By birth she is my daughter, and I will do anything within my means to rescue her from the bloody Japs.'

Travers pushed himself away from the desk and went to the map on the wall. He glanced at the reported location. 'It will be bloody difficult, Jack,' he mused. 'We can't spare any personnel or resources. You might be best waiting it out until we win this war and hoping that the Japs don't get a chance to hand her over to the Germans.'

'That's not likely. The Germans must want her pretty badly to be going to so much effort to get her,' he replied. 'I don't imagine the Japs have been treating her well, but it'll be nothing compared with what the Huns will do to her. Bill, I need your help to get her back before it's too late.'

'She's an American citizen,' Travers said. 'It's really a matter for them to organise a rescue mission. After all, the report also identified another Caucasian prisoner and, from what I have heard, the Yanks think it is most likely one of their staff officers who was on the same flight.'

'Bill, you and I both know that the Yanks are only interested in defeating the Japs in the Philippines. As far as they're concerned, New Guinea is just a backwater to be mopped up at a later date. By then it will be too late for Ilsa. We have to act now.'

Bill Travers returned to his desk, pulled open a drawer to retrieve a military form and proceeded to write on it. When the form was duly signed he passed it to Jack.

'That is your movement order to catch the next plane to join our boys up north,' he said. 'You have instructions to coordinate intelligence on my behalf in the region your daughter is being held. Needless to say I am not condoning any operations to rescue any Allied personnel. You have a month before you are to return to Moresby. You will coordinate with our man on coastwatching duties and will take all orders from Captain George Vincent in command of our detachment. Just don't make it as hard for George as you do for me – he's a good bloke.'

Jack's face widened in a broad smile of gratitude and he thrust out his hand. 'Thanks, cobber. When this is all over I'll shout you beers for a month.'

'Yes, you will, Jack,' the major replied. 'And put me at the top of your list. You've called in so many favours you'll be buying beers for the rest of your life – and I can't wait that long.'

Jack grinned again. 'I suppose I had better get back to the office and collect my kit then,' he said, gripping the precious piece of paper as if it were the winning slip on a long shot.

'Get out and good luck,' Travers said with a sigh and turned to the requisition forms on his desk.

Jack raised his hand in a salute and walked out.

★

Major Karl Mann kept his eyes closed until he heard the reassuring crack and felt the bite of the parachute straps against his body. Overhead he could hear the drone of the aircraft engines leaving him to enjoy briefly the coolness of the air high over the Malayan jungle as he descended.

Far below he could make out the smoke rising up to indicate the drop zone clearing. Within moments the air changed and he felt the heat rising from the ground. He readied himself for the impact with the earth. The pilot had judged well and Karl allowed his limp body to roll with the contact. Several Asian men rushed forward to assist him, and with them were three taller bearded Europeans, one of whom Karl knew.

The Chinese guerrillas were a fearsome sight, with their array of modern weapons and ancient long knives at their waists. Karl knew from his briefing that the Allied mixed team of SOE and OSS men was training and leading Chinese communist troops against the Japanese Army in Malaya.

Karl was helped to his feet and he watched as more parachutes appeared like flowers in the sky, to float earthwards with much needed stores of ammunition, food supplements and medical stores for the small guerrilla army operating deep behind enemy lines.

'Well, old chap,' said a heavily bearded and bronzed soldier. 'Welcome to our little private war at the arse end of the earth. You didn't happen to bring a crate of cold Aussie beer with you, by any chance?'

The speaker was a captain Karl had met in the commando training camp in Victoria years earlier. He had been a barrister before the war and now dispensed his own justice at the end of a .45 calibre Thompson submachine gun.

Captain David Carlton was as big and broad as Karl but, Karl noticed, the time in the jungles and hills of Malaya had taken a toll on the captain's health. Under the tan was a pallor associated with fever, and Karl could see that he had lost a lot of weight since they had last met.

'Sorry about the beer, Dave,' Karl said, dusting off his uniform and recovering his Owen gun. 'Good to see that you're still alive. I heard a rumour you copped it back in New Guinea.'

'That would not surprise me,' Carlton answered with a sigh. 'When Featherstone sends you off on a mission, you may as well be dead to the world. But I hear you won't be with us for very long. Your Froggie friend is back at camp awaiting your arrival. He's just returned from a trip across the Gulf of Siam to God knows where.'

Karl followed the column of jungle fighters as they carried the supplies from the drop zone. He found himself beating through the thick undergrowth of tropical rainforest, anxious not to be left behind. They were not only under threat from potential ambushes from Japanese patrols but also from man-eating tigers and deadly snakes, so Karl moved cautiously behind the silent men until they broke into another clearing, overlapped by the canopy of giant trees. Here he could see a few Chinese women armed as heavily as the men sitting in cramped huts made from forest materials. They glanced at him with little curiosity then went about their duties, preparing meals with rifles slung over their shoulders.

Karl was escorted to a hut made from bamboo and thatch.

'Just make yourself at home,' Carlton said, waving into the gloomy hut adorned with a few tattered maps. 'This is our HQ and mess area,' he added, plonking himself down on a log and beginning to examine his ankles and legs for the leeches. There was always a danger that the wound a leech inflicted could turn septic in the tropical conditions of the forest.

Karl followed Carlton's example and found numerous leeches engorging themselves on his ankles.

'Good afternoon, Major,' the Free French officer said, appearing at the doorway. 'If it would be convenient, Captain Carlton, I would like to talk to Major Mann alone.'

'Sure thing, cobber,' Carlton said, heaving himself from the log and wandering out into the compound. 'I'll introduce you to the rest of the mob when you're through with Captain Pham.'

Karl turned to the Vietnamese officer. 'I heard that you did a run across the Gulf.'

'Yes, I was able to pay fishermen to transport me to the coast of my homeland without incident, and from there I made my way to Saigon to ensure that our contacts are in place. Before the end of the week you will travel with me across the gulf in a fishing boat.'

'Just like that,' Karl said with a note of sarcasm. 'I presume we'll receive a warm reception.'

'The people you will meet with accept you as a German engineer,' Pham said. 'I have all the papers required for you to move around freely – so long as you are able to convince those you meet that you are who you claim to be. I will accompany you as your interpreter. The rest is up to you.'

It all sounded so straightfoward, Karl thought, but something about the whole operation worried him. There were too many loose ends, as if Featherstone had not told him the whole story.

'In the meantime,' Pham said, 'we are guests of Captain Irving Goldstein, an American from their OSS. He is in command of this section.'

'A real Allied spirit of cooperation,' Karl said, scratching at a leech.

'Captain Goldstein has been very helpful in getting me to the coast; he has been instructed by his government to provide all the assistance we require,' Pham replied. 'I don't like his choice of allies in the Chinese communists. My guess is that after the war is over the British will be fighting these people, as will be my government. The communists will settle for nothing less than complete domination of a postwar world – both in Asia and Europe.'

The Vietnamese officer's reflections grated on Karl as he looked around at the men and women prepared to risk all in the crusade to defeat the hated Japanese Empire. Any suggestion that the Germans and the Japanese would only be replaced by another enemy once this war was over was too dispiriting to contemplate, so he shrugged and returned to his leech search-and-destroy mission.

NINE

The days in hell passed slowly for Ilsa. She was brought food, mostly by Fuji, and allowed a short time out of the cage. Ilsa was at least grateful for the fact that she had not been raped or beaten by her captors, but she wondered at the absence of the American colonel, who had been taken from his cage days earlier and had not returned.

On one seemingly endless day, Ilsa was sitting with her back to the wooden cage when she became aware of a stirring in the village. It was late afternoon and she noticed that the Japanese soldiers were gathering in the clearing, bringing the sullen villagers with them.

It was then that Lieutenant Yoshi appeared in his spotlessly clean uniform, wearing his sword at his waist. The soldiers on parade were brought to attention, and Ilsa

watched as the Japanese commander gave a speech. She
noticed Fuji standing at the end of one of the ranks, and
he stepped forward when the Japanese officer had finished
talking. He addressed the gathered villagers in a dialect she
had learned was universal to the people across Papua and
New Guinea; it sounded a little bit like English, but she
thought it had German words as well.

There was a disturbance from one of the huts, drawing the attention of the villagers. Ilsa gasped. Two soldiers
were dragging the American colonel from the hut. His
arms were bound behind his back; he had a black rag tied
around his eyes and he was stripped to the waist. His piti-
fully thin body was covered in sores and welts and his chin
rested on his chest. The colonel was dragged to the centre
of the clearing and Ilsa watched, horrified, as he was forced
to his knees. The Japanese officer slid his sword from the
scabbard, stepped back and lifted the shining blade above
his head. The American remained silent, head bowed,
obviously knowing what his fate was to be. He did not cry
out or beg for mercy but simply muttered something Ilsa
could not hear; she guessed he was praying.

The sword came down, hacking into the back of the
American's neck and severing his head from his body.
A cry of '*Banzai!*' went up from the gathered soldiers as
they watched the execution of their enemy.

Ilsa thought she might be sick. She looked away from
the headless body twitching on the ground, bleeding out a
great red gush. She swore, using words that she had never
used before in both German and English, and then broke
down and cried.

She did not look up as the colonel's body was dragged

away and the soldiers stood down from the spectacle intended to impress both them and the villagers with Japanese justice.

That night Fuji came to her with her ration of rice and fish.

'Why was the colonel murdered?' Ilsa asked as she took the bowl of rice and fish pieces floating in a dark liquid.

'He was executed, not murdered,' Fuji replied. 'He had no further use to us and would have become a burden.'

'Will I be executed?' Ilsa asked.

Fuji frowned. 'You are enjoying our hospitality until our German allies take you,' he answered. 'Until then, you will be treated with courtesy. Tomorrow, Lieutenant Yoshi wishes to speak with you. You will have the opportunity to wash before you meet with him.'

Fuji's statement chilled Ilsa to the bone. She had seen at first hand the butcher's cruelty and was now feeling real terror of what might await her in the presence of the enemy commander. Suddenly the thought of food made her feel sick, despite her hunger. She placed the bowl on the earth by her feet and considered a way of killing herself. Maybe she would be able to cut her wrists with a piece of sharpened bamboo she had stripped from the cage.

As if sensing her fear, Fuji crouched and spoke softly to her. 'He will not harm you. He has orders to deliver you to our German allies in good health.'

Ilsa was slightly reassured and nodded her thanks. Fuji straightened up and left her alone with her fears.

★

Inside his billet, Fuji met his friend Petty Officer Oshiro, who had returned from radio piquet.

'The Americans are making progress in the Philippines,' Oshiro said, passing Fuji a small bowl of sake. 'But our comrades are making them pay for every foot of ground.'

They were alone in the native hut that served as their quarters.

'We are losing this war,' Fuji said, accepting the fiery rice liquor.

'That is defeatist talk,' Oshiro reminded Fuji with a note of sarcasm. 'How can our master race be defeated by big-nosed barbarians?'

Fuji swilled down the last remnants of the sake and placed the bowl on a small table he had crafted from jungle timber in his spare time.

'I fear that it will only be a matter of time before the enemy attack my homeland,' Oshiro sighed.

'Remember, that is defeatist talk,' Fuji mocked, and received a baleful look from his friend.

'My family will be in harm's way,' he said sadly. 'And here you and I are at the arse end of the world, sitting around in a place our army and navy have forgotten. We were told that we were to go on a special mission and all we do is sit around this village, cleaning our weapons and guarding one American woman. The commander should kill her and release us to join our forces defending the homeland.'

Fuji shrugged. 'Maybe we will survive the war and return home to our people.' Papua had been his home before the war. How would he be received back at Port Moresby if the Allies won the war? Once, he would never have entertained such a question. Defeat had seemed impossible early in the war, when the armed forces of Japan had swept virtually unopposed south across the Pacific and Asia. But this was January 1945 and the war had gone badly for Japan. Fuji knew he would have no home if the war went against them.

A year earlier a letter from his mother had reached him via the international Red Cross. She had written to him from an internment camp on the Australian mainland; she said that she and his father were being treated well. The officer who had passed on the letter to Fuji had said with contempt that his mother's words were propaganda from the enemy, who had no doubt forced his mother to say such an unbelievable thing. Fuji had bowed and agreed with the officer but had known enough about the Australians to guess that her words were probably true.

His mother had also said that Mr Jack Kelly had ensured they were looked after and this was what had confused Fuji. Why would his old enemy be kind to his family, knowing that their son was a dangerous foe? There had been a time before the war when Fuji's father owned a small boat building business near Port Moresby. Lukas Kelly had caused his father to lose face when Lukas had stepped in to defend a native worker from an unjustified assault. The incident of Lukas striking Fuji's father may not have meant much to the Europeans but it had brought great shame on Fuji's family. Fuji had vowed never to forget the grave insult and carried the grudge with him into the war.

But Fuji had lived long enough with the barbarian Australians to understand that they were a tough but compassionate people. When they recovered their bodies, had they not granted full military honours to the Japanese submariners killed in the midget submarines that had penetrated the defences of Sydney Harbour?

As Fuji accepted a second cup of sake he reflected on the fact that the man he hated most in this world was his commanding officer. He had sworn to kill him, yet he knew this was not possible whilst Lieutenant Yoshi remained in command of their small unit behind enemy lines. That would endanger the lives of them all and he was not prepared to sacrifice his fellow soldiers for his desire for personal revenge. That could wait.

Fuji drank sake with his friend until he noticed that the walls were closing in and the floor was beginning to spin. Eventually he let sleep take him from a world at war, but even his sleep was without peace, filled instead with images of violent death.

*

The following day a guard came for Ilsa and beckoned for her to follow him to a creek. Ilsa knew that she was supposed to wash whilst he watched her but she shook her head when he tried to force a bar of soap into her hand. The guard got angry and waved his rifle at her in a threatening manner, but she refused to take off her rags in front of him. Besides, she thought that if she was filthy, Lieutenant Yoshi, who was clearly fastidious about cleanliness, would be disgusted by her and less likely to rape her.

Defeated by her determination not to bathe, the guard marched her back to the village, where he took her to a hut on stilts that had had a small verandah added to the front.

Here he was joined by Fuji, who looked ill. When Ilsa was close enough to smell the alcohol on his breath, she realised that his condition was self-inflicted.

'I am to translate,' he said without any greeting. 'When you are in the lieutenant's presence, you must bow and not make eye contact,' he instructed. 'Do not ask questions and you will not be badly treated. Do you understand?'

An order was barked and the guard prodded Ilsa with the butt of his rifle to climb the steps to the office. She did so with Fuji close behind.

There was no door and Ilsa could see Lieutenant Yoshi sitting behind a desk made of oil drums and a flat piece of timber. She stopped just beyond the doorway and bowed from the waist. Ilsa could almost feel the cold cruelty of the immaculately dressed Japanese officer fill the small room, and she remained bowed until Fuji told her otherwise.

'You may straighten up but keep your gaze away from our commander's face,' he said quietly.

Ilsa obeyed and stared down at the woven-reed floor.

'Our commander wishes to know if you are being treated well,' Fuji translated.

'Tell him that I do not complain about the circumstances of my imprisonment,' Ilsa said. She was terrified but was determined not to show it. Instead, she adopted the demeanour of a subservient woman, as she had read Japanese women were expected to do in the company of men.

'The commander wishes to know why you are so important to the German allies,' Fuji continued.

To this question Ilsa did not have any real answer – except that she was the daughter of a German intelligence officer who had defected to America before the war.

She had been too young at the time to be told anything about her father's work, and when she was old enough, that part of his life had seemed so distant and unreal she had never asked him any questions, and he had never raised the subject himself. Ilsa tried to give a truthful answer, explaining that she, too, was mystified.

As her answer was being weighed up by Lieutenant Yoshi, Ilsa could feel the sweat trickling down her spine. Outside she could hear the grunt of pigs rooting for scraps under the stilted huts and the laughter of children playing games.

After a long silence Fuji again translated. 'Our commander says that soon you will be gone from us and you will no longer be of any importance to him. He says that you will continue to receive the best of treatment whilst in his care.'

Ilsa bowed in acknowledgement of this statement.

She was marched out and returned to her cage. There she slumped to the ground and buried her head against her knees. Time had begun to lose all meaning and she wondered if she would still be alive when the Germans came for her. This hell came with a steaming green prison deep in a place so far from help that only despair could find its way here. She feared there was no hope for her but she was determined to stay alive as long as she could.

She started to shiver; she had never felt so cold, despite the stifling heat of the day, yet her skin was hot to the touch. She recognised the signs with dread. Malaria might yet claim her life before the interventions of men could.

★

Sergeant Jack Kelly climbed out of the Douglas transport and stretched his legs. He was relieved to be on land after the bumpy, gut-wrenching flight across the towering mountain range of the Owen Stanleys, where updrafts had bounced the twin-engined transport around as if it were no more than a toy.

The steaming heat of the valley filled with long kunai grass wrapped him in an instant sweat. He hoisted his kitbag over his shoulder and went in search of the detachment of PIB soldiers he knew were camped a short distance away. He was fortunate to be able to hitch a lift on an American jeep driven by a PIB clerk. He was dropped off at the edge of the encampment and met by a smartly uniformed Papuan soldier standing sentry. The man grinned at him broadly.

'Masta Jack!' he exclaimed. 'You come back to us.'

'Hello, Private Ramos, you been well?' Jack was pleased to see him. Ramos had accompanied him on many patrols and was a good soldier, with a liking for detaching Japanese heads with a machete.

'Been well, Sergeant,' he replied. 'Captain Vincent is in HQ.'

Jack thanked the sentry and made his way to the centre of the encampment. He passed soldiers cleaning weapons and lying around tents; some of them recognised him and greeted him warmly. He could see from their appearance that these men had returned from an arduous patrol, and in the distance Jack could hear the drone of aircraft taking off and landing at the nearby airstrip laid down in the valley.

'Sergeant Kelly, I see you have returned to us,' a voice boomed and Jack saw the solidly built PIB captain striding towards him. Captain George Vincent was a big man with a ruddy face. Before the war he had been manager of a copra plantation near Lae and, like Jack, he had served his term with the PNGVR. 'Travers was a bit vague on why you've been posted back to us, but if I know you, Jack, you'll be up to some kind of mischief.'

Jack pulled the face of a man hurt by such an insinuation, then thrust out his hand. 'How are you, George?' he asked and the big man grinned as he took Jack's hand. The formality of rank had little place amongst men who had worked beside each other before the war and shared the dangers of the early days, standing alone to defend their country before the Australian government had been able to rush reinforcements onto the Kokoda track.

'Okay, Jack, why have you come back when you had a cushy job down in Moresby, sorting papers under a cool fan and with unlimited access to cold beer?' Vincent asked. 'All I got in the signal was that you were going to put together a small mission in our area of operations.'

'I need your help to put together a task force to rescue some prisoners the Japs have captive west of here, about a couple of weeks' march,' Jack told him.

'You mean the ones a patrol spotted a few weeks back?' Vincent asked. 'We're a bit short on personnel for those kinds of ops, and from what Corporal Gari reported, he thought the Nips were at least a platoon strength of Special Landing Force troops. God knows why the Nips would have men like that up the coast, where they can do no one any harm. I suspect the Japs are under the impression they'll be back in force any day now and then their boys will be able to act as a forward base. They must be dreaming.'

'I'll need to borrow a few of the boys to assist me and at the moment my son has his boat anchored north of us, putting ashore supplies. I'm sure that you can clear it with Moresby to allow him to transport us up the coast to save time.'

The captain rubbed his face with the palm of his hand, as if attempting to wipe away the dilemma of going through the paperwork of bureaucratic clearances. 'Okay, I'll get clearance and I can give you a section of nine men for one week. But you must know the statistics as well as I do – you need at least a three-to-one ratio to attack an entrenched force.'

'Do I get Corporal Gari?' Jack asked. 'He's worth at least ten men.'

'You get Joseph,' George sighed. 'But you also submit a plan for your mission and don't hold back on what your objectives are. I want to know why this mission is so important to you.'

'One of the prisoners is my daughter,' Jack said softly.

'Bloody hell, Jack!' he snorted. 'Are you sure?'

'Pretty well sure,' Jack answered.

'I didn't know you had a daughter,' Vincent said sympathetically.

'One of those unexpected things from my past,' Jack answered vaguely.

The captain didn't ask any questions. 'Well, get yourself to the lines then. I'll leave it to your discretion as to how you organise your show. You have my authority to draw weapons, rations, radios and Corporal Gari with eight men of your choosing. I'll have call signs allocated by 0600 tomorrow when you brief me on your mission in full. Any questions?'

'She's pretty jake,' Jack answered. 'And my thanks for

everything. We'll see if we can bag a few Japs along the way, and I promise to get all the boys back safe and well in your tender care.'

'See that you do, Sergeant Kelly.'

Jack did not waste time. Every hour counted and he barely threw his kitbag on a field stretcher before going in search of Corporal Gari. The mission had the green light and Jack – not a religious man – said a silent prayer that he would not be too late to save his daughter.

★

Ilsa felt a raging thirst and when she opened her eyes, she realised vaguely that she was no longer in the cage but lay on a woven-straw mat inside a hut.

'You have a bad fever,' Fuji's voice said. 'Lieutenant Yoshi had you brought here until the fever goes away.'

Ilsa attempted to sit up but felt too weak to do so. 'Water,' she croaked, and Fuji held a canteen of warm, brackish water to her lips.

'You probably have malaria,' he said in a matter-of-fact way. 'It is killing more of our troops in this campaign than your army's bullets.'

Ilsa let the water run into her mouth and wished she had something for the pain that seemed to be splitting open her head. At least the hut was out of the sun, she thought, and then she became aware that it was raining outside and was doubly grateful to be out of the wet. 'Is your commander going to allow me to stay here?' she asked.

'I think so,' Fuji replied. 'There is nowhere you can escape to, anyway.'

138

Ilsa nodded. Escape was the last thing on her mind right now as she fought the debilitating fever. She had been briefed that Papua New Guinea harboured every kind of tropical disease known, from dengue fever to scrub typhus. Disease was causing more casualties amongst troops on both sides than actual combat.

Fuji exited the hut and Ilsa was left alone throughout the day, coming in and out of fever. She woke near evening to a guard bringing her a bowl of food. With effort she sat up and slowly ate the food, knowing that even this meagre nourishment would help her regain her strength. In the gloom of the native hut she could see that the flesh had wasted from her body. What skin she had on her bones was marked by sores and insect bites. She wondered what Clark would think of her if he could see her now, and the tears flowed down her sunken cheeks as she remembered how it had been before this terrible time. Her mind wandered through flower-soaked fields in Montana, where Clark had taken her to meet his family when they had fallen in love and the war was something on the other side of the world.

Gradually, as she drifted back from the past into the present, Ilsa became aware that someone was watching her from a dark corner and she started to feel afraid. She peered hard into the gloom and realised with a flood of relief that it was a little girl. She must have crawled in through a gap in the floor.

'Hello,' Ilsa said with a weak smile. The little girl stared back at her with big brown eyes. Ilsa guessed she was probably around four or five years of age. 'What are you doing here?'

The little girl was naked and sat with her thumb in her mouth, observing Ilsa with a serious expression.

'Come here,' Ilsa said gently, gesturing with her hand, but the girl remained in the dark corner, afraid to approach. 'I will not hurt you.'

Eventually Ilsa was able to coax her across and the little girl reached out to touch Ilsa's matted hair. Then she sat down beside her and continued to suck her thumb. Ilsa felt a burst of warmth in the presence of another human who did not threaten her with harm. Although she knew the child did not understand her, she continued to talk softly to her until the girl stood up and left.

Ilsa sighed. At least there was one person amongst the villagers who was not afraid to make contact with her.

TEN

The next morning the same little girl returned and walked cautiously through the front entrance with a handful of wild flowers for Ilsa, who was deeply touched by the gesture. She was reaching out to take the gift when a shadow fell over the doorway.

Ilsa looked up to see one of the men she recognised as a friend of her interpreter, Fuji. She had heard Fuji call him by name – Oshiro. He had a broad, friendly face and the few times he had brought her the daily ration he had been kind and gentle. When he saw the little girl standing beside Ilsa, he broke into a wide smile and said something Ilsa guessed to be a friendly greeting. He even bowed at the waist to the startled child, who watched him with an expression of fear, as she was clearly in a place she had been told by the adults of her village never to go.

Ilsa glanced at Oshiro and smiled, sharing the gentleness of the moment.

The Japanese man kneeled down and offered a stick of beef jerky to the girl. She took it hesitantly, and he indicated for her to bite on the dried meat.

Just then there was a noise in the doorway. Ilsa's heart almost stopped beating – the Japanese commander stood blocking the entrance, his face a mask of rage.

Oshiro came to his feet and saluted smartly.

Lieutenant Yoshi looked past his subordinate to the child, now backing away fearfully towards the rear wall. The Japanese officer dropped his hand to the hilt of his sword. Oshiro cried out urgently. Ilsa did not understand Japanese but she could tell from the enraged voice of the commander and the pleading voice of his subordinate that a heated discussion was going on. Ilsa wondered at Oshiro's bravery, then noticed that his hand was covering the hilt of his commander's sword, as if trying to restrain him.

A shouted command from Lieutenant Yoshi brought two Japanese soldiers scrabbling to his assistance. They seized Oshiro, who did not attempt to resist. Without another word Lieutenant Yoshi stormed out of the hut, the other three following him.

Ilsa hardly dared breathe again. Thankfully the little girl had slipped away during the confrontation. Ilsa guessed that in the brief but terrifying time the incident took to happen, Oshiro had saved the little girl's life.

Within minutes she could hear the sound of soldiers being called to assembly and she struggled to her feet to

peek through a gap in the thatched wall. The Japanese soldiers were being addressed by Lieutenant Yoshi, who was
standing on a wooden crate in front of them. Ilsa could see
that Oshiro was now stripped down to a loincloth and was
being spread-eagled on the hot earth, his arms and legs
tied to wooden pegs in the ground. He lay face up and the
soldiers stepped back, leaving him to bake under the tropical sun.

Fuji was called out and stood beside the officer to
address the villagers, who had also been forced to attend
the field punishment. Ilsa did not understand what he was
saying but she could hear a tremor in his voice.

Lieutenant Yoshi dismissed the parade and then stepped
off the box; within minutes Oshiro was alone in the
clearing.

That evening Fuji brought Ilsa her food ration.

'Is your friend being punished?' she asked as he placed
the bowl on the floor in front of her.

'Yes,' Fuji replied. 'He has been sentenced to three days
and nights without food or water for daring to interfere
with the actions of a superior officer and for assaulting
him.'

'Your friend did not assault anyone,' Ilsa retorted. 'He
was begging your Lieutenant Yoshi not to harm an innocent child.'

'That does not matter,' Fuji said bitterly. 'Oshiro knows
better than to interfere with the wishes of a superior officer.
His punishment could have been worse.'

'Worse than what he is suffering now!' Ilsa exclaimed.
'In this heat he will be lucky to survive two days without
water.'

Fuji turned his back and shrugged. 'Oshiro knows our military law and is an Okinawan. They are a tough people. He will live.'

Ilsa was not so sure, and when the second night arrived she could hear the weak calls of a man beginning to suffer delirium. She found herself praying for rain that night and then wondered that she should care for the fate of an enemy soldier, one of her captors. Her prayers were answered anyway because a few hours later there was a short but heavy downpour.

Ilsa hoped that Oshiro was able to drink some of the rain and survive just one more day and one more night.

*

Fuji was summoned to his commander's office in the early evening. He saluted smartly, standing rigidly to attention.

'Petty Officer Fuji,' Lieutenant Yoshi said, seated at his makeshift desk. 'I remember you when you were rescued in the company of a native girl I saw it as my duty to execute.'

Fuji felt his face redden at the memory of the 'rescue'. He had been on a mission to his home district around Port Moresby, to make contact with an influential traitor to the Australian government. He was supposed to be extracted by a Japanese submarine but when that didn't happen, Fuji and his lover, Keela, attempted to reach friendly territory in a native canoe. They wound up on an island patrolled by the Japanese Navy, and a marine team led by Yoshi found them in a sad state. Without heeding the explanation from Fuji, whom he suspected of being a deserter, the

Japanese officer personally beheaded Keela on the white sands of the island beach.

Fuji felt both rising rage and a sick fear. Fuji had wondered whether the navy officer would remember his face. Now he knew.

The officer rose menacingly from behind his desk and walked to within inches of Fuji, staring into his face. 'You are a warrior of the Emperor, and even if you were not born in Japan, you wear the Emperor's uniform. Who do you swear your loyalty to – the Emperor or a dead barbarian girl?'

Fuji could see the menace in his officer's eyes but he knew his duty. 'My oath is to our Emperor,' he said tightly.

The officer stared at Fuji as if contemplating something. 'I can see that you would like to kill me, Petty Officer,' Lieutenant Yoshi said. 'But we are at war and your personal desires are of no consequence. You will die for the Emperor if I command it.' He raised his hand to dismiss him, and Fuji saluted, bowed and retreated for the doorway.

Outside, he found himself reeling from the encounter. Once again he was confused by his thoughts. On the one hand he was a warrior of the Emperor, sworn to obey and die. On the other hand, Yoshi was responsible for the brutal and unnecessary death of the one person who had brought gentleness and love into Fuji's life. Love was not an emotion easily dismissed.

In the gathering darkness, Fuji was aware that Oshiro was still pegged out in the clearing, moaning weakly, and for a fleeting moment Fuji considered overpowering the guard and cutting his friend loose. They could flee into the jungle to wait out the war. But the thought was merely an impulsive dream, he knew that.

★

Jack found his son sitting on a case of .303 ammunition. Supplies had been offloaded onto a small beach adjoining a mangrove swamp, and the cases of food, ammunition and medical supplies were being carried by New Guinean porters along the same track Jack had used to reach the coast.

Lukas was flipping through a sheaf of order forms, ticking off his cargo. He glanced up and when he saw his father he broke into a broad smile.

'Hello, Dad, what the hell are you doing up here?'

'Nice way to greet your father,' Jack replied, crushing his son in a great hug. 'I've come to requisition your boat – and your services – for the next couple of weeks.'

Lukas looked curious. 'Want a drink before you tell me what this is all about?'

'What have you got?'

Lukas stuffed the paperwork into a canvas pouch and led his father down the beach to a small dinghy. They climbed in and Lukas rowed out to the *Riverside* anchored a short distance offshore. Jack could see that the vessel's heavy machine gun was manned by Mel Jones. Mel greeted Jack with a wave and helped them aboard.

'Thought you were down in Moresby,' the American grunted, thick cigar clenched between his nicotine-stained teeth.

'Up here to do a job,' Jack replied. 'You and Lukas will be helping me.'

The American shrugged and returned to scanning beach and sky for any possible threat. Lukas led his father below into the cramped cabin, where he reached for a bottle of gin. 'No tonic, I'm afraid,' he said, pouring generous tots into enamel mugs and passing one to Jack. 'What's this about requisitioning my boat?'

Jack found a small seat on the starboard side whilst Lukas remained standing in the stifling cabin filled with charts, cooking utensils and medical supplies. A spent brass cartridge case rattled on the floor when the boat shifted slightly on the gentle tide.

'There's something I have to tell you,' Jack said, taking a long swig of the fiery liquor. And for the next ten minutes he explained what had happened to Lukas's half-sister, who was now a prisoner of the Japanese not far from where they presently sat. Lukas listened in silence and Jack could see a certain amount of hostility in his son's face. This was not going as well as he'd hoped.

'So I guess you expect me and my crew to risk our lives to rescue her,' Lukas said when Jack had finished talking.

Jack thumped his mug down beside him, spilling what was left. 'Don't be so bloody selfish, son!' he exploded. 'You might resent her, but she's still your half-sister.'

'We hardly know the woman, Dad. Yes, she's your daughter, but you're asking me to risk good men for her. You're the one who's being selfish.' Lukas turned his back on his father and climbed out onto the deck.

Jack could hear him stomping around up there and guessed that his son was torn by his strong sense of duty to his boat and crew, balanced against the life of just one woman – despite her blood connection to them both. Jack knew that in the brief time his son had known Ilsa, he had liked her and was not altogether being selfish. This was war and his son had been entrusted to keep his boat operational, and his crew alive. Jack knew that Lukas was putting duty before emotion for the moment. But he also knew his son and how he reacted to these situations. Jack let out a long breath of air, running his hand through his thick greying hair. Lukas would come to his senses; he just had to give him time.

Sure enough, ten minutes later Lukas stepped into the cabin with an apologetic look on his face. 'I'm sorry, Dad. I guess I am a bit jealous that you'd go to all this effort for a daughter you barely know. But you're right, we have to do something. If she is a prisoner of the Japs we can't just leave her to her fate.'

Jack could see the genuine concern in his son's expression. 'I'm not going to insist on you coming on this mission, Mel can handle the *Riverside*.'

'Like hell he can,' Lukas snapped. '*Riverside* is mine – and stays under my command. I am coming with you. Besides all else, Ilsa is my sister.'

Jack placed his hand on his son's shoulder. 'If anything happened to you, my world would cease to have any meaning,' he said gently.

'Thanks, Dad,' Lukas answered. 'It means a lot to me to hear you say that.'

Jack was torn. He needed the *Riverside* to ship them up the coast, but he couldn't deny that he would be putting his son in danger in his attempt to rescue a daughter he hardly knew. But he also knew that Lukas was a chip off the old block and would refuse to be left out of the mission.

'We ship out before first light tomorrow,' he said. He began rustling amongst charts stacked in a pile on the navigation table. When he found the one that he wanted he spread it out on the small table and both men leaned over it.

'You will transport us to this point,' Jack said, jabbing at a section of coastline. 'From there I will take my section inland and hit the Jap village.'

'How far inland?' Lukas asked, peering at the chart.

'According to one of my men, the camp is in a small village about half a mile from the shore. There are around a dozen Japs, most probably special troops left behind our lines to play havoc with our communication.'

'How many am I transporting?' Lukas asked.

'A section,' Jack answered and his son looked up at him with concern.

'You will be facing what you think is a highly trained Jap platoon with just nine men.'

'Ten, if you count me,' Jack said.

'God almighty!' Lukas swore. 'The Japs will eat you alive.'

Jack thought his son was probably right; he knew Gari and his men were courageous, but courage was not enough when the odds were stacked against you.

'Maybe I can scrounge up a bit of artillery to support you,' Lukas said.

'What have you got?' Jack asked.

'We have a three-inch mortar and bombs stashed away – I was supposed to drop them off a few days ago but they got forgotten somehow. We should be able to get some use out of that.'

'Do you know how to use a mortar?' Jack asked, raising an eyebrow.

'Yeah, you just drop the bombs down the hole at the top and make sure it's pointed away from you,' Lukas grinned.

'You'll have to bring it ashore and set it up so that it's within range of the village,' Jack said thoughtfully. 'The three inch is limited in range. What kind of ammo?'

'Mostly high explosive – and a few white phosphorus bombs. No illumination.'

'That doesn't matter – we'll hit the Japs right on dawn,' Jack said, pleased at the sudden but very significant addition to his armoury. Even if his son proved to be a lousy mortar man when the time came, which he doubted, the sound of bombs going off in the jungle would help confuse and rattle the enemy.

'Well,' Jack said, 'the rest of the briefing can be done when we kick off tomorrow morning. I'll bring the boys down the track and bivouac off the beach tonight. Maybe we can finish the bottle under the stars.'

'Sounds good,' Lukas answered, staring down at the chart and already calculating what he would need to make the journey to the target and back again safely. They'd have to go carefully. Despite the Allies pushing the Japanese back to their homeland, the Imperial Japanese Navy was still a force to be reckoned with.

*

On the outskirts of Sydney a group of high-ranking military officers converged on a colonial farmhouse that had been requisitioned by the government for the duration of the war. The house was built of sandstone and its wide verandahs were covered in European ivy, providing welcome shade from the hot summer sun. The broad gravel driveway to the house was crowded with vehicles discreetly marked as military by their tactical signs. The men who had been chauffeured to the meeting place wore the uniforms of the United States and Britain. Amongst them was Captain Featherstone, who dismounted carrying a leather briefcase handcuffed to his hand. Neatly tucked in a holster under his shirt was a Webley Scott revolver.

Featherstone was met by a smartly dressed United States Marine Corps sergeant who politely asked for his identification then checked his name against his list. The sergeant gave him a smart salute and ushered him into the house.

Inside the meeting room, Featherstone was assailed by cigarette smoke and the smell of human sweat.

'Hello, Featherstone,' an American colonel said, passing him a crystal tumbler of gin and tonic. 'I believe this is your drink.' The man had solid shoulders and greying crewcut hair. He looked tough and Featherstone knew his looks were not deceiving. Colonel Ben Basham was a former USMC officer who had seen service in China before the war and was a veteran of the trenches in the last war. He was an officer in the American equivalent of Featherstone's service – the Office of Strategic Studies.

Featherstone accepted the drink and thanked the colonel. Without taking a sip he placed his drink on the great polished timber table at the centre of the room and unlocked the handcuff securing the briefcase. There were several men milling around talking in subdued voices.

An American brigadier entered the room and called the meeting to order. Each man took his place at the table marked by a small sign indicating name, rank and position. The cards indicated that most of the men attending were officers of the American OSS or British SOE. Conspicuously absent was any Australian representation.

Featherstone sat down next to Colonel Basham and the meeting got underway without the military formalities normally associated with briefings. Each man reported on his section's mission, then a civilian with an American accent was introduced by the brigadier as a representative of President Roosevelt. He was a youngish man, prematurely balding and wearing thin-framed spectacles. He had about him the air of a Yale or Harvard graduate, and his expensive, well-tailored suit hardly had a sweat mark on it.

He began by congratulating those at the table for their successes, which was only politic, Featherstone thought.

'Now, to the matter of Ho Chi Minh in Indochina,' he continued, looking directly at Featherstone. 'Our president is impressed with Ho Chi Minh's guerrilla war against the Japs. Mr Roosevelt is concerned that there is a rumour our French allies are plotting to dispose of him at the first possible opportunity. I hope that they are not getting any assistance from Mr Churchill.'

Featherstone was aware that the eyes of the meeting were on him and was startled by the fact that the Americans would raise the matter in such a public way. He reached for his drink, taking a sip before replying.

'Churchill has little interest in matters outside Burma, Malaya, Hong Kong and Singapore in this theatre of the war,' Featherstone replied casually. 'Whatever the French are scheming is a matter all their own. As you may well know, France is the traditional enemy of Britain.'

There were several smiles and chuckles around the table. Featherstone was deliberately keeping the discussion as light as possible. The fact was, he knew that the French officer assigned to accompany the Australian officer into Saigon was an avowed enemy of Ho Chi Minh; he was quite capable of an assassination attempt.

'You know that the president's policy is of opposition to imperial interests in the Far East – after the war is won,' the young man continued. 'From what we know of Ho Chi Minh, he is more nationalist than communist. Some in our State Department feel he would be a helpful ally in this part of the world when the war is over.'

Featherstone refrained from commenting that the Americans were preparing to reoccupy the Philippines, and that would put them on a par with any imperial ambition of Britain and France. The United States had, after all, seized the country from Spain at the turn of the century. 'I must confess, sir, that we have not considered France's position in respect to their imperial possessions before the war,' he lied, 'but I will look into it.'

'So you are not aware of any plot to assassinate Ho Chi Minh?' the American asked.

Featherstone was not aware of any plot to kill the Vietnamese guerrilla leader, but it must surely be a possibility.

'I am not aware of any plot that concerns our organisation to kill this Indochinese gentleman you regard so highly,' he replied.

The civilian representative nodded and turned his

attention to another matter, leaving Featherstone to wonder why he had been confronted with the issue at all. As he sat through the meeting, he went over everything he knew about Karl Mann's mission and found himself thinking that the man might be in even more danger than anyone had anticipated.

When the meeting was over and the various representatives began dispersing to their cars, Featherstone approached Colonel Basham.

'Ben, could I have a moment of your time?' he asked quietly.

'Sure,' Colonel Basham responded, waving off his driver, a pretty young woman in an army uniform. 'What can I do for you?'

'What is this about Ho Chi Minh and the French?'

Basham glanced around to ensure that their conversation was not being overheard. 'You guys are being used by de Gaulle and his cronies,' he said. 'The French only think of their own interests, you know that. We don't trust de Gaulle. We figure if he ever gets into power he will run France as a dictator. I would watch your back, if I were you.'

Featherstone nodded and watched as the American strode away to his car. He suspected that the Americans had somehow broken the strict security surrounding his operation to insert Karl Mann into Saigon. If so, Pham must be working with the Yanks. The British intelligence officer snapped the handcuff back on his wrist and walked to his car. He had the uneasy feeling that Karl Mann was as good as dead in an operation compromised almost before it had begun.

ELEVEN

Weeks had passed and Karl was bored. He had asked to accompany the Chinese guerrillas on raids and ambushes but had been firmly informed by the OSS and SOE officers that they had strict instructions to keep him out of harm's way. So Karl had been forced to remain in camp and the only time he was able to leave was when the guerrillas changed location to avoid being discovered by the Japanese.

However, during this time he had more contact with Pham, who uncharacteristically revealed his contempt for the Chinese partisans.

'The Chinese have always been the enemy of my people,' he spat, watching a Chinese guerrilla commander pass by. 'They have always come from the north to invade my country but have always been forced back to their own lands. We will do the same to the Japanese.'

'From what I have heard from our Yank OSS comrade here, a fellow by the name of Ho Chi Minh is doing a pretty good job of that,' Karl reflected, leaning back against the log they shared and sipping his mug of tea. He was surprised at the dark look that came over the Frenchman's face. 'I gather you do not agree.'

Pham glanced at Karl. 'He is a communist and his Viet Minh will cause problems for us all – including you in the west. Do you know that Ho Chi Minh is not even his real name? He was born Nguyen That Thanh and decided to adopt his present name, as it means "the bringer of light". There will be no light. He will only bring death to my country, but the Americans who support him cannot see that, despite the fact that Ho was a founding member of the French Communist Party back in the twenties and trained in Russia. Indochina belongs to France and while Ho Chi Min is alive we will not know peace.'

Karl could hear the passion in Pham's voice and began to sense that this little-known part of the world was facing even more turmoil than he had realised. 'I get the impression that you would like to see the Viet Minh gone from your country,' he said cautiously.

Pham smiled. 'As you will be glad to see your present Chinese comrades gone from Malaya. When the war is over they will oppose the return of the British.'

'As I am an Australian, what the Poms do with Malaya after the war is really not much of a concern to me. But right now the communists are doing a bloody good job of harassing the Japs,' Karl replied. 'And that is all that counts at the moment.'

'You are a true soldier, Major Mann,' Pham said quietly. 'You fight a tactical battle without considering the strategy of war. The Japanese have changed attitudes in Asia and you will not have peace when we defeat them. We will find ourselves fighting the very same people we are working alongside.'

Karl had finished his tea and stood to return to his hut. 'For a junior officer, you appear to have a very good insight into global strategy,' he said, but Pham did not respond.

The next day Pham informed Karl that the coded signal had come through – they would be leaving that night for the coast. From there they would take a fishing boat across the Gulf of Siam to the Mekong Delta.

Karl made the rounds of the camp, bidding his fellow European officers farewell.

'Keep your back to the wall,' Captain David Carlton said, gripping him by the hand. 'Don't take your eye off that French bastard – I don't trust him one little bit. Bon voyage and see you in the future for a cold beer.'

'Thanks,' Karl answered with a smile. 'I have a feeling that the cold beer is a long way off yet.'

That evening, Karl, dressed as a Malay peasant in sarong and straw hat, departed for the coast with Pham and a small escort party of Chinese guerrillas. Despite his disguise, Karl stood out because of his size. At least Pham's disguise might fool a Japanese patrol, but not Karl's.

They travelled cautiously through the pitch darkness, the Chinese knowing their territory like the backs of their hands. In the morning they camped at what Pham said was only another day's travel from a small Malay coastal village where a local Chinese merchant had arranged to provide a fishing boat to take them across the Gulf of Siam. Japanese naval patrols had dropped off due to the vigorous activity of American submarines attempting to strangle all supplies to Japan from their previously conquered territories.

Little conversation passed between Pham and Karl. Captain Carlton's warning echoed in Karl's thoughts as he watched Pham move like a leopard amongst the Chinese he detested. Both men were armed, Karl with a revolver and Pham with a submachine gun. If it came to a shootout Karl was at a distinct disadvantage. As he sat with his back to a tree, eating his ration of rice, he tried to dismiss the crazy idea that Pham was a potential enemy. After all, they were both fighting the same enemy, albeit for different reasons.

There was a sudden stir amongst the Chinese fighters. The leader of the escort party, a tough, battle-scarred man who had lost three fingers on one hand, was signalling to his men to be on alert. Karl immediately drew his revolver and scanned the clump of rainforest trees that provided their protection.

Pham glanced over his shoulder and mouthed to Karl, 'Japs.'

The sentries posted on an outer perimeter had spotted the patrol of seven Japanese soldiers wandering towards the trees across a rice paddy. It was obvious from their relaxed manner that they were not expecting trouble; their arms were slung and they were chatting amongst themselves. However, if they continued into the trees they might easily walk straight into them.

Karl slid over to Pham. 'What in hell do we do now?' he whispered.

'The Chinese have orders to draw off the Japs,' Pham said, straining to spot the approaching patrol. 'You and I will slip past them and make it to the village.'

'Good plan,' Karl nodded, looking over at the Chinese guerrilla leader urgently signalling to his men to take up fighting positions.

Karl could now hear the chatter of the Japanese soldiers and within seconds he saw the first break through the foliage, almost on top of them. The first soldier was followed by a second and third before the gunfire erupted. The first target to be killed was the soldier carrying the radio set and another burst of fire destroyed the link to their HQ.

'Now!' Pham said, rising to his feet and sprinting in a crouch through the trees.

Jack followed, gripping his pistol and hearing the exchange of gunfire behind them. In his haste, he tripped on a tree root, falling heavily, his pistol wrenched from his hand by the impact. He rolled onto his back and, to his horror, saw a young Japanese soldier standing only a couple of feet away. Karl could see the young soldier's fear and confusion. He must have become separated from the rest of his patrol, but he still had his rifle. His eyes widened at the sight of the big man lying defenceless at his feet and, despite his obvious terror, the soldier raised the rifle to his shoulder and took quick aim at Karl.

The stutter of a light machine gun rent the air and the soldier's expression changed. The bullets from Pham's Sten had missed but the shot from the Japanese soldier's rifle had gone wild, throwing up a small spout of dirt next to

Karl's head. Karl did not hesitate but used all his strength to hurl himself to his feet and straight at the young soldier, who was attempting to chamber another round. Karl knocked the man from his feet and smashed his fist into his face. Then, without hesitating, he drew back his hand and slammed the edge of his knuckles into the soldier's throat. The young soldier gagged, his eyes bulging, and tried to call out. Karl reached for the finely honed commando knife he carried under his clothes and plunged it deeply into the man's chest, burying it to the hilt. Blood gushed from the dying soldier's lips and the life faded from his eyes.

With some effort, Karl withdrew the deadly knife and looked up to see Pham standing a couple of feet away.

'Thanks,' he muttered, wiping the blade on a tree root. Pham had saved him from certain death and for that Karl was very grateful indeed.

'Hurry,' Pham said, turning and hurrying away.

Retrieving his revolver, Karl followed. He was in the Frenchman's debt now. He would not forget that Pham could have left him to his fate and made for the coast by himself. From there he could have continued with his own mission, but instead he had chosen to save Karl.

Behind them they could hear the continuing sporadic gunfire of the skirmish and Karl realised that the guerrillas were drawing the enemy away from them.

The two men hid themselves outside the village until night fell; then Pham led the way to his contact, whose store was at the edge of the small settlement. They were met by a frightened old man, who ushered them inside.

'Jap man everywhere,' he said, glancing around furtively. His store was stocked with a meagre supply of rice bags, trade goods and herbal medicines. 'Soon they come here.'

Karl knew that the Japanese exacted a bloody and cruel toll on the Chinese population suspected of assisting in acts of sabotage. They were putting this old man and his family in peril.

'Is the boat ready?' Pham asked, seemingly oblivious to the old man's dread.

'Yes, boat ready. My son will take you across the Gulf.'

'Good,' Pham responded. 'We will go now.'

Relieved, the Chinese trader closed his door and led the two men through the deserted streets to the beach, where a large motorised fishing boat lay at anchor a little way offshore. He signalled with a kerosene lantern, and a small dinghy was launched and rowed to where they stood waiting. A young Chinese man gestured for Karl and Pham to climb aboard and the two men were rowed in silence to the waiting boat.

Aboard, they were met by two other men, who helped them onto the deck. Even in the dark Karl felt uneasy as he recognised Malay being spoken. He had been briefed that the Malay people were mostly pro-Japanese and known to betray escaping prisoners of war.

'They are Chinese,' the son of the merchant said, seeing his discomfort. 'We speak Malay as well as English. I learn from my father, who had good business with the English before the war.'

Reassured, Karl found a secure spot amongst the fishing nets and settled back to snatch some badly needed sleep. But as he dozed off under a brilliantly clear sky, the image of the terrified young Japanese soldier dying with Karl's knife buried in his chest snapped him back into wakefulness. Karl rubbed his eyes. He had personally killed many Japanese but he sensed that this one would haunt him for the rest of his life. The soldier had been so young and so afraid. It was the first time he had seen a Japanese soldier as a human being, just as frightened of dying in some foreign country as he was. He cursed, settling back to close his eyes, knowing that sleep would elude him this night.

*

Sister Megan Cain loved her work in the Medical Air Evacuation Transport Unit. Her role as an evacuation nurse with the RAAF meant saving lives and that's why she had become a nurse in the first place. She was standing aboard the twin-engined transport plane; racks of seriously ill and wounded soldiers ran along each side of the cramped interior of the aircraft. She was the only nurse on this flight and she had six patients in her care, one of whom was particularly special to her, as he was the air force doctor who had saved her life when she had been struck with scrub typhus in the heavily forested region of the island they had been working from, transporting patients to hospitals in Milne Bay and Port Moresby.

Flight Lieutenant Charles Crawford lay on his back, sweating and feverish. A fellow physician had diagnosed dengue fever and ordered his evacuation to Port Moresby. Crawford was a handsome man in his mid-thirties, and before the war he had had a prosperous practice in Sydney's Macquarie Street.

Megan felt the bumps and shudders as the aircraft fought the hot thermals coming up from the tropical land over which they were flying. Dr Crawford moaned and Megan placed a cool, damp cloth on his forehead – it was all she could do while they were in transit. In his delirious state the doctor reached out and caught her hand. Hoping that none of her other patients would require her attention, she remained by him until he relaxed his grip and let her go.

Megan stood back, feeling guilty. She knew from the other nurses' gossip that Dr Crawford was a divorced man with no children. Apparently his socialite wife had left him for another man when he had enlisted. He was a tragic and romantic figure to the nurses who worked with him, and Megan knew him to be a gentle, caring man who was highly regarded for his professional skill. It had been he who had quickly diagnosed Megan when she'd become ill, and it had been he who had held her hand during the feverish hours when it seemed possible she might die. After her recovery she had noticed his looks of interest and had felt herself return that interest. Megan had to acknowledge the fact that she was strongly attracted to the doctor and that only made her feel more guilty about Lukas.

'Sister,' croaked a young soldier with malaria. 'Could I have some water, please?'

Megan retrieved a bottle of chlorinated water for her patient, who half-sat up to drink the bitter liquid. She held his head so that he could sip the water and found herself thinking about Lukas. Worse still, she found herself comparing Lukas with Charles Crawford.

The two men were so different. Lukas could have honourably returned to Australia years earlier after his service with his father's regiment, but he had opted to stay on in the dangerous job of running the gauntlet of enemy naval and air forces to resupply isolated positions in the islands. He was very much like his father – a fearless fighter who would have been at home with the old pirates of yore – and that was very much his appeal. Megan suspected that Lukas was more interested in fighting than settling down. Since that terrible day when she had miscarried their baby, something had changed in their relationship. Megan no longer felt close to Lukas and without real intimacy their relationship could not heal from their loss. When Megan felt she could not stand her grief, Charles had been the one to comfort her. And she had found in him the support she so desperately needed.

Charles was an established and successful doctor, handsome and rumoured to be very well off; he was steady and reliable, and not in the least likely to get bored with family life after the first shine had worn off. Megan knew that Charles would stand by her; no matter what happened. More than that, however, she had strong feelings for him and sensed that the two of them would be happy and content together. After this war was over, Megan wanted a quiet life; she'd had more than enough of her share of adventures. Somehow, though, she suspected Lukas would be bored by that.

The aircraft hit another thermal and the water from the bottle splashed over her young soldier. She went to apologise but he smiled weakly.

'That's all right, sister,' he said. 'Saves me having a bath when we get to Moresby.'

She smiled back and felt a lump in her throat. She had seen so many young men mutilated or sick beyond hope who had never complained of their condition. They were just glad to see a smiling female face and feel a soft hand on their brows before they died. She was, to her patients, the mother, wife or lover they would never see again.

Within the hour the Moresby airfield loomed under the transport aircraft and the undercarriage touched down on the hot surface. Megan gave instructions as her patients were lifted from the aircraft to be conveyed to the hospital. As she watched Charles Crawford being wheeled into the ambulance she knew she had made a hard decision. She loved Lukas but she understood deep in her heart that their relationship had changed. They wanted different things from life and he couldn't be the husband and father of her children that she needed. Now she had to tell him, which was going to be one of the hardest things she had ever done in her life.

*

The *Riverside* ploughed its way through the tropical waters without incident. The engine thumped away as regular as a heartbeat. Lukas had been able to locate firing tables for the mortar, which he studied carefully, attempting to memorise critical elevations and traverses for the tubelike weapon he had once heard his father refer to as an 'educated drainpipe'; an expression he had picked up in the trenches of the last war.

'We're about a day from the target area,' Mel Jones grunted, wiping oil from his hands with a dirty rag and looking over Lukas's shoulder at the firing tables. 'You reckon you'll do any good with the tube?'

'Hope so,' Lukas replied. 'It's the only artillery support we're going to have on this crazy mission.'

'Speaking of being crazy,' Mel said, tucking the oily rag in his waistband. 'Here comes your old man.'

When Lukas looked up he noticed for the first time how grey his father's hair was becoming.

'Got it all worked out?' Jack asked with a smile.

'We'll find out when I drop the first bomb down the tube,' Lukas answered, closing the tables. 'Mel says we're about a day from the village.'

Jack was suddenly serious and he squatted down on the deck beside his son.

'That means you will have to steer a course to put us east of the village,' he said. 'We will have to find a secure place to land and then make our way on foot to the village. We'll need to carry out a recon before launching our raid.'

'Do you have a plan?' Lukas asked.

'I will have one, as soon as I carry out the recon,' Jack replied. 'We can't just barge in firing from the hip or the Nips might kill their prisoners. Private Rabasumbi will go with me on the recon while the rest of the section will remain with you, guarding the boat. When we return I will issue orders.' Jack was suddenly distracted by something. 'What's that?' he asked, reaching forward to touch a small leather pouch hanging from a leather strip around his son's neck.

'I keep Megan's engagement ring in it,' Lukas answered self-consciously. 'It's a kind of good-luck token.'

Jack nodded his understanding. 'You'll be all right,' he

said gently. 'I'm your dad, and it's my job to look after you, remember that.' Lukas felt his father's strong hand on his shoulder. 'I only have one son, and he is bloody precious to me.' Lukas could hear the emotion in his father's voice. 'But what you and I are doing is a family thing. Ilsa shares our blood.'

'I know, Dad,' Lukas said, touched and surprised by his father's uncharacteristic display of emotion. 'You and I will get her back – no matter what.'

Jack took his hand off his son's shoulder and wiped at his face with the back of his hand. 'Bloody sun makes your eyes water,' he said.

★

Lukas took the helm for the last leg up the coast, seeking out a safe place to anchor. The sun was low on the horizon but night was still an hour away when one of Jack's PIB men shouted from the bow. He had spotted something and Jack hurried forward with his binoculars.

A native canoe manned by two men came into view.

'Probably out fishing,' Jack said to Corporal Gari, who had taken up a position next to him. 'Better to get to them before they reach shore and alert any Japs in the area.' He turned to Lukas and beckoned towards the canoe, now making its way to the shore.

Lukas opened up the throttle and the *Riverside* strained to run down the fleeing canoe. Within a few minutes they had overtaken the two terrified New Guinean men in the canoe. Jack could see a couple of large fish at their feet. He yelled to them to stop and the two frightened men automatically raised their hands in surrender. Jack spoke to them in pidgin and the men responded in the same language.

'Are there Japanese soldiers in your village?' Jack asked after ascertaining where they were from. They both said yes and that the Japanese were bad men.

Jack knew that the New Guineans would have said the same about them had positions been reversed.

'Don't trust them,' Corporal Gari growled, fingering the trigger on the Bren gun trained on the helpless men. 'We should kill them now, before they can row to the village and warn the Japanese.'

Jack considered this proposition. It was war and these men were a threat to his mission. 'I will give you men two shillings each if you row back that way and only return to your village in one day's time,' he said, retrieving two silver coins from his pocket and holding them up for examination. 'If you return any earlier, I will kill you.'

The two fishermen did not need to consider the conditions of the bargain, saying straightaway that they would prefer the money.

'Do the Japanese men have any white prisoners?' Jack asked, still holding the coins.

'One man they behead,' one of the fishermen answered, licking his lips. 'They have a white woman still.'

Jack felt his heart skip a beat. Ilsa was still alive, or had been when the men had left the village early that morning to fish. Jack continued questioning the men and learned how many Japanese he was up against; they told him that the Japanese were dissatisfied with being left behind. They could not tell Jack much more, and he would still have to carry out his reconnaissance of the village. Jack threw the money down to the two men, who eagerly caught it and just as eagerly pushed off, paddling as fast as they could in the direction Jack had indicated.

'They will betray us,' Corporal Gari muttered in disgust.

'I don't think so,' Jack said, noting the ripples of tide close in shore. 'The wind and tide are against them, and it will take at least two days for them to return if they continue in the direction I told them to go.'

Corporal Gari gazed after the canoe and nodded with grim satisfaction.

★

'Petty Officer Fuji!' Lieutenant Yoshi bellowed. 'Report to me immediately.'

Fuji scrambled to put on his shirt and trousers. In the bunk beside his own, Oshiro was still sleeping, recovering from his ordeal days earlier. Fuji had been able to take his friend's shifts without their commanding officer noticing, but the double duties had taken a toll on him and he was groggy as he slipped on his boots.

Stumbling outside into the rain, Fuji covered the short distance between his hut and that of his commanding officer. He climbed up the steps and stood outside the entrance, awaiting further orders.

'Come in, Petty Officer,' Lieutenant Yoshi commanded.

Fuji entered the room and bowed at the waist in the most respectful manner he could.

'I have had a message from naval headquarters. We are finally to be rid of our prisoner today,' the lieutenant said.

'Now we can get on with serving our Emperor in the way we were trained and not as mere gaolers. It is your duty to prepare the woman for handover.' He then went on to explain what Fuji must do.

Fuji heard the words and wondered why he should feel regret for the prisoner's fate. After all, she was one of the enemy.

'Yes, sir,' Fuji replied and left the hut to do his duty.

TWELVE

Lukas had been lucky enough to locate an anchorage in the mouth of a swampy creek hidden amongst mangroves. The rain that pelted down raised a mist, further concealing the *Riverside*. Lukas had sent the crew and PIB men ashore to cut saplings to hide the boat, and when they had finished she was almost invisible to those ashore and at sea.

Lukas ensured all weapons were stripped, cleaned and made ready for action, and he was pleased to see his father nod his approval at such careful preparation.

'Rabasumbi and I will go ashore and conduct a recce,' Jack said, arming himself with his Owen gun and spare magazines of ammunition. He strapped a large knife, honed to a razor's edge, to his webbing belt, along with a couple of Mills bomb grenades primed for use. 'Corporal Gari will be in charge of the boys while I am gone.'

Private Rabasumbi armed himself with a Bren gun, grenades and a deadly sharp-edged machete. On top of his personal weapons, the PIB soldier carried a cumbersome radio. It was one of three that Mel Jones had been able to barter from a marine unit months earlier. The radios only had a range of around three miles with the aerial fully extended, but they could be carried by one man. At thirty-eight pounds it was a considerable load for a soldier, but Private Rabasumbi had carried heavier loads in the past.

'Take it easy, old man,' Lukas said with a grin as his father and the PIB soldier clambered over the side of the boat and splashed into the shallow, muddy water of the creek. The rest of the men scanned the waters, rifles ready, for any sign of the big saltwater crocs that inhabited these mangroves.

'Just remember the tide,' Jack said over his shoulder. 'You don't want to be hung up in the creek.'

Lukas felt a little annoyed that his father would remind him of something so simple. He felt like a little boy being taught how to handle his trading schooner. Then he realised from the expression on his father's face that he was only worried for him and he regretted his irritation. He was worried for his father, too. Who knew what the recon mission would find – there could be a platoon of Japs out there, just waiting for his father to step into their ambush. Lukas shuddered. It didn't bear thinking about.

★

Jack and Rabasumbi began squelching their way through the tangle of mangroves, the glutinous mud sucking at their boots. They fought their way inland, the rain showing no sign of letting up, and eventually encountering solid ground. They trudged on, following a compass bearing that would take them towards the Japanese outpost. According to Jack's calculations they would arrive at the village midafternoon, when they still had light to observe the enemy dispositions and plot an effective means of assault.

Both men moved cautiously in the thick underbrush, thankful that the weather would help muffle the sound of their movement.

Private Rabasumbi was at home in the jungle. As a boy and young man he had hunted wild pig and cassowaries for food. Stealth had been the secret of success, and now he used the same principles to hunt his enemy. Just before they reached their target, Rabasumbi stopped and signalled the enemy was ahead.

Jack froze. Now Rabasumbi pointed them out he could see two heads under capes, just above a well-concealed parapet of fallen logs. Both men watched carefully, identifying a Nambu machine gun post. This enemy was well prepared, Jack thought, and was pleased to have decided on this careful reconnaissance before deploying his small section of men for an attack.

Jack and Rabasumbi carefully made their way to another position, slithering on their bellies until they were certain they were out of sight of the Japanese crew manning the machine gun. From here they proceeded to observe the southern flank of the cluster of thatched buildings. Japanese soldiers were scuttling between huts in the rain, capes over their heads, oblivious to the fact that they were being watched by their enemy.

★

Even as Jack settled into his OP with Rabasumbi, Mel Jones heard something that had brought terror to him years earlier, when he was on the Atlantic convoys. It was a sound he would never forget, and now he leaned against the bow, scanning the flat grey sea through a veil of steady rain, trying to find the source.

'Get over here, Luke,' he said quietly.

'What is it, Mel?' Lukas asked, assuming a position beside the burly American and taking the binoculars from him.

'See if your one good – and young – eye can spot anything out there . . . about a quarter mile away.'

Lukas took the glasses and adjusted the focus, peering as best as he could through the sheets of rain. Then he saw it and his blood froze. It was just the dimmest outline of a surfaced submarine.

'Yank or Jap?' he said softly.

'Neither,' Mel replied. 'It's a Kraut U-boat. I know that sound anywhere. I heard it once too often in the Atlantic, when the goddamned sons of bitches would surface at night to shell us.'

'German!' Lukas exclaimed and remembered that the Germans were still active in the Pacific, albeit in very small numbers. 'What in hell is it doing out there?'

'Just pray that it doesn't spot us,' Mel replied.

'You sure what we're looking at is a U-boat?' Lukas queried. 'What if it's a Yank sub?'

Mel leaned back from the bow railing. 'If you look carefully you will see that its deck gun is manned by three sailors, and I know the outline of a German 88. At least it hasn't got one of those goddamned 105s mounted.'

Lukas strained his eye and could see that his engineer was right. The distinctive outline of the dreaded German 88 gun was apparent, and it was manned. Off the U-boat's bow he could see a small dinghy, rowed by two people, making its way towards the beach. When Lukas swung his glasses to the deck he noticed that people were moving around, but he could not make out what they were doing.

Lukas knew he had the element of surprise on his side, and to bag a U-boat would be the pinnacle of his fighting career. If the Germans were firing the deck gun from a rolling deck, the sub would have to be close to their target to get an accurate shot in, and if they did so it meant they could not dive. If he opened fire on the surfaced sub the commander would have to choose between fighting or diving for safety. Lukas knew the sub was in shallow water, and the U-boat commander would probably have to remain surfaced until it could reach deeper water. He would naturally have to order his deck gun crew below if he were to make a crash dive to run for deeper water.

On the other hand, Lukas could simply remain hidden in the creek without exposing his boat to the German submarine. After all, his mission was to support his father's rescue attempt, not bag a U-boat.

Mel had already signalled to the men on the *Riverside*

to remain absolutely silent, lest the sound travel across the water and alert the gun crew to their presence.

'We have to give it a go,' Lukas said quietly. 'This is a once in a lifetime opportunity.'

'Are you crazy?' Mel exclaimed. 'We can't take on a U-boat with just a .50 cal as our heaviest weapon!'

'We have a mortar, and just one hit on the hull would either destroy or cripple the sub,' Lukas said.

'You don't have any real experience with the mortar,' Mel reminded him. 'Besides, we're rolling against the tide and the balance for the tube would be out of whack. I say that we just sit it out and radio a report to the fly boys. Let them hunt her down.'

'I'm going to take the mortar ashore. We'll set up on firm ground away from the *Riverside*,' Lukas said, quickly working out the details of his impromptu plan. 'That way the location of the boat won't be compromised, and my guess is that a mortar fired from shore will be hard to spot. From what I know of U-boats, they don't even have a range finder and have to rely on line of sight to engage a target.'

'You're crazy, you know that?' Mel grunted, then added, 'I can act as your forward observer – if you take a radio.'

Lukas turned to his engineer; he could see the resignation in his face, but there was excitement too.

'I always wanted to get even with those Kraut bastards,' Mel said with a determined smile. 'I saw a lot of good Joes die in the freezing seas of the North Atlantic, and we never once had the chance to fight back. Now we have one of those sons of bitches sitting out there, charging its batteries, without any clue it might be mincemeat in a few minutes. This is a chance to get our own back.'

Lukas slapped his friend on the shoulder. 'Good on you, cobber,' he said, watching the dim outline of the enemy submarine. He quickly selected two of the heftiest of his father's soldiers for mortar duty and informed them of his plan. He gave orders for all mortar bombs to be brought on deck and their charge bags protected against the rain. Lukas personally grabbed one of the two remaining radios and clambered overboard, followed by his men with the mortar, who were in turn followed by others carrying the precious ammunition.

Lukas prayed that the sub would not move away as he fought his way through the mud until he found a spot in the mangroves where the sand had packed hard. Out of the corner of his eye he noticed a huge croc slither into the water but his adrenaline was pumping so hard he did not pay it much heed. The most dangerous creature he was focused on right now was the commander of the German U-boat.

Lukas quickly set up the tube on its base plate and bipod support, realising that the sub would most probably steam out of range as soon as the first bombs began falling. He remembered just a few critical elevations related to ranges and ammunition type. He had a plentiful supply of high-explosive shells, so he did not need to be concerned about conserving ammunition. He quickly traversed the tube and elevated it to calculate the distance he figured the sub was offshore. Squatting by his mortar, Lukas established radio contact with Mel, who had a good view of the target.

'Firing now,' Lukas said, dropping the first bomb down the tube. With a loud popping sound and a puff of smoke, the mortar bomb was launched into the rain-sodden sky, barely missing overhanging branches of a mangrove tree. Lukas waited, preparing a second bomb. He hardly heard the mortar round explode on the surface of the sea.

'You were around three hundred yards high and about the same wide of the sub,' Mel's voice crackled over the radio. 'The sons of bitches are running around on the deck like chooks with their heads cut off.'

Lukas quickly made corrections to the mortar barrel and dropped the second bomb down the tube.

'Going the wrong way with your fall of shot,' Mel's voice came over the radio. 'And it looks like the sons of Nippon are going to make a run for it. The gun crew are leaving their post.'

Lukas made a quick calculation in his head and fiddled with the ranging devices on the mortar traversing and elevation adjustment. Down went another bomb, and long seconds later Mel's voice came over the radio. 'That was closer. You were around twenty yards short, and about the same wide.'

Lukas made another adjustment, dropped a bomb and waited.

'Short and wide again,' Mel said sadly. 'The Kraut looks like he's going to dive for it. I think we've lost this one.'

Lukas sighed. It had been worth a try and at least he had got in some practice with the mortar. Now it was time to return to his boat and await his father's return.

★

Hours earlier Ilsa had been shaken awake by a grim-faced Fuji.

'You must prepare yourself to go,' he said, standing over her.

Ilsa rose, wiping down her ragged clothes in an instinctive way as if she had been informed she were going to a party, not to an uncertain fate.

'Where am I going?' she asked.

'I am to take you to the beach, where there is a boat to take you on a German submarine. After that, I do not know.'

So she was not being taken to her execution, as she had resigned herself to, but instead conveyed to a German submarine.

Two guards appeared and Ilsa's hands were tied behind her back. They gestured with their rifles for her to leave the hut, and then marched her along a trail winding through groves of scrub until they reached a small beach where a native canoe with an outboard engine was waiting. Through the sheets of rain, Ilsa could see the dark shape of a submarine at anchor in the small inlet. The canoe puttered out to the submarine, where Ilsa was helped up the side and into the hands of a couple of very young German sailors.

'This way, miss,' one of the sailors said, and Ilsa turned to Fuji, who sat in the canoe looking up at her.

'I wish you well, Miss Stahl,' Fuji said as he pushed away from the hull of the U-boat.

Ilsa found his farewell strangely touching, and nodded her appreciation. Despite his being the enemy, she had come to know him as a sad and lost man who had ensured she had been treated as well as possible. She turned to the

German sailors and was escorted to a hatch on the sub's deck.

One of the German sailors untied her wrists and helped her climb down the ladder to the interior of the U-boat. She was immediately assailed by the familiar stench of men living close together in cramped conditions.

Ilsa could see in the expressions of the sailors she passed a certain amount of sympathy for her physical condition. She had lost a lot of weight, and her face was gaunt with the shadows of malnutrition and fever. Her hair was matted but her large eyes still burned with a luminous defiance. Ilsa knew it was her duty to keep alive and face each situation as it arose.

The sailors took her to a cabin, which she guessed must have belonged to the captain, as it had a single bunk and the tiny room held a photo of a young woman with two beautiful children at her side. Ilsa sat down on the edge of the bunk and a sailor stood by the open door until a lean young man with short-cropped blond hair appeared in the doorway. He wore a clean uniform decorated with an iron cross, and a well-worn and battered naval cap turned down at the sides.

'I am Commander Michael Schmidt,' he introduced himself. 'This is my boat.'

'Ilsa Stahl,' Ilsa said without attempting to rise from the bunk. 'I am an American war correspondent and a prisoner of war.'

'I know who you are, Miss Stahl, and we do abide by the Geneva Convention, despite the fact our enemy attempts to discredit us by saying otherwise. You will be afforded all privileges accorded to a prisoner of war, and I think our cook will be able to prepare you a good meal. I am sure that a bowl of sauerkraut and sausage will be to your liking.'

'Thank you, Captain,' Ilsa replied, realising that she was speaking in her mother tongue of German. 'It has been a long time since I had such a meal.'

'Coffee?' the U-boat commander asked.

'Yes, thank you,' Ilsa replied.

'When you have eaten I will have you escorted to another section of my boat to be your quarters for the duration of the journey. I will ensure that you are well treated by my crew and—'

Suddenly a slight shudder passed through the sub's hull. The captain immediately left the room, shouting orders. Ilsa could hear the boat's engine go to full power and, after a few minutes of moving, felt the incline in the room. It was obvious from the clanging of metal and running footsteps outside the cabin that the men of the German sub were going to action stations.

Seconds later a stronger shudder rocked the boat, and Ilsa began to think that maybe they were under attack, but from what, she couldn't begin to guess.

*

Jack was confused. He could hear the crackling conversation between his son and Mel Jones over their radio, and realised that his son was receiving artillery-like corrections. What in hell was Lukas firing at?

When it appeared that the fire mission was over, Jack broke in to question what had happened. Lukas gave a scant report.

'We have to get back to the *Riverside*,' Jack whispered to Rabasumbi, who informed him that he had heard the distant sound of explosions, muffled by the constant soaking rain.

Checking carefully for any enemy around them, both men slithered a safe distance on their bellies, then got to their feet and began their trek back to the *Riverside*. Whatever had happened was sure to alert the Japanese outpost to their presence in the area, and Jack had a sick feeling it would jeopardise their mission.

★

Fuji raced back to the village as fast as he could. He had barely returned to shore when unidentified mortar fire had rained down on the U-boat. The German sub was lucky the fire had not been accurate and it had been able to escape – for a moment there, Fuji had thought it was doomed, and Miss Stahl with it.

Back in the village he briefed Lieutenant Yoshi on the attack. The commander listened carefully and then issued his orders. They would send out a large patrol to locate the mortar base plate.

A surge of exhilaration went through Fuji as he contemplated returning to the war that seemed to have passed them by. It had become obvious to him that HQ in Rabaul had forgotten them, and no longer needed them for whatever behind the lines operation they had originally planned. At least now Fuji and the other highly trained men could track down their enemy and kill every last one of them.

★

'Why on earth did you think you would have a hope in hell of hitting a German sub with indirect fire?' Jack demanded of Lukas, barely restraining his rage. 'You had more hope of finding a needle in a haystack.'

Lukas poured his father a hot coffee laced with a generous tot of whiskey, and then did the same for himself. They sat forward away from the crew, under the protection of groundsheets that hardly kept them dry. The night was pitch black and no lights shone from the *Riverside*, which rocked gently on the incoming tide.

'I had to do something,' Lukas answered sheepishly. 'The target rated as a high priority. If we had sunk her we might have prevented a lot of people from being killed by her torpedoes in the future.'

Jack knew his son's actions had been impulsive but he could not maintain his anger at him. Maybe he would have chosen the same course of action if he had been in Lukas's shoes; his son was right – a submarine was a deadly weapon and the good of many must be balanced against the good of one.

'You had a go and it didn't work out,' Jack relented. 'Matter closed.' He took a sip of the strong black coffee. 'Now, launching a raid is going to be difficult but, oddly enough, your actions might have helped us. If I were the Nip commander I would already have a patrol out searching for us. They'll have a good idea of where we are and it is only a matter of time before they find us.'

'Do we pull out and abort the op?' Lukas asked.

'No, we use the distraction to our own ends,' Jack replied. 'If the Japs have sent out a patrol, their village defences will be significantly reduced. Rabasumbi and I have a good idea of the village layout and Jap positions, so I will take a small force of myself, Rabasumbi and four of my men to the village. We'll move in a flank to avoid their patrol, which I presume will be coming this way and should be around this area by morning. That means we will have to set up an ambush tonight, which should keep the patrol pinned down while we make an assault on the village. Mel will remain aboard and allow himself and the *Riverside* to be spotted, while you will have the rest of my section and your boys set up out in the mangroves.'

'It's a risky plan, Dad,' Lukas said. 'They might not walk into the ambush. They might destroy my boat. But I trust your experience and judgement, so let's call everyone in and brief them. I think we should get this show on the road.'

'Good idea,' Jack said. 'We should have your men in position before midnight to ensure the Nips don't catch us asleep.'

The crew and PIB soldiers were mustered in the rain and informed of the plan. None questioned it and Mel just grunted his understanding.

'You keep the .50, Mel,' Lukas said. 'Maybe you will be in a position to give us covering fire when the time comes.'

The briefing over, Jack supervised the collection of weapons and Lukas dragged out his mortar. He would use his old mortar base plate location again, as the lack of foliage overhead allowed the bombs to ascend without interference.

Although it was risky, Jack made a decision to use torches so the ambush party could set up their positions;

he made a calculated guess that the enemy would still be a way off, the heavy undergrowth and pouring rain slowing them down as it had him and Rabasumbi. He appointed Corporal Gari to command the ambush, and it was after midnight when he was satisfied the ambush was in place.

With his small party of heavily armed men, Jack slogged his way through the jungle in inky blackness. Just before dawn the rain eased, and soon afterwards Private Rabasumbi signalled that they were very close to the village. Just then Jack heard the first distant crump of an explosion from the direction of the *Riverside*, indicating that he had been right about the enemy's movements. Jack found himself madly praying that his son would be safe.

He glanced at the luminous dial of his watch and noted that it was just after 0545. It was now or never, he told himself, and whispered his final orders to his men, who had quietly gathered around him. The first target was the Japanese machine gun post. Jack knew it would be manned at all times, as it covered a track into the village. Private Rabasumbi volunteered to take one of the men out into the bush and flank the gun; the elimination of the machine gun crew would be the signal to launch the assault on the village. Which hut Ilsa was being held in could only be ascertained once they cleared the village.

Rabasumbi and the soldier accompanying him melted into the jungle while Jack nervously fiddled with his Owen gun. Village dogs were barking now, sniffing the intruders on the outskirts, but their barking was silenced by the explosive blast of a grenade coming from the direction of the machine gun post.

'Okay, boys, up and at them,' Jack said, rising from the

wet, stinking earth and brushing aside the sodden foliage that had concealed him and his men.

He sprinted straight for the hut he had earlier observed being used by the Japanese soldiers as a billet and was at the entrance when the first bleary-eyed soldier emerged, armed with a rifle and wearing nothing more than a loincloth. Jack cut him down with a burst of fire, bullets slamming into the soldier's chest and stomach, throwing him on his back. Jack quickly pulled the pin from a grenade and held it for a couple of seconds to allow the internal fuse to burn down, before tossing it through the open doorway. The blast ripped through the flimsy sides of the building, and he could hear a man screaming inside.

There was no way back now, and Jack was aware that he and his men would have to kill every Japanese they came across, without giving any quarter.

THIRTEEN

The rain had eased, leaving a steamy mist rising throughout the mangrove swamp. Lukas lay on his stomach next to his precious mortar tube, gripping a .303 Enfield. He peered into the mist, straining to hear any sound that was out of place. He knew that his father had laid out an L-shaped ambush position covering the most likely approach, and about a hundred yards away the *Riverside* lay at anchor, Mel standing by his machine gun.

The waiting was terrible, and every sound made Lukas start with fright. To reassure himself he touched the little leather bag around his neck, feeling the engagement ring inside. He swore to himself that he would return and place it on Megan's finger as soon as they had completed this mission; he might even consider taking an administrative job back in Moresby, which he knew would please her.

Lukas sensed that the Japanese were coming, and the only thing he and Jack's men had on their side was surprise.

He did not see the first Japanese soldiers enter the ambush zone, but Corporal Gari did, initiating the attack with a long burst from his Bren gun; immediately afterwards Jack heard the ripping sound of rifles engaging the enemy in the thick tangle of mangroves.

Whilst setting up his mortar, Lukas had agonised over his elevations and traverses, and now he prayed that his calculations were correct. He dropped the first bomb down the tube, and the projectile soared skyward to drop back into the mangroves. The explosion was about two hundred yards out and, using his hearing, he ascertained that he had dropped the bomb in the place he had calculated would intersect the route the enemy would take to engage them. Muffled screams of men caught in the explosion drifted to him.

'Bloody beauty!' Lukas whooped and dropped another bomb down the tube.

★

Petty Officer Oshiro, leading the patrol of ten men, had been taken by surprise. One of his forward scouts had spotted the concealed boat, and Oshiro had given orders to form a line of assault to attack the boat, which was seemingly manned by only one guard on a heavy machine gun. It was when they were making their cautious approach that all hell broke loose. The soldier next to Oshiro collapsed, almost cut in two by a burst of machine-gun fire that erupted from very close by. Oshiro cast about desperately for the rest of his patrol, as bits and pieces of foliage were whipped off the stunted, tough trees around him.

The ambush had been cleverly concealed, Oshiro thought despairingly, and immediately knew that he would have to fall back and try to outflank his hidden enemy. But as he did so, the first mortar bomb exploded only yards away and cut down three of his men, and it was quickly followed by another explosion that took the life of another man, shredding his arm from his body and tearing off the top of his head.

The rifle and machine-gun fire continued to tear through his patrol, but the mortar was inflicting the worst of the casualties. Oshiro did not know if the fall of shot was being directed, but he knew he must eliminate the mortar.

'Get on your feet and advance to our left,' he shouted to the remainder of his men.

More bombs fell but now they were random, as if the operator of the mortar were probing for the survivors of the enemy patrol.

More by luck than calculation, Oshiro saw movement through the mangroves. He sent up a silent prayer of thanks to the ancestral gods because he could see the mortar man fiddling with the sights on the mortar, preparing to fire again. Oshiro leaned forward and fired his rifle. The bullet smacked up a squirt of mud beside the mortar operator, who reacted by snatching up his rifle and looking around to identify where the shot had come from.

Oshiro fired again and saw that his enemy had rolled

to the ground behind a log that appeared to have been put in place for his protection. Oshiro noticed one of his men moving up beside him; he, too, had seen the mortar and was firing off rapid rifle rounds at the log, pinning down the operator. Oshiro knew the only way he could get to the enemy behind the log was to move in closer and use a grenade.

Oshiro moved closer until he was only about ten feet away, and lobbed his grenade towards the log. He was satisfied to see that it had fallen on the other side, but when he glanced up he suddenly realised the mortar was covered by the big American .50 calibre machine gun mounted on the boat, just visible through a gap in the mangroves. The gun was pointed in his direction and Oshiro did not understand the words the gunner was yelling.

Oshiro was vaguely aware that the explosive sounds around him were the thumb-sized heavy projectiles from the enemy machine gun ripping apart the foliage – and his own body. He felt no pain as he fell to the ground, only a strange sense of relief that his war was finally over.

*

Lukas heard Mel scream the words, 'Look out! Grenade!' and he turned his attention away from his mortar. For a split second, Lukas caught sight of the Japanese soldier throwing the grenade and then the man seemed to explode in a red mist, as the heavy .50 calibre rounds ripped through his upper body.

The small metal object arched through the air as Lukas instinctively flung himself down behind the log between himself and the bullet-riddled Japanese soldier. But, alarmingly, the grenade fell on his side of the downed tree, only a few feet from him. Type 91 or 97, Lukas thought, and lunged towards the grenade to toss it over the log away from him. He was on his knees when the grenade exploded with a blinding flash and ear-splitting bang.

Lukas was hurled back against the log and lay crumpled in a world of shock. Then the terrible pain hit him and he knew that the small but deadly hand grenade had done its job. He did not know exactly where the fragmented metal casing had hit him, but it seemed all his body had taken the full impact.

He rolled painfully on his back to stare up at a clear patch of blue sky above and tasted blood in his mouth. Mel was still screaming orders to him. 'Keep your head down!' he could hear.

For some strange reason, Lukas remembered a time that he and Karl had scored a try together playing rugby at their boarding school in Sydney. It had been a cold day in June, and Karl was playing front row in the forwards, whilst Lukas hovered near by as a breakaway. Their team work resulted in a greasy ball being slipped from the scrum into Lukas's hands and a break in the opposition defence. With his speed, strength and agility, Lukas made it through to the try line to score.

Then Lukas found he was thinking back to when he was a young man, and his father stood beside him as he learned to handle the navigation of one of their trading schooners. He had felt so proud at how his father praised his sailing skills.

Lukas gasped; the pain was terrible and more blood

filled his mouth. He knew that he was mortally wounded and reached for the small leather pouch attached to his dog tags. He wrapped his hand around the satchel containing the treasured ring intended for Megan's finger, and reassured himself that it was his lucky talisman, and that so long as she loved him, he could not die.

'I'll get to you,' Mel roared above the sluggish chatter of the big machine gun, raking the foliage around Lukas. 'Just hang on.'

Lukas continued to grip the bag containing the engagement ring. He spat a mouthful of blood and sighed. 'Megan,' he whispered, closing his eyes and slipping into an unconscious world where the body-racking pain mercifully faded to nothing.

★

Jack could feel his heart pounding with slippery, sweating fear as he glanced around to ascertain the next threat. Already the Papuan villagers were spilling from their huts, screaming their terror and running towards the shelter of the surrounding forest. When Jack turned around he could see his men going from hut to hut, cautiously probing inside with their bayonet-tipped rifles. Occasionally gunfire was followed by screaming and then silence. Jack was about to congratulate himself on the clearance when, suddenly, a Japanese officer wielding a sword emerged from behind a building and sprinted towards him.

Jack raised his Owen and fired but it clicked on an empty chamber. Absolute fear gripped Jack as he reached for the only weapon he had – his long combat knife.

The enemy officer was only yards away when he slowed to a stop, samurai sword held in both hands and raised above his head. His face was contorted with rage and he was yelling something at Jack.

Jack knew he was dead if he attempted to run; the officer would cut him down from behind. He knew his puny knife was no match for that sword, but still he stood his ground, crouching in the knife fighter's pose.

'C'mon, you yellow bastard!' Jack spat, edging sideways, aware that the blade poised to take his life could descend from any angle.

Suddenly there was a shout – the words sounded like a woman's name, but Jack couldn't be sure – and the Japanese officer lurched forward as if pushed from behind. Jack leaped back to avoid the samurai blade, which still slashed him with its point, opening up a wound across his chest. He lunged forward with his knife, burying it in the officer's chest. The man struggled but the bullet had done its job and, after a few twitches, he lay dead at Jack's feet.

Jack looked up to find a Japanese soldier standing above him, his rifle raised. He blinked and looked again. Surely that couldn't be Fuji Komine? What was he doing here? And why the hell had he shot his commanding officer to save Jack's life?

'My mother has written that you have personally ensured my parents' welfare,' Fuji said, as if reading Jack's mind.

Jack was completely confused. 'Why?' he asked and his question could have meant so many things.

Fuji gave a slow smile. 'Maybe because we are both Papuans,' he answered and laid the rifle stock against his cheek to take aim. The crack of the rifle came an instant before the pain. Jack felt the bullet rip through his thigh, causing him to lose balance and collapse into the mud of the village clearing.

He shouted out in pain, and when he rolled over he could see that Fuji was gone. Instinctively he knew that he had deliberately aimed his shot to wound rather than kill him. He had no idea why Fuji would kill the officer and spare him. Whatever the reason, though, Jack was grateful to be alive.

Seconds later he looked up into the face of one of his men, who was crouching over him with an expression of concern.

'No more Japanese man left alive in the village,' he reported. 'We ask one of the villagers we caught about the white woman and they say she taken away yesterday to the beach.'

'God almighty,' Jack groaned. 'We were only hours late. The German sub must have been here to pick her up.' He couldn't believe it – they had missed Ilsa by less than a day. He didn't dare think about the consequences for her; in fact, he barely allowed himself a moment to register the information. The raid might have been a success, but there was still a lot of work to be done, and he would not stop until he had returned to the *Riverside* and found out whether or not his son was safe.

Jack was relieved to discover that none of the men in his party had been killed or wounded. After a quick sweep of the village for any useful documents or equipment, he made his way back to the *Riverside*, limping with the aid of an improvised crutch and leaning on the shoulder of a PIB soldier.

As he neared the location of the boat he saw the devastating results of the ambush. Dead and mangled Japanese soldiers lay where they had been struck down and already the flies were buzzing around them in the humid air. Jack was greeted by Corporal Gari and Mel Jones, both looking grim, and Jack knew immediately that something had gone terribly wrong.

'How many did we lose?' he asked, leaning heavily on the shoulder of the PIB soldier.

'Just one, Jack,' Mel replied and stepped forward. 'I'm sorry. It was Lukas.'

For a moment Jack thought he had heard incorrectly, and he shook his head in denial. He pushed himself away from the PIB soldier and leaned on the crutch, staring wild-eyed at the American.

'Lukas took the full blast of a Jap grenade,' Mel continued gently. 'He got the mortar working and broke up the Jap patrol, killing a lot of the bastards in the process. He's over here. We haven't moved his body yet.'

Lukas's body was covered with a canvas sheet and Mel gently lifted it away. When Jack looked down at his son's body, he saw that it was covered in blood from the many shrapnel wounds the grenade had inflicted.

'I personally killed the son of a bitch who did this,' Mel said. 'Lukas was one of the best goddamned men I ever had the honour of serving with.'

Jack collapsed to his knees beside the body of his son, ignoring the searing pain from his own wound, and gently stroked his son's thick crop of matted hair. He saw the leather pouch around Lukas's neck and removed it, placing it in the pocket of his trousers.

'We bury him at sea,' Jack said quietly. 'I know that's what he would have wanted.'

The men gathered around the young *Riverside* captain and set about conveying his body to the boat. He was laid out on the deck and, after sending off a radio report, Mel set the boat on course to return to their base down the coast.

A few hours later, out in the open sea, Mel had Lukas's body sewn up in the strip of canvas and weighted with a couple of mortar bombs. The boat came to a stop on a gently rolling sea and Lukas was committed to the deep, as the American engineer read out a passage from a battered Bible. 'Yea though I walk through the valley of the shadow of death . . .'

The body disappeared out of sight below the surface and Jack just stared at the sea. Mel turned over the engine and the *Riverside* continued her voyage. Jack remained on deck until night came, then went below to share the last of the bottle of whiskey Lukas had stowed.

Jack could not cry. He felt too numb. The mission had cost his son's life and had failed to rescue his daughter. There were no words to describe the grief and regret he was feeling. Death had been his constant companion through two world wars, and during his time prospecting in the dangerous territories of hostile tribesmen of Papua and New Guinea, but he had never grown used to it. Even the pain he'd felt at the loss of his beautiful wife Victoria was nothing compared with his pain at losing his son and his daughter. He didn't think he would be able to bear it.

When the bottle was empty, Jack stumbled onto the deck to find a place away from the crew. Gazing at the myriad stars now visible in the clear night sky, Jack was reminded of how he once used to sit on their trading schooner, teaching his son about the constellations of the Southern Hemisphere. Eventually the tears began to trickle down Jack's cheeks and then turned into a flood as he sat sobbing quietly. A few hours before dawn, he stretched out on the deck and fell into an alcohol-troubled sleep, while the boat rolled and pitched on its voyage to safety.

When the sun rose on the next day, Jack reminded himself that he had a job to do, despite the terrible grief he knew he would have to conceal from those around him. The war was not over and the men in his command trusted him to keep them alive.

After five days at sea, Mel guided the boat into the bay It was busy with small craft unloading supplies for the forward sections of the PIB unit camped inland. Offshore sat a destroyer guarding the small fleet.

Jack knew that his wound was not healing well; his leg had swollen and he suspected the gunshot wound in his thigh was infected.

'Got to get you to a hospital so that they can give you some of that new penicillin stuff,' Mel said, examining the wound after the bandages had been removed.

'Guess you could be right,' Jack agreed, although he hardly cared what happened to him now.

Against his protests that he wished to walk, Jack was littered to the PIB encampment.

'Too bloody sick, Sarn't Kelly,' Corporal Gari growled. 'The boys will take you.'

When Jack was received by the unit regimental aid post, his name was recorded on a list of those requiring hospitalisation down south, and he was in luck, as a medevac flight was due out that afternoon.

Until then he lay on a cot inside a big tent with its sides rolled up to catch what little breeze there was wafting through the tall stands of kunai grass. Captain George Vincent stopped by to offer his condolences on the loss of Lukas. Jack appreciated the gesture but didn't want to talk about his son's death. Vincent, sensitive to that, talked instead about Jack's mission.

'Some of the papers your boys picked up were interesting,' he said, taking a seat on a wooden crate beside Jack's cot. 'It appears that the mob you and your boys cleaned up were a special squad, sent behind our lines to secure a base for future operations. The intercepted Nip signals out of Rabaul confirm that your daughter was one of their captives. I'm so sorry that you missed her.'

'It appears that a German sub was sent to pick her up,' Jack said in a hoarse voice. He was starting to feel feverish; the throbbing in his leg seemed to be growing worse – it was incredibly painful now – and he was experiencing a great thirst. He unsuccessfully groped for a water canteen beside the field stretcher. 'You don't know if any of our intelligence people know anything about the Hun U-boat?'

'Sorry, Jack,' Captain Vincent replied, reaching down and passing the canteen to Jack. 'That's a navy matter and you would have to ask them.'

Just then a couple of PIB soldiers came to take Jack to the airfield. There was a tropical storm brewing over the mountains, and the pilots wanted to get going before the storm hit. Jack was loaded aboard the transport and, within hours, found himself under a creaking fan in a Port Moresby hospital.

He was examined by doctors, who immediately put him on a course of antibiotics, giving orders to have his wound cleaned and bandaged each day. By the second day the throbbing in his leg had subsided a little. He lay in his bed with its clean white sheets, thinking about his son. He hoped he would be able to rejoin his unit, but a visit from his commanding officer in Moresby soon quashed that idea – upon discharge he was to return to PIB HQ to resume his work in intelligence.

On the third evening, as the sun was setting, Jack noticed a couple of American air force officers strolling through the ward.

'Hey, captains,' he called, recognising their rank by the insignia on their chests. 'You got a moment?'

The two officers approached Jack's bed.

'What can we do for you, Aussie?' one of them asked. He was typical of the young, clean-cut and confident men who flew for the American air force.

'I was just wondering if either of you two gentlemen know a Captain Clark Nixon; a flyer like yourselves.'

The two men glanced at each other before answering.

'You knew Captain Nixon?' one of them asked.

'Yeah, a good bloke,' Jack said and slowly became aware that the American officer had used the past tense. 'Is he okay?'

'I'm sorry,' the American pilot replied. 'Clark's crate was shot up on a mission in the islands. No survivors.'

Jack sighed. The bloody war just kept taking people from him. 'I'm sorry to hear that,' he said and the pilot nodded.

But the second pilot turned to his comrade. 'That was Grant's crate, not Clark's,' he corrected. 'Clark has been rotated stateside as an instructor, lucky son of a gun.'

Jack felt pleased to know that the young American officer was safely out of the front lines. He hoped that one day they might meet again. If all had gone well, Clark Nixon would have been his son-in-law. He would have to write to him today and tell him what had happened to Ilsa, why the mission had failed. He didn't relish the prospect. 'Thanks, cobber,' Jack said, settling back against his clean sheets. 'Keep your bloody heads down and good luck.'

The two pilots nodded their thanks and moved on, leaving Jack to reflect on how things might have been had it not been for the misfortunes of war that had cost him his beloved Victoria, his son and his daughter. For a moment he found his mind wandering to his best friend's widow and her son – Karin and Karl Mann. They were as close to family as he had left now. Jack had always liked Karin, who had been like a second mother to Lukas when he was a young boy. He would go to Townsville in person to tell her about his death; she deserved that.

The overhead fan continued to creak, and the night was mixed with the moans of men reliving the hell of the jungles and the footsteps of a nurse gliding gently amongst them with soothing words. For Jack Kelly, no words or soothing touch could ever take away the pain.

FOURTEEN

By the end of a week in hospital Jack Kelly was becoming restless. He had received visits from old mates and his boss, Major Bill Travers, who assured him that his job in Port Moresby was just as important as that of being with the troops in the field. But the loss of Lukas had changed Jack. All he wanted was the chance to return to the fighting, to be absorbed by the comradeship of men facing danger on a daily basis. Nothing else seemed to matter.

One evening he saw Megan enter the ward. He was surprised to see her – he didn't know she was back in Moresby. He struggled to sit up, then noticed that she had not seen him but had stopped by a bed at the end of the ward, occupied by an RAAF medical officer recovering from dengue fever. She sat herself in a chair by the patient's bed and they began to talk; he could see that they were deep in conversation. After about half an hour, Megan rose, bent over and kissed the man.

'Megan.' Jack called softly and she turned, gave a big smile and hurried to his side.

'Oh, Jack, it is good to see you again,' she said.

'It's good to see you too,' Jack responded.

Megan removed his medical records from the end of his bed and scanned them. 'How does a man of your age get shot in the thigh?' she frowned. 'And how is Lukas?'

'You haven't heard?' Jack asked.

'Heard what?' Megan replied, still frowning.

'Lukas was killed a couple of weeks ago or so, up north,' Jack said.

Megan paled and seemed to sway on her feet. 'Oh God, oh no,' she moaned. 'How could that happen?'

'I got him killed,' he said softly. 'It was my fault. He was on a mission with me up north, and it all went wrong.' He began to cry.

For a moment Megan looked too shocked to speak; then she reached out to wipe away the tears running down his cheeks. 'Jack, you can't blame yourself. Lukas was too much like you. He wouldn't have done anything he didn't want to,' she said. 'He had too much courage for his own bloody good.' She started to tremble but did not break down.

Jack continued to cry silently. His son was supposed to have shared his life with this beautiful young woman. They were supposed to get married and have children. Jack would have had grandchildren. But all that was gone now.

'I saw you visiting that RAAF doctor,' Jack said. 'Is he a member of your unit?'

'Yes,' Megan answered, but could not look Jack in the eye.

'You must be very fond of him, from the way I saw you talking together,' Jack said gently.

'Dr Crawford is a fine physician, we're lucky to have him in our unit,' Megan replied stiffly.

Jack was perceptive enough to see the flicker of guilt in her face, but he did not feel angry. Instead he thought of the irony of war, that it should spare Lucas the loss of the woman he had loved so fiercely in life.

'I have to go, Jack,' Megan said, rising from the edge of the bed and giving him a hug. She looked very close to tears. 'I will visit you every chance I get when I'm in Moresby.'

'I would like that,' Jack replied.

When she was gone, Jack reached over to the small cupboard by his bed and opened a drawer. Inside was the small leather pouch with the ring Lukas had planned to give to Megan. He untied the thin leather string attached to the ring and tied it tightly to his dog tags. At least Jack would carry a reminder of happier times when the future had more certainty.

★

Megan stumbled out of the hospital. The night air was warm and she stopped to stare at the star-filled sky above, tears rolling down her cheeks. Lukas would never see that sky again. He was dead. Now she would not have to break the news to him that she had chosen another man. In a way she was relieved that he had been spared that pain, but somehow she felt even guiltier that she had been falling in love with someone else while Lukas was living the last weeks of his life. She felt a terrible pain in her chest and bent over, wracked with sobs. She had loved him and now she would never be able to tell him how sorry she was.

★

It had been a few weeks since the raid on the village by the PIB. Petty Officer Fuji Komine sat at the edge of the beach under the shade of the tall trees. The day was hot and very humid, and the waves lapped feebly against the tiny beach. A line of dark clouds broiled on the horizon, promising a heavy afternoon downpour.

The last of Fuji's supplies were dwindling. He had slipped away into the forest after he shot Jack Kelly in the thigh, then returned to the village when he was sure the raiding party had left. He had been able to retrieve a quantity of hidden Australian currency from the unit pay store and this had been useful in purchasing food from the villagers, who had slowly returned to their homes after the raid.

A few days after it, when he had felt it was safe to venture out, Fuji had searched the route Oshiro and his patrol had taken. He had located the area of an ambush – the signs on the ground were unmissable – but all the bodies were gone. He saw crocodile tracks all around the area, which gave him a pretty good idea of what had happened to his friend's body and those of the others killed that day.

Now, sitting by the sea and staring north, he pondered his future. He was a realist and knew that the western powers would eventually defeat Japan. He was also astute enough to know that if his supply of coins ran out, the villagers would probably kill him, as he would no longer be of any use to them. Fuji was careful to change his campsite on a daily basis to avoid them catching him in his sleep and killing him.

He knew that his options were limited. He could attempt to sit out the war by hiding in the bush or he could do the honourable thing and commit *seppuku*. But Fuji also had to admit to himself that he was not such a devoted warrior of the Emperor that he was prepared to kill himself. He considered his third option. He could trek east and find a village under Australian control, and surrender to his enemy. To his comrades he would be a coward but he had had enough of the war and yearned to see his parents once again. Fuji considered stealing a native canoe as to journey east would expose him to the enemy naval forces which may rescue him under the laws of the sea. To stay alive was important if he were to keep his promise to his old friend.

Fuji sighed and stood up. It was time to relocate and set up his new camp before the rain came.

★

Ilsa's journey aboard the U-boat had been uneventful. She had been treated well, and a regular diet of nutritious food had put a little flesh on her bones and the ulcers on her body had begun to heal.

The captain and crew had been courteous, and a few submariners even sympathetic. From the snippets of information Ilsa was able to overhear, it appeared Berlin was facing imminent attack from the Russian juggernaut. The morale of the crew, however, was still high; they were returning from a successful mission harassing Allied shipping along the east coast of Australia.

Ilsa had been able to ascertain that she had been a prisoner of war for over three months and she wondered if anyone knew that she was still alive. She had requested the U-boat captain to notify the International Red Cross that she was a prisoner, but he had politely refused, saying that he was under strict orders to maintain radio silence. Ilsa did not believe him, as she had once seen the radio officer transmitting and receiving messages in his tiny nook in the sub's hull.

The captain would not tell her their destination, but a sailor she had befriended said that the submarine was scheduled to go to Singapore for resupply but their course had been altered and they were to ship into another port.

'Are we returning to Germany?' Ilsa asked.

'No,' the sailor replied. 'It is too dangerous. I am not sure what we will be doing – only the captain knows our future operations.'

'Do you know where the next port will be?' Ilsa persisted.

'Only our captain and second-in-command know the answer to that question, Miss Stahl,' the sailor replied, glancing around to ensure that they were not being observed in conversation. 'All I do know is that we will be going to another port somewhere in the Far East.'

Ilsa wondered why she should even care where they went. All she knew was that when they arrived, the Gestapo would be waiting for her.

Then, one day, the U-boat surfaced and Ilsa was fetched from where she was held captive. She was told that she had reached her destination and would be handed over to the German authorities.

Ilsa was taken up on the deck and she blinked into the blaze of the tropical sun. When she looked around she saw that the U-boat was cruising in muddy waters and that off its bow lay what was obviously a great delta. She could see many small boats where men wearing wide conical hats to protect them against the sun were fishing with nets in the murky waters.

'I am sorry to say you must leave us here, Miss Stahl,' the captain said, standing with his arms behind his back. 'You will be taken ashore here and handed over to our Gestapo liaison officer.'

'Is this Singapore?' Ilsa asked, taking in the heavy scent of rotting vegetation and human waste as they approached a wharf manned by half-naked Asian coolies and armed Japanese guards.

'No,' the captain replied. 'We have come to the port of Saigon.'

'French Indochina,' Ilsa gasped. 'But why?'

The captain excused himself and turned to speak with his second-in-command. 'I am sorry, Miss Stahl, but I have duties to attend to. I wish you good luck.'

Alone on the deck beside the sub's 88 mm deck gun, Ilsa was flooded with confused thoughts. She knew that Saigon was the capital of the southern French colony of

Indochina and that the Vichy French had been allowed
to continue their government under the watchful eye of
the Japanese occupiers. Ilsa had no idea what was going
to happen to her, but if she were being handed over to
the Gestapo, she would probably be interrogated and executed. She shuddered, wondering why she had survived
her ordeal with the Japanese only to face more suffering
and probable death at the hands of the Germans.

The U-boat slid into a space beside the wharf and when
Ilsa looked up, she could see the distinctive figure of a
European man wearing a white hat and white suit. He was
staring down at her with a grim expression; beside him
stood two Japanese soldiers. Ilsa felt sick. It was obvious
that the old adage applied: she had gone from the frying
pan into the fire. Now no one would ever learn of her fate.
She thought about Clark and despaired.

*

The Berlin road was nothing but a giant rubble heap bor-
dered by grey stone buildings pocked by shrapnel and
bullets. Captain Herff clutched the briefcase containing
the falsified papers identifying him as an ordinary soldier
in the German army. He knew that Berlin was only days –
if not hours – from being engulfed by the Red Army, and
he also knew that his only hope of survival was to escape
to the American front lines, where, it was said, the Americans treated their prisoners according to the rules of the
Geneva Convention.

A massive explosion blasted dust, bricks and parts
of dead bodies into the air and blew Herff off his feet.

Winded, he lay on his back, still clutching to his chest the briefcase with the precious papers. The noise was deafening: artillery rounds exploding, the constant chatter of machine guns and crack of rifles. He could hear people screaming somewhere. Slowly, Herff pushed himself to his knees. He could see an alleyway that he knew led to the railway, which might provide protection from the shelling. He groaned. A detachment of Russian soldiers had appeared only metres away, between him and his escape route. He could see that they were all heavily armed with submachine guns and festooned with grenades; probably a forward unit. Worse still, he could see that they had spotted him and they peeled off in his direction.

'Hands up!' a female voice called in German and Herff obeyed, rising unsteadily to his feet.

Three Russian soldiers, one of them a woman, approached with their weapons levelled at him. He had enough knowledge to know she wore the insignia of a political officer; she looked to be in her mid-twenties and was in fact very pretty, with startling blue eyes and high cheekbones.

'I am a German soldier who has lost his unit. I was attempting to find a unit to surrender to,' he said to the young woman, who watched him with hostile eyes.

'Papers,' she demanded, holding out her hand. Herff reached inside his briefcase, and produced the papers and photo identifying him as a German soldier from an infantry regiment. The woman scanned the papers and looked up at him.

'You are not dressed in the uniform of a soldier,' she said in a cold, flat voice. 'We have been instructed to locate any SS who might be attempting to elude capture.'

Herff felt a cold chill of fear. 'I . . . my uniform was in such bad shape that I changed into civilian clothes.'

The girl continued to stare at Herff, oblivious to the roar of shells passing overhead. 'Take off your shirt,' she ordered.

Herff hesitated.

The young woman rammed the short barrel of her machine gun into Herff's stomach with such force that it knocked him to the ground. He knew he must obey or be shot. He sat up, and struggled to remove his heavy coat and then his shirt.

'Up,' the woman commanded and Herff rose to his feet to stand half-naked before her. The woman glanced over his body, her eyes settling on his right arm below the shoulder. Herff had gone through a lot of pain to have the incriminating SS tattoo removed from his arm.

'You are SS,' the woman said with hate in her voice. 'Your attempt to conceal your identity has not worked. We have found others with the same wound.'

'It was a wound I received a few days ago,' Herff protested but he could see by her demeanour that the Russian woman was not fooled – or simply did not care. 'I am a soldier in the army – not SS.'

The woman raised her submachine gun level with Herff's head. 'You have been found guilty of being a member of the SS and sentenced to death by this people's court.'

Herff raised his hands as a plea to the Russian and, for some strange reason, had a fleeting thought that halfway across the world Ilsa Stahl would be facing death too – he had sent the order through to Saigon only a few days ago.

He had known that her death was a useless gesture but he had ordered it anyway.

The submachine gun bucked in the Russian woman's hands, and the bullets tore into Herff's head, neck and chest. As Herff felt the life go quickly from him, he had a picture in his head of Ilsa Stahl's body jerking in the last moments of her slow death at the end of a piano wire.

FIFTEEN

The Gestapo officer was a fit-looking man in his late thirties, with blue eyes and oiled raven-black hair.

'I am Captain Kurt Wessel,' he said to Ilsa after she had ascended the ladder to the wharf. 'You are my prisoner and I welcome you to hell.'

His words chilled Ilsa to the core.

'I am an American war correspondent and must be accorded the rights of the Geneva Convention,' she countered, with as much defiance as she could muster. The Gestapo officer only smiled coldly.

'As far as your American friends are concerned, you are probably dead,' he said, pushing Ilsa towards a black French sedan car with a Japanese driver behind the wheel. She was ushered into the back seat and Captain Wessel slid in beside her, while the two Japanese soldiers stood aside to allow the vehicle to drive away.

Ilsa sat in silence throughout the trip, taking in the wide boulevards of a Far East city reminiscent of Paris. Eventually they pulled up in front of an imposing colonial building and Wessel ordered her to get out. Ilsa knew that she had nowhere to run in a city occupied by the Japanese, and where she could not speak the language of the local people, as well as not being able to speak French.

'I must apologise for your reception, Miss Stahl,' Wessel said unexpectedly. 'But one of those monkeys on the wharf understood German.'

Confused, Ilsa stared blankly at the German officer.

Without another word, he directed Ilsa inside the building. Vietnamese clerks sat at desks shuffling papers; they hardly looked up as Wessel escorted his prisoner in. He snapped something at one of the clerks, who disappeared for a moment before returning with a squat, vicious-looking Japanese officer. The man had severe pockmarks on his face and his dark eyes were cold as death.

'This is Colonel Hitachi,' Wessel said quietly, saluting. 'He is my superior in Saigon and I think he plans to have me killed if Germany is defeated. But he does not understand German.'

'Do you think Germany will fall to the Allies?' Ilsa asked, glancing with fear at the Japanese officer watching her as a snake watches its prey.

'It is inevitable,' Wessel replied. 'I only pray that the Americans and British get to Berlin before the Russians. The Russkies will not be so generous in their treatment of us after what we have done to their people and country.'

Wessel said something to the Japanese officer, who nodded and walked away. The German officer returned his attention to Ilsa.

'I know who you are, and it was my role to execute you. However, if you wish to live, you will have to trust me and also provide me with the assistance I need to escape this foreign hell. The French can have the place back, for all I care. When Germany falls, the Gestapo will be at the top of the list of wanted. In your position as a journalist, I think, you will be able to pull strings to help me and my family escape to America.'

Ilsa understood that if she cooperated with this German secret policeman, she had a chance of surviving. 'I will not be able to help you whilst I am a prisoner of war,' she said.

'Let me work things out and we both might survive the war,' Wessel said, taking her elbow and guiding her through a door into a dimly lit passage. It housed a row of cells that stank of human excrement and vomit. Ilsa gagged and put her hand over her mouth.

'I am sorry I must bring you here but I will endeavour to keep you out of Colonel Hitachi's hands for as long as I can,' he said.

A short Vietnamese gaoler wearing a pair of oversized dark trousers and a white shirt stood at the end of the corridor. Wessel gestured to him, and the man came forward with a set of keys on an iron ring. He led them past empty cells with their doors wide open, until they came to the last cell in the row. It was a windowless room made of concrete, with nothing more than a filthy straw mattress and bucket inside. The solid timber door had a small observation opening, which was the prisoner's only link to the world outside the prison cell.

'This is the best I can offer for the moment,' Wessel said as Ilsa stepped inside the small cell. 'On a whim, the colonel has emptied the gaol by having all the prisoners of the Imperial Japanese Empire executed yesterday. He is completely insane, but that does not prevent him from being the chief of the *Kempeitai* here.'

The Gestapo officer stepped back and the door was closed, leaving Ilsa alone in the darkened cell, until a light was switched on and filled the cell with a bilious brightness. When she was once again alone, Ilsa experienced a despair deeper than she had ever known before. At least when she had been a prisoner in the jungle, she had had the stimulation of life going on around her. In this desolate place she felt as if she had truly entered the reception area for hell.

That night it became obvious that prisoners were being brought in to occupy the empty cells. She could hear shouting, cries of misery and the clanging of doors shut, until an eerie silence fell on the building, broken only by moans of anguish.

Ilsa finally fell into an exhausted sleep and was woken a few hours later by the high-pitched screams of a woman in agony. Ilsa huddled in the corner of her cell, hugging her knees to her chin and praying that God would protect her from whatever evil was causing so much pain to this poor woman.

The next morning, peering through the opening in her cell door, she saw a European woman, battered and bleeding, being thrown into the cell opposite her own.

She wondered whether this was the woman who had been screaming last night. The door clanked shut and Ilsa waited until she was sure the corridor was empty.

'Can you hear me?' she called softly in English through the aperture in her door. 'Who are you?'

Ilsa did not receive a reply and was disappointed. In the brief glimpse she had caught of the woman she had recognised her as once a beautiful woman, and in a small way it comforted her that she was not alone in this hell.

She returned to a corner of her cell and slumped against the wall. A few minutes later she could hear the other woman sobbing. 'If you can hear me, please let me know,' Ilsa called quietly.

Eventually the sobbing ceased and a thin, strained voice replied, 'Who is calling to me?' Ilsa was startled to hear the woman speak in German.

'I am Ilsa Stahl, an American war correspondent,' she replied in German. 'I was born in Germany.'

After a pause the other woman's voice trailed to her. 'My name is Herlinde Kroth and I am a German citizen. My father is a high-ranking intelligence officer.'

Ilsa felt her hopes shatter completely. If this were what the Japanese were doing to their allies – including the daughter of a high-ranking German officer – what real hope did she have?

★

The stench of death had been everywhere. Bodies of men, women and children had lain in the village streets, only recently dead but already resembling skeletons. Karl and

Pham had moved cautiously. There had been no sign of Japanese soldiers so close to Saigon – nor any evidence of the French administration.

Karl and Pham had landed on the western side of the Indochinese peninsula in the region known as Cochin China. There they had been met by a relative of Pham, an old man with a wispy grey beard and stooped by age. He was practically toothless, and tears ran down his wizened cheeks when he met his nephew.

That night, Karl, dressed in a white shirt and dark trousers similar to the disguise worn by Pham, had sat around a fireplace eating spiced fish with the old man's family. Karl had not been able to understand the conversation going on around him, but he had sensed that all was not well.

'A couple of weeks before we arrived here,' Pham had told him afterwards, 'the Japanese forced the French army to surrender and interned the government administrators. The Japanese have forced the peasants to grow jute and peanuts instead of rice, and have seized any supplies of rice they can find. The people are starting to starve.'

For the next few weeks the two men had moved from village to village on foot, avoiding Japanese patrols. Moving through the countryside of rubber plantations and thick scrub, they had seen the result of the desperate Japanese policy of forcing an enslaved nation to supply its war needs. People everywhere were starving. The gold coinage the men carried ensured that they were usually able to buy what little food there was available for sale, but sometimes they went hungry too. Karl's European appearance did not raise much suspicion and he did not have to try to pass as a German engineer. It seemed he was perceived as just another Frenchman on the run to avoid internment or as one of the French nationals the Japanese trusted as collaborators.

With the fall of the French administration in Indochina, the original plan to enter Saigon and make contact with French officials secretly working for the Free French forces was disrupted. Now they would have to make their way to the town of Tây Ninh, north of Saigon, to make contact with members of the Cao Dai cult. The Cao Dai had sprung up after the First World War, espousing a spiritual movement that included a mix of secular and religious ideals. Amongst its saints were Buddha, Joan of Arc, Jesus Christ, Sun Yat-sen and Victor Hugo. The cult had suffered persecution under the French administration and members had appealed to the Japanese occupiers for protection. Pham knew that their best chance to make contact with the German woman being held by the dreaded *Kempeitai* was through a member of the cult who was related to his uncle.

When they reached the hamlet town of Tây Ninh, Pham took them to a well-tended brick home built in the French style, with white stone walls surrounding a well-kept garden and fishponds; an oasis from the death and misery of the streets. They were met by the servants of the owner, a Vietnamese medical doctor trained in Paris, who enjoyed Japanese patronage.

Pham and Karl were requested to wait inside a spacious room adorned with pictures of the Japanese Emperor. They sat on a comfortable divan, while a pretty young servant girl wearing a long white dress served them coffee.

In a matter of minutes a man around Karl's age and wearing a white suit and tie appeared. He had gold-rimmed spectacles and was prematurely balding. Pham rose and spoke softly in Vietnamese as the man looked Karl up and down.

'I speak English, Major Mann,' the white-suited host said. 'I am Doctor van Nuyen and I believe that you have the authority to speak for the British government.'

Karl stood to address the Vietnamese doctor, surprised to hear that Pham had so elevated his status.

'I have been sent here to make contact with a German national,' Karl said and the doctor raised his hand.

'I know of this,' he said. 'But you must not know that Germany is on the verge of surrendering to the Allies. The war in Europe is almost over. Berlin is in its death throes at the hands of the Russians.'

Stunned, Karl allowed a few moments for the news to sink in. If what he was told were true, then his mission really had no meaning. He and Pham had been isolated from any outside news for so long that a war had ended on the other side of the world and they were only just learning of it now.

'You are sure of that?' Karl countered.

An expression of annoyance darkened the Vietnamese doctor's face. 'We are not all ignorant chinks, Major Mann,' he calmly replied. 'I am certain the Germans have been defeated, and it will only be a matter of time before the Japanese leave our lands to retreat back to their own.'

'Won't that be, as we would say, inconvenient for you?' Karl questioned.

'Please, sit down and I will have food prepared for you,' the doctor said politely. 'My cook is the best in town.'

Karl sat back down on the divan.

'I am useful to the Japanese, as I am a man skilled in medicine,' Nuyen explained. 'But I am also a loyal subject of our Emperor Báo Dai and know that we need the French to return, to establish stability. If they do not return and take power, Ho Chi Minh and his Viet Minh will enforce their communist state on us, and it is not in the nature of us freedom-loving Indochinese to accept dictatorship. This is a complex society of competing groups. Your comrade, Pham, is a Catholic. I am a follower of our great founder, of Ngo Van Chieu's ideals of Cao Dai. We are also living in a devoutly Buddhist country. Yet we all agree that communism is not the answer. The Japanese have kept stability – until now. When their defeat comes we will still need them to resist the Viet Minh in the vacuum that will be created before the French return. That is why I retain a relationship with our enemy.'

Karl understood that the Vietnamese doctor was on the side of the French, and this reassured him a little. He was playing a dangerous game, though. If Ho Chi Minh gained power after the war he would almost certainly be executed as a collaborator.

'I am still under orders to make contact with the German woman,' Karl said. 'Can you help me?'

'I will try,' the doctor replied. 'I have contacts in the *Kempeitai* who may help. But in the meantime I will arrange to hide you both. I have a room in the building where you will be safe from prying eyes.'

Pham said something in Vietnamese and the doctor replied in English for Karl's sake.

'My servants can be trusted,' he said. 'They do not wish to join the many around us starving to death.'

For the next few days Karl and Pham enjoyed the excellent food, hospitality and protection of the doctor. It felt strange to be living in such comfort after weeks of hardship, and Karl felt guilty that they were being so well fed when so many were starving outside these walls.

After a week, Doctor van Nuyen returned from Saigon with the news Karl had been waiting for. 'There is a German woman being held in the *Kempeitai* prison in Saigon,' he told Pham and Karl. 'But I do not know who she is. I have also been informed that the police are holding an American woman.'

Karl frowned. If this were the woman he had been sent to make contact with, her circumstances had changed dramatically. To be suddenly imprisoned did not speak well of the current unstable situation in the country.

'It does not seem that you will be able to complete your mission,' Pham said to Karl.

Karl reflected on this. He was isolated in a country very alien to him; he had only a rudimentary grasp of French and no Vietnamese at all. If the Germans were on the verge of defeat, his false identity papers as a German engineer would be of no use to him. He was faced with the dilemma of continuing with his mission or simply attempting to get out of the country, both of which would require Pham's assistance.

'I have to verify that the German woman being held by the Japanese is the one I seek,' Karl said.

'It is better that you return to Malaya,' Pham said. 'Making contact with the *Kempeitai* is suicidal. The doctor has told me the Japanese are rounding up anyone they suspect of holding defeatist ideas. Even members of the

Cao Dai are being interrogated. The commander of the secret police in Saigon is a brutal and sadistic man, who needs little excuse to have those in his custody tortured and executed.'

'I have come this far,' Karl said. 'I have to at least attempt contact with the German woman to ascertain if she is of any use to us.'

He turned to the doctor. 'What is the attitude of the Japs to the French in Saigon?'

Nuyen shrugged. 'Maybe a certain amount of indifference. The local French population is lying low, trying to avoid the attention of the *Kempeitai*.'

'Do you think you could get me papers identifying me as a Frenchman?' Karl asked and both men looked at him as if he were insane.

'I can do that,' the doctor replied. 'But I do not think it will work.'

'If I am in the streets and stopped by Japanese patrols, all I will have to do is produce the papers and use a few words of French,' Karl said. 'I doubt the average Jap would know the difference between French and German, and if they do I will say that I am from the Alsace region, where we also speak German.'

The Vietnamese doctor stared at Karl for a moment and broke into a smile. 'All Europeans look the same to us,' he said. 'You might get away with it.'

Pham did not have the same optimistic expression. 'I would keep that cyanide capsule very close, if I were you. If the Japs take you prisoner, Colonel Hitachi will torture you himself.'

Karl tried not to think about that. Instead he wondered

about the radio transmitter he had been told about during his brief back in Australia. That seemed a lifetime ago now. Apparently, though, the French resistance in Saigon kept a radio to maintain communication with Allied intelligence. The transmitter was constantly being moved to avoid detection by the enemy. Karl had been given the name of the operator, and he wondered now whether the man was still at liberty or had been interned and perhaps killed.

'I have the name of a Frenchman in Saigon,' Karl said, addressing the doctor. 'I will need your help to find him.'

The doctor appeared anxious and Pham seemed surprised at Karl's mention of a French contact.

'Saigon is a dangerous place now,' the doctor said. 'You are asking much.'

'I understand,' Karl said. 'But from what I know of you, you are a true French patriot.'

Pham said something in Vietnamese to the doctor, who nodded, then turned back to Karl.

'I will help,' he said. 'I will need the papers that identify you as a German engineer. We will alter them so that you are a French citizen. It will take at least a week and until then you will be safe here.'

Karl thanked the doctor. He knew he would be risking his life, but he was not prepared to leave Indochina until he knew whether or not his mission was still viable.

*

Several days after she had been imprisoned – she wasn't exactly sure how many; one day drifted into another without much distinction – Ilsa was visited by the Gestapo officer. Until then she had seen no one but her gaoler, who would bring her a daily ration of rice and fish, and allow her out of the cell to empty the bucket into the sewerage system that was out in a concrete yard within the prison compound. It was then that Ilsa saw the copious amounts of fresh blood on the cement, and the clouds of flies drinking from the red patches. She guessed that the yard was being used for executions but had not heard any gunfire. Ilsa shuddered. The condemned were being beheaded.

One day she had met Herlinde Kroth face to face for the first time. They had not spoken since that initial exchange; Ilsa thought that perhaps Herlinde had been moved to another cell too.

They were fortunate enough to be left alone while their guard sauntered away on another task. Both women sat down in a quiet corner of the open courtyard and struck up a conversation. Ilsa could see that Herlinde had been badly treated by her captors.

'Why are you imprisoned?' Ilsa asked, gently touching the other woman's hand.

'I was betrayed,' Herlinde replied, and Ilsa saw that the young woman had a beauty barely concealed by her cuts and bruises. 'My lover betrayed me to the Japanese.'

'What could you possibly have done to have deserved this fate?' Ilsa said.

Herlinde glanced away and then looked back at Ilsa. 'You are an American despite your German birth. You live under a system of fair laws, but here the enemy make up their laws to suit their own means. My French lover told the Japanese that he suspected I was going to defect to the Americans or British. That was all they had to know to . . .' Herlinde did not end her sentence but stared with vacant eyes at the opposite stone wall of their prison court-yard. Ilsa guessed that what the Japanese had done to her was more than she could bear to remember and squeezed her hand in a gesture of understanding.

Herlinde turned to Ilsa. 'Why are you here and not in a prison camp for women?'

'It is a long story,' Ilsa answered, wanting to avoid going into detail about her father's history. 'But I think that we may have an ally close at hand who will be able to help us both.'

A bitter smile crossed Herlinde's swollen face. 'You cannot trust anyone here,' she said. 'Just look at me. Henri said that he loved me more than his own family but when it came to deciding between his family and me, I was expendable. He used me to barter with the Japanese for his own skin.' Herlinde looked up then and turned even paler under her bruises.

Striding towards them, accompanied by the guard, was the dreaded commandant, Colonel Hitachi. Ilsa felt terror at the sight of him and she saw that Herlinde was trembling.

'You,' he said in heavily accented French. Ilsa and Herlinde glanced at each other.

'You,' Hitachi said again, stepping in front of Herlinde. 'Come.'

Herlinde struggled to her feet, her head down, and was escorted across the courtyard into the building.

Later, back in her cell, Ilsa had called out loudly, 'Her-linde!' but she had received no reply. After that she had been left alone until Captain Wessel's visit.

The Gestapo officer stood inside her cell, smoking a cigarette; he offered Ilsa one and she took it, despite the fact she did not smoke.

'I have organised for a message to be sent through the International Red Cross to inform your country that you are alive and are a prisoner here of the Japanese in Saigon,' he said, lighting Ilsa's cigarette. 'So far Colonel Hitachi has left you alone because you have officially been a prisoner of my department.'

Ilsa took a long suck on the cigarette and let the nicotine flow through her body. She suddenly felt self-conscious about the fact that she must have smelled rank to anyone as clean as this man. She had not been able to wash since the time on the U-boat and had once again lost weight; her skin was covered in sores from the bites of the myriad insects that came in her cell at night.

'Thank you for informing my country that I am still alive,' she said and meant it.

'I expect a favour in return,' Wessel said, looking Ilsa directly in the eye. 'You probably do not know it but Germany has fallen – we have surrendered and are no longer an ally of the Japanese Empire.' He blew smoke into the stale air of the cell while the gaoler hovered outside the door. 'I always thought that sending you to us was a waste of time – it was obvious you would have been too young to know much about your father's pre-war activities – but Himmler insisted. I have heard that our noble leader has killed himself now the Fatherland has been defeated.'

'What favour can I grant you?' Ilsa asked.

'At the moment Colonel Hitachi has ignored my status as a member of a defeated nation, but I will be on a list for arrest by the Allies and could be executed for so-called murderous activities committed by my department. You are a well-known and respected American journalist and I will need you to stand as a character witness to my good behaviour. You will be able to tell your people how I have ensured your wellbeing whilst you were my prisoner.' Wessel crushed the stub of his cigarette under his heel. 'I need you to promise me that you will speak on my behalf to the Americans.'

Ilsa finished her cigarette and let the smouldering stub fall to the concrete floor. 'I cannot do that if I am a prisoner in this place,' she said.

'What if I get you out of here?' Wessel said softly.

Ilsa looked at him with interest. 'How could you do that?' she asked. 'I doubt you hold much influence with the Japanese now that Germany is defeated.'

Wessel stepped closer to Ilsa. 'I have ways, and if I satisfy my part of the bargain to get you free of this place, I expect you to honour your deal to protect me against any misguided American or British sense of judicial revenge. I would also require assistance to resettle in Spain. As a fellow Fascist, General Franco is sympathetic to our plight.'

Ilsa knew that she would do anything to be out of this place, knowing it was only a matter of time before the Japanese came for her.

'If you can get me out of here, along with another woman, Herlinde Kroth, I will honour my side of the bargain,' Ilsa answered.

The German Gestapo officer looked pained. 'Kroth is a prisoner of Colonel Hitachi,' he said. 'It would be madness to interfere in matters of personal concern to him. She is a traitor and has been working against the Japanese Empire. She has confessed during interrogation as to her complicity with the English.'

'Herlinde is a German citizen; surely you have an interest in protecting her from the Japanese.'

'That no longer matters now we are a defeated nation,' Wessel replied. 'All that matters is that we survive. If you do as I say, I can save you. I cannot save Kroth.'

For the first time in months Ilsa considered the possibility that she would survive to return to America. This would be possible because of a man she would rather have seen executed for what she knew he must have done, as a Gestapo officer, to innocent men, women and even children. But Ilsa would have signed a contract with the devil himself if it meant being freed. She had the discomforting feeling that she'd done just that.

SIXTEEN

Captain Featherstone prided himself on his ability to remain emotionally detached from those he commanded. He was acutely aware that many of the missions he assigned men to would prove fatal; he couldn't do his job effectively if he weren't able to send men to their deaths. But he found it difficult to be completely removed when it came to Major Karl Mann, although he could not explain exactly why.

He sat in his Sydney hotel room, enjoying the luxury that both his rank and family fortune could buy, and pondering the sheet of paper stamped *Top Secret*. The sealed document had been delivered to him by an American courier wearing the uniform of the Signals Corp.

A Miss Ilsa Stahl, respected war correspondent for a

well-known New York newspaper, had been listed as a prisoner of war, currently being held by the Japanese in the Indochinese city of Saigon.

Featherstone looked to the signatory and could see that it had been authorised for release by a known colleague in the American OSS. What really caused him to sit up, almost spilling his Scotch, was the paragraph detailing how the said female American journalist was the first cousin to an Australian army officer seconded to his department, Major Karl Mann.

'Good God!' Featherstone exclaimed, rising from his big leather chair.

Why had the OSS sent him this information, Featherstone asked himself and knew that the message was some kind of bait by the Yanks. He just had to work out what it was they wanted. They seemed to know about Mann's presence in Saigon; perhaps they wanted to use him to extract Stahl.

He would find out, but there was something else he felt he must do first. Call it being sentimental, but what he had just learned fitted like the missing piece of a jigsaw puzzle. He took out paper and an envelope from his briefcase and began writing.

A few hours later, Colonel Ben Basham met Featherstone in a small park overlooking the harbour. It was one of those parks tucked away from public view, and both men wore civilian suits. Evening was falling and Featherstone stood gazing out at the flotillas of warships at anchor.

'Hello, Ben, old chap,' Featherstone said when the American colonel approached, puffing on a large cigar.

'Featherstone, pleased to see that you understood my

message,' Basham said, accepting the British officer's hand-shake. 'I'm pleased to see that we can talk.'

'What exactly did your message mean?' Featherstone asked, taking out his packet of cigarettes.

'We know that your Aussie major is in Saigon – or at least in the area,' Basham said.

'How would you know anything of the sort?' Feather-stone countered, cupping a cigarette in his hands as he lit it with a Zippo lighter.

'Your man was up in Malaya, and one of our men was on the same team Major Mann was temporarily posted to. It was not hard to find out where he went after leaving the team,' Basham said. 'We also know all about that Frenchie officer he was with – Indochinese, pro-French, orders to assassinate a couple of high-ranking Viet Minh operatives in Saigon. It seems that the French badly want their old colony back after this war.'

Featherstone baulked at this revelation from his Ameri-can counterpart. The mission had been full of holes from the start, and under pressure from London he had reluc-tantly given support to something he saw as not in British interests.

'What has all this got to do with our operation in that part of the world?' Featherstone asked, suspecting he knew.

Basham removed the cigar from his mouth and rolled it in his fingers. 'Miss Stahl works for a very prominent newspaper in New York and they want her back at all costs. And it just so happens that the owner of the paper is a good friend to our new president, so we have orders to make it happen. Which is where you come into the picture – you have the only person within goddamned of the forsaken place. Indochina will be of no consequence to us after this war, but the owner of the paper will be very important to the future aspirations of our new president.'

'Are you suggesting that Major Mann attempt a rescue of Miss Stahl?' Featherstone asked, gazing out at the shipping now being cloaked by the last rays of the setting sun. 'That was not his mission.'

'Featherstone, old man, we have always known that you limeys were out to snatch an anti-Hitlerite from Saigon for debriefing, but I can tell you unofficially that she was executed by the Japs just a few days ago. Major Mann's original mission is over and now, in the spirit of Anglo-American cooperation, you would be doing us all a favour by reassigning him to Miss Stahl. I'm sure he'd be grateful – after all, she is a blood relative.'

Featherstone shrugged. 'I am afraid that I have lost all contact with Major Mann since he left Malaya. I am not sure whether he is dead or alive.'

Colonel Basham took a long puff of his cigar. 'You'll find a way to contact him, I'm sure. And there's something else we want from him.'

'What is that?' Featherstone asked with a note of suspicion.

'We would look very favourably on your man eliminating that Frenchie officer, before he goes upsetting the apple cart,' Basham said casually. 'Our president is still taking advice on whether to side with the Viet Minh in any future declaration of independence. Frankly, I can't see that happening because Ho Chi Minh is a goddamned commie, but there you go. If Mann can guarantee Pham is dead, we will be in a position to lend assistance to extricate him from

Indochina. All I have to do is make contact with our agent in Saigon and the support will be provided by Uncle Sam.'

Featherstone was silent for a moment. 'I understand what you are telling me and I will reassign Major Mann – if we have any future contact with him,' he conceded. 'However, what if we are unable to extract Miss Stahl?'

'Well, the matter is officially in your hands, and we can report back that we did everything we possibly could to save the lady,' Basham shrugged, 'but you Brits bungled the job. Plausible denial.' He tilted his head at Featherstone and then turned and walked away.

Featherstone lingered for a moment, lighting another cigarette, and reflected on how quickly the world was changing. Britain, once the most powerful nation on earth, was being quietly shuffled aside by a brash but energetic young nation of former British colonists. The Russians were even now occupying half of Europe, and when the war was over, which would be very soon if the rumours of a new bomb were true, the noncommunist world would be confronting a new and formidable enemy. Britain and America would be forced to work together, and Featherstone didn't relish the prospect.

With a sigh he dropped the glowing stub of his cigarette to the grass and crushed it out under his shoe.

*

Jack Kelly was surprised to see a letter addressed to him on his desk.

He had been discharged from hospital once the bullet wound had started to heal and, thankfully, he could walk without a limp. His grief was still with him but his intelligence work kept him occupied. At times he wondered if he had been born without human feelings because he could still function as a soldier. But he also knew that he had become hardened to the death. He loved his son more than anything else on earth, but his long experiences of war had also taught him to cope. Jack was able to block this terrible episode from his mind during the day, and only at night in the privacy of his bed did he let himself remember. Then he would break down and sob.

The envelope was typed, and when he opened the letter he immediately noticed it had no address or even signature. All it had was seven extremely import words . . . *Do not despair, your daughter is alive.*

Jack slumped into his swivel chair, rereading the note. 'What in bloody hell,' he said softly.

He picked up the envelope and noted that the letter had a Sydney postmark, but nothing else identified where it had come from, or from whom. But the words echoed in his mind and then filled him with hope. Ilsa was alive!

Jack sat under the slowly whirling fan and stared at the map of the world. If what the note had said was true, where in the hell was she?

*

The long night dragged on. Sweat trickled down Ilsa's body. She tried not to scratch at the infestation of lice and flea bites, but the itching was unbearable. She kept praying that the German officer would honour his word and somehow free her from this nightmare.

She strained to differentiate every sound echoing in the corridor outside the cell door. There were the usual noises of men and women crying and moaning and the occasional clank of a cell door, followed by the high-pitched wailing of some poor soul being dragged away for torture or execution.

Despite her alertness, Ilsa found herself nodding off. She did not know how long she had been asleep when the door to her cell slammed open.

For a moment she thought it was Wessel, but then she realised with horror that it was Colonel Hitachi, and behind him was a Japanese soldier with his rifle and bayonet.

'Get up!' Hitachi screamed.

Ilsa had trouble rising, she was so petrified. She managed to get to her feet by leaning back against the wall and pushing herself up.

'You come with me,' he ordered and Ilsa obeyed, now beyond hope.

The guard gestured into a much larger, dank cell and Ilsa felt as if she would either vomit or faint when she realised the dimly lit room stank of human excrement and blood. In the centre of the room was a simple wooden table with two chairs – and one of the chairs was covered in a sticky-looking substance Ilsa guessed was blood.

'Sit down,' Hitachi barked, gesturing to the bloodied chair, and it was then that Ilsa noticed the naked body hanging limply from a rope swinging from the ceiling. Ilsa hardly recognised Captain Wessel, as his face was a bloody and pulped mask. Ilsa doubled over and retched.

'As you can see, Captain Wessel is now dead,' Hitachi said, leaning menacingly forward. 'It seems your friend was planning to . . . how you say . . . spring you from here. But Captain Wessel has been under suspicion from my department since the fall of his country to the enemy. I am afraid that he was not a very brave man when it came to being subjected to his own methods of gaining information from reluctant prisoners.'

How fluent the Japanese officer was in the English language filtered through Ilsa's terror.

'May I compliment you on your excellent English, Colonel,' she said and her flattery caused the Japanese officer to blink.

'I learn when I live in Hawaii before the war,' he replied. 'Captain Wessel tried to rescue you and I want to know why you are so important that he would risk my anger.'

'I am not important,' Ilsa replied. 'I am just a war correspondent and a prisoner of war – that is all.'

Hitachi moved very fast for a man of his bulk, and Ilsa felt the heavy blow of the back of his hand, sending her flying from the chair. She hit her head on the stone floor and saw a red haze. So, death was going to come to her as it had to the Gestapo officer; she could only pray it would be quick. Ilsa felt hands roughly lifting her to her feet and she was then slumped back in the chair.

'You answer question with truth or you will beg for death with your screams,' Hitachi said.

Ilsa could taste blood in her mouth and her head was reeling.

'I am a war correspondent and American citizen,' she whispered. 'My father was once a member of the Nazi party in Germany, but he defected to the United States when I was a child. I do not know why the Nazis would want to question me.'

Her answer seemed to please the interrogator as he leaned back in his chair, placing his hands on his belly. 'Himmler was a stupid man. He used his country's resources to wage war against the Jews, and that helped our German allies lose the war. When we inflicted terror on the Chinese at Nanking, it sent a message that resistance was futile. We did not kill for the pleasure of killing.'

Ilsa heard the words but her head was still spinning. 'I will answer any question you ask me,' she said. A Japanese soldier entered the room and moved nervously to Hitachi's side. He said something that Ilsa didn't understand but brought a frown to the Kempeitai officer's face.

Hitachi rose from his chair and turned to the armed guard hovering in the shadows at the edge of the room. He said something and the guard stepped forward. Ilsa felt a surge of panic but Hitachi turned to her and said, 'You will be taken back to your cell. I have a matter to attend to.'

Ilsa rose from the chair unsteadily and allowed the guard to prod her with the tip of his rifle towards the doorway. She stumbled back to her cell and, for the first time, felt pleased to be back inside. At least she was out of that room of pain and death, even if it were only for the moment.

Ilsa collapsed into a corner, with her knees up around her chin and gripping her legs. Her body trembled uncontrollably and she wondered how long she could remain sane now that all hope of getting out of this hellhole was well and truly crushed. Only then did she consider means of killing herself. It would be better to die by her own hand than experience the fate of Captain Wessel.

★

Karl Mann could feel every nerve in his body stretching to breaking point. He was deep in Saigon and in the company of Pham, whose knowledge of the city was all that was keeping him alive. The two men, dressed in civilian clothing, made their way through an open marketplace filled with men and women wearing broad-brimmed conical hats. The air was filled with a thick, pungent smell Karl could not identify. From the market, they stepped out onto a broad boulevard and he was struck by how European the buildings were in this far-flung colony of France.

A convoy of Japanese military lorries prevented the two men from crossing the street and, as they waited for it to pass, Karl was surprised to see that the Japanese seemed oblivious to him. But when he glanced up and down the crowded pavements, he could see other Europeans amongst the Vietnamese, and presumed that they were French nationals.

'The man we will meet is a Chinese merchant whose shop is off the street,' Pham said under his breath, lest he be heard speaking English. 'He is Viet Minh.'

'Can we trust him?' Karl asked, surprised.

'At the moment we have a common enemy,' Pham replied. 'The Moslems I served with in North Africa had a saying – the enemy of my enemy is my friend. It is very appropriate for these times in my country.'

Karl followed Pham off the broad, tree-lined boulevard into what was no more than an alley, until they came to a doorway marked in Chinese and French, identifying the occupant as a healer and seller of medicinal herbs.

Both men stepped inside the tiny shop that was filled from wall to ceiling with jars of strange items hardly recognisable to Karl's western eyes. There was in the air a strong smell of incense, which he was familiar with from his time staying with Doctor van Nuyen.

Karl was surprised to see a man of about his own age standing behind a cluttered counter – he had half-expected to be met by a wizened old man with the look of an Asian Merlin. Pham spoke in Vietnamese and Karl knew that he would be exchanging code words to identify them to the Viet Minh operative.

'This is our man,' Pham said, turning to Karl. 'He does not speak English, but he has invited us to join him inside his house for tea.'

Karl followed the Chinese herbalist through a curtain, into a tiny room where a young woman was sitting with a baby in her arms. She looked alarmed when she saw Karl and Pham said something to reassure her.

'I told her that you are not French,' he said. 'I told her that you are British. She is the wife of the herbalist.'

Karl smiled at the young woman, who hugged her baby close to her breast; then her husband said something to her and she left the room. Pham said that they were to sit down on the floor.

Within minutes the wife returned, placing a tray of glasses and a pot of tea on the floor between the men before leaving again.

The herbalist poured tea and passed the glasses to his guests. Pham began conversing with him in what Karl guessed was Vietnamese. After a pause in the conversation, Pham turned to Karl.

'He says that he no longer has the radio transmitter because of the danger its presence meant for himself and his family. It has been taken to another area of the city, but he does not know where.' Unknown to Karl, the vacuum created by the Japanese turning on their former French Vichy allies had been filled by Ho Chi Minh's forces in the southern part of the country. The Viet Minh took the opportunity to seize resistance arms and equipment, sometimes killing their former allies against the Japanese occupiers. The valuable radio transmitter was now in Viet Minh hands, and any agents for the OSS and SOE were keeping a low profile. This left Karl and his operation under the scrutiny of the nationalist Indochinese.

'Ask him if he knows anything about a German woman being held by the Japanese in the Saigon prison.'

Pham turned to the herbalist and questioned him. 'He says that he has heard there is a European woman being held by the Japanese, and the last thing he heard was that she is still alive, although Colonel Hitachi is not prone to keeping his prisoners alive for very long.'

Karl's hopes were dashed. With the radio he might have been able to send a coded message south, to be picked up and relayed to Featherstone. He wanted clarification of his mission, or a reason to abort it and get the hell out of Indochina.

As far as Karl was concerned, he had an obligation to make contact with the woman – despite the fact Germany had been defeated. 'Ask him if the Viet Minh have any armed forces in Saigon,' Karl said.

Pham raised his eyebrows but turned his attention back to the herbalist, who was sipping his tea. Karl could see that the question caused the Chinese man some discomfort, as he squirmed in his cross-legged position.

'He says that a request for armed forces could only be cleared by Ho Chi Minh himself, and he is up north. But I know the Viet Minh do have armed guerrillas in the city,' Pham explained.

Karl smiled at the herbalist. 'Tell him to somehow make contact with Ho Chi Minh and get permission to use any forces he has here for an operation against the Japanese. I have no doubt that this Colonel Hitachi has some Viet Minh in the prison.'

Pham translated and Karl could see that the herbalist was considering the suggestion. He spoke slowly when he gave his answer.

'He says that it will take a little time for any message to be sent north, but he thinks Ho Chi Minh would look favourably upon an operation against the enemy in Saigon. It would be good for the people's morale in the south, and there are Viet Minh leaders being held by Hitachi. He wants to know if you have a plan.'

'Tell him I will have a plan,' Karl replied. 'I promise that we will do a lot of damage to the Japanese if he gives me the men and weapons I need.'

When the meeting was over, the herbalist gave Pham the address of a safe house where they were to wait. Karl left with a buoyant feeling of hope. Finally he might have the chance to strike at his enemy; he was sick of sitting around for wasted weeks, drinking tea and all the time looking over his shoulder. He was back in the war and, with any luck, he'd soon be able to make up for lost time.

*

Ilsa had almost become used to the tormented screams of the prisoners around her as they were dragged past her cell. A huge cockroach nibbled at her leg and she barely had the will to flick it off. Wessel was dead and all hope of escape gone. Even the little comfort she had found in Herlinde's company was gone – when she had badgered her Vietnamese gaoler with Herlinde's name he had run his finger across his throat, which had left Ilsa in no doubt as to the woman's fate. It was only a matter of time before she herself was killed. She comforted herself with the knowledge that Wessel had been able to contact the International Red Cross, informing them of her whereabouts. At least Clark would know where she died.

She spent hours thinking about him; it was a place to retreat to, away from all this torment. She would remember how strong his arms had felt around her, think of the gentleness in his touch and voice. Often these memories were taken over by visions of huge, juicy steaks sizzling on the barbecue plate at his parents' Montana ranch and Ilsa would feel guilty that those memories seemed even stronger than the memory of Clark's face. Her ration was barely enough to keep her alive and she thought with bitterness that she would probably starve to death before she was executed.

Her gaoler came to her cell and pushed a tin plate of rice in fish sauce across the floor to her. Ilsa fell on the meal, eating with her hands and licking the dish while the guard stood back watching her. He seemed to be struggling to say something and finally one word tumbled awkwardly from his lips.

'Hope,' he said before retrieving the plate and closing the door behind him.

Ilsa thought she had heard wrongly. Why on earth would the man say that? She dismissed the incident as a figment of her imagination – after all, malnutrition had a way of causing hallucinations – but that night she found herself clinging to one word . . . *Hope.*

SEVENTEEN

They were all around him and Fuji cursed himself for remaining in this campsite for too long. He had traded some of his Australian shillings for food, then hidden away in the bush again. But the men of the village had realised their Japanese occupiers were not returning and they were growing bolder. They wanted Fuji's money and would not hesitate to kill him for it.

Fuji lifted his rifle and checked the last three grenades to see that they were primed. It was near dark and he could feel the hair on his neck stiffen. A tiny crack of a twig from the thick bush around him and the ominous silence of the native birds warned him that he was being stalked.

The arrow thumped into the tree trunk behind him, missing him by inches, and he swung around, spotting the fleeting shadow of the archer. Fuji brought up his bolt-action rifle and fired. The range was only around ten yards and the bullet took the archer through the side of his head. He did not scream but simply crumpled, dropping the long hardwood bow strung with a strip of thin bamboo.

Chambering another round, Fuji crouched, scanning the deepening shadows of the rainforest and spotting movement only twenty yards away. Three, maybe four warriors were moving to outflank him and he reached for one of his precious grenades. It would be difficult because of the thick foliage – grenades thrown in these circumstances had a nasty habit of bouncing back on the thrower. But Fuji could see a space and he tossed the grenade under-arm to where he calculated the warriors would be. The grenade exploded, shredding leaves and causing a man to scream in pain.

Fuji pulled his long bayonet from its scabbard and clicked it into place on the end of his rifle, then slipped cautiously into the shadows of the forest. He stumbled on two semi-naked men attempting to drag their wounded comrade through the bush. They did not see the Japanese sailor behind them until it was too late and Fuji lunged from cover, his bayonet burying itself deep in the chest of one of the warriors. The warrior had swung around, raising a machete, but he had not had time to use it, instead only exposing his chest. Blood poured from the dying man's mouth as he feebly attempted to wrap his hands around the barrel of the rifle, but Fuji simply twisted the long knife in his chest, inflicting even more damage.

The second man fled into the gathering dark.

Fuji allowed the warrior's weight to drag the rifle down

to the ground, then placed his foot on the dead man's chest, dragging out the bayonet with a sucking sound.

He turned his attention to the man he had wounded with the grenade. He could see the fear in his eyes, and he did not hesitate. With a quick lunge he sank the bayonet into the man's throat with such force that the tip of the blade exited his neck. The man struggled, flopping around until his life ebbed from his body.

Fuji felt no emotion – other than gratitude for the fact that he was still alive. He had killed the men who had come to kill him and take his money. He listened carefully for sounds of any other attackers, but could hear none. No doubt the remaining warrior would be halfway back to the village to tell of the devil guarding the silver coins. He did not think any others would wish to risk death for the sake of the coins, but he knew payback would be a consideration once the men spoke to one another in the meeting house. It was time to leave but he had no means of escape other than by sea. And if he did escape, he had no choice but to surrender. He knew the war was as good as lost.

He was determined to keep his promise to Oshiro to return to his family; he would tell them he had died a hero's death. He knew it was an impossible task, but he would stay alive to try.

Fuji groped his way back to his campsite, gathered up his last remaining supplies and, in the dark, made his way to the place he knew the fishermen from the village launched their canoes.

He slept in the jungle adjoining the beach and when the sun rose, he noticed a canoe at the edge of the forest. Gathering up his bag of supplies, he made his way down to the beach and the unattended canoe, all the while listening out for the sounds of the village coming to life. He dumped his bag in the bottom of the wooden vessel, pushed it into the calm waters lapping at the beach and jumped in. There was a wooden oar lying at the bottom of the canoe and Fuji began paddling as quickly as he could.

The craft was well built and sliced through the rising waves as Fuji put distance between himself and the shore. Soon he was well out to sea, and the canoe rose and fell on the ocean swell. When he looked over his shoulder he could see the great forested mountains rising up over the water.

Fuji knew that all he had to do was keep starboard to the shore and paddle until night came, when he would once again go ashore to camp. A promise to a dead comrade kept him alive, helped by his own innate toughness as an experienced warrior of the Emperor.

*

The safe house was located in the Chinese quarter of Saigon, and the people who lived and worked in the area had anti-Japanese sentiments. Karl admired the courage of people who resisted occupation at such great cost to themselves.

Karl was sipping from a bowl of tasty spicy soup when a messenger came to speak with Pham.

'Hitachi has decided to transport your German woman to Japan but the messenger, who has contacts in the prison, says that she is an American prisoner of war,' Pham translated.

'American?' Karl queried, wiping his mouth with the sleeve of his long cotton shirt. 'You sure he got that right?'

Pham turned to the messenger, a boy barely in his teens.

'He says an American woman who is also German. But does not know her name.'

Karl frowned. 'Does he know when the transfer is to be done?'

'He says that the woman will be taken by convoy to the docks, to join a ship going to Japan in the next twenty-four hours.'

'I don't know what is going on but I know we cannot wait for an answer from up north as to my request for a force of Viet Minh. It looks like we will have to ambush the convoy before she gets to the docks.' Karl knew that this mysterious woman might not be Herlinde Kroth, but he was not prepared to leave until he found out for sure. He was a determined soldier and did not want to let Featherstone down; besides, if the woman were an American prisoner of war, the prison would be a living hell for her, and he had a soldier's duty to try to rescue her.

'What you are asking is almost impossible,' Pham groaned. 'We don't have the resources to stage an ambush, and even if we did, how would we extricate ourselves afterwards?'

'You said *almost* impossible,' Karl retorted. 'We figure out the *almost* bit and then prepare ourselves for the operation.'

Pham picked up with his chopsticks a piece of green vegetable from his bowl. 'I will talk to Dr Nuyen. I think he will be able to supply us with some weapons and maybe a few men. He is currently in the city, working at the hospital. I will go to him there.'

Karl smiled, thrusting out his hand to Pham. 'Thank you,' he said gratefully. 'When this is done, we can get out of this bloody place and go home.'

Pham accepted the proffered hand. 'You forget,' he said. 'I am home.'

As soon as the meal was finished, Pham left with the young messenger and made his way to the city hospital, leaving Karl alone to ponder how he would carry out his operation. He had obtained a map of the city and surrounding villas from the Chinese resistance fighters, and now he rolled it out amongst the food bowls on the short-legged table. Karl had already identified the location of the prison, and he ran his finger along a road that led directly from the prison to the docks. Not only was he thinking of places to spring his ambush, but also their means of escape. He had at least one major military principle on his side – surprise. Deep behind enemy lines, the Japanese would never consider that anyone would be foolish enough to take them on; the transfer would be considered routine, with a minimum of armed guards. The young messenger had known the expected time of the convoy and was sure that he had the route. But a good soldier also carries out a reconnaissance of any area of operations. As soon as Pham returned, they would go out in the night – despite the curfew – and make notes on all they could.

Time, however, was at a premium, and Karl wondered whether it would be possible to put together an operation like this in such a short space of time. Even if he could, how successful would it be? After all, he might be able to snatch the woman from the Japanese but where would they go after that?

★

Jack did not want to go on leave, but his old friend and superior Major Bill Travers had insisted and now he found himself on an aeroplane flying to Townsville in northern Queensland. He at least knew the town and was looking forward to catching up with Karin Mann, Karl's mother and the widow of his best friend, Paul, who had been killed on a mission to New Britain earlier in the war.

After landing, Jack hailed a taxi to Karin's house, which was on the outskirts of the town. The battered old sedan pulled up in a cloud of dust in front of a modest wooden house built high on timber pylons, in the manner of many houses of the tropical north. He hoisted his kitbag over his shoulder and paid the driver, who scowled at him when he did not tip.

'Bloody Yanks give a man a bit more,' he growled, then grated the transmission into gear and drove away.

For a moment Jack stood staring at the house, which was surrounded by a few stately gums. There was a chicken coop to one side and about half-a-dozen chooks scratched around in the front yard.

'Jack!'

Jack glanced up at the verandah and for a moment felt the strange sensation of having come home.

'Karin,' he said as she lifted the hem of her long skirt to hurry down the stairs to greet him.

They met at the bottom of the stairs and Karin threw herself into his arms in a tender embrace.

'It is good to see you again,' she wept and Jack felt just a little self-conscious at causing this beautiful woman to cry. 'I have had no news and didn't know if you were dead or alive.'

'I'm not a big writer,' Jack apologised sheepishly, pushing Karin back gently to look into her face. It seemed that she had hardly aged, looking much younger than her fifty years. Her skin was unmarked and still retained a European smoothness. Her long golden tresses showed streaks of grey but her eyes were young, although her smile was sad.

'What of my little boy, Lukas?' she asked.

Jack had been dreading this.

'Lukas was killed,' he choked and saw the colour drain from her face.

'When? How?' she gasped.

'A couple of months ago, up north,' Jack answered, holding her elbows lest she faint. 'I was with him.'

'Oh, Jack,' Karin sobbed. 'He was so young. This war is taking everyone I have ever loved – first Victoria, then my wonderful husband, and now my little boy. When will it end?'

Jack held Karin as she cried, near to tears himself. Finally Karin had cried herself out, and she took Jack's hand and led him up the stairs to the verandah.

'I will make us a cup of tea,' she said, using the end of her flour-spattered apron to wipe away the tears from her face.

Jack dropped his kitbag on the verandah. Breezes played

amongst the gum trees and the sun shimmered on the horizon as he removed his slouch hat and sat down in a big, comfortable cane chair. Karin returned with a silver platter, teapot, milk jug and two dainty teacups. She placed the tray on a rickety table that Jack idly thought should be fixed.

She poured the tea, and handed Jack a cup.

Neither of them spoke as they sat side by side, lost in memories. They remained so until the sun settled into a thin shimmer of heat haze to the west.

'I'll turn down your bed,' Karin said, rising from her chair. 'You will stay here tonight.' Jack was about to protest that he could walk back to town but she stopped him by raising her hand. 'I have lamb chops for dinner, and I know that you like lamb chops.'

Jack smiled his gratitude. There had been so many times that Karin, Paul, Victoria and he had sat on the verandahs of their respective plantations in Papua, playing cards, drinking and laughing. They had danced together, and shared both the good and the bad times as families. But that had been a lifetime ago, between two terrible wars, and they could never return.

That night Karin came to Jack's bed and lay down beside him, and cried for the loss of those years, while he held her and felt his own pain.

In the morning he got up and fixed the rickety table on the verandah.

*

Karl was aware that they were taking a grave risk carrying out the recon during curfew hours, but Pham knew the city like the back of his hand, even in the dark, and they were able to avoid the Japanese roadblocks and patrols.

By early morning they were huddled around the map of the city, safely back in the Chinese quarter, and Karl was fixing the location of the ambush.

'We will need help,' Pham said. 'I have been informed that we can get the assistance of four Viet Minh fighters for the operation.'

'That will be enough,' Karl said wearily, feeling the need for sleep creeping up on him. The adrenaline-charged hours dodging the Japanese patrols had taken their toll on both his energy and nerves. 'What kind of weapons do we have?' he asked Pham.

'From what I have been told, we have a couple of rifles and three submachine guns – British Stens, I think – as well as a few grenades.'

Karl stared at the map, thinking that in a few hours the lines marked would become real streets to him. Pham had worked on the withdrawal, and organised for them to be conveyed by a waiting car to a village on the outskirts of the city via a route rarely patrolled by the Japanese, as it had until recently been in the jurisdiction of the Vichy French police.

It was a simple plan: hit the convoy, predicted to be one truck accompanied by a police car; release the German woman and escape to the village. Karl knew that if they moved quickly, and no one betrayed them, they had a chance of being successful; but he was also acutely aware of the military maxim that all well-planned operations had a way of going astray as soon as the first shot was fired.

Never had Karl felt this uncertain about an operation.

So many things could go wrong. He was conducting a mission in a foreign land with people he hardly knew. He did not really know whether he could trust Pham, or the Viet Minh fighters; he did not know whether the weapons they were being given were reliable. What he did know, though, was that he needed to snatch some sleep if he were to be ready to meet and brief his tiny army of liberators.

EIGHTEEN

Jack armed himself with hammer, saw and axe, and went about fixing things up around the house. He felt at home here, and in Karin's bed. Paul had been dead for over three years, and Jack and Karin comforted each other in their loneliness.

Stripped down to his shorts and with sweat glistening on his body, Jack swung the log splitter against iron-hard wood. Just then Karin appeared on the verandah with a tray of tea and scones.

Jack glanced up, saw her smiling down at him and reached for his shirt before joining her on the verandah.

'Do you have any idea where Karl may be?' Karin asked, pouring him a cup of tea. He had told her about the last time he had seen her son, in Moresby with Lukas, and that he was off on an operation he couldn't tell them about. She had listened apprehensively, as though not wanting to hear the worst. Now she seemed ready for more information, except Jack didn't have it.

'I don't, I'm afraid,' he answered. 'But I do know that Karl can look after himself. He'll be home to you before you know it.'

Jack felt a little guilty about not telling Karin the whole truth – Karl's mission was both very secret and very dangerous, but this was not something he wanted to share with an anxious mother who had already lost a husband to the war.

'Karl wrote to me and said that if he did not return, I should contact a British naval officer by the name of Captain Featherstone,' Karin said, cupping her mug of tea in both hands.

'Did he say anything else about this pommy officer?' Jack asked.

'Only that he had worked for him before, in Palestine,' Karin said. 'Do you think you could use your contacts to find this Captain Featherstone?'

Jack had had an inkling that Karl was working for the British SOE, from rumours picked up from old mates working with the very secretive special forces based around Cairns. That meant that this Captain Featherstone must be one of his bosses, and Jack had heard the man's name mentioned at the wharf in Port Moresby before Karl had disappeared on his last assignment. 'Even if I found him I don't think he would entertain the idea of telling me anything.'

'Karl has done more than any soldier is required to do,'

Karin said and Jack could hear the pleading in her voice. 'It is not normal for soldiers to have no contact with their families. Mrs Eggleston down the road receives letters from her boy in New Guinea, so why should I not hear from my only son?'

Jack knew the answer to that, but to explain would only add to Karin's fears. 'I will try,' he answered. 'But I can't promise anything.'

'Thank you,' she responded, leaning over and touching his forearm. 'Paul always said that you were capable of moving mountains when you had a mind to.'

'I miss the bastard,' Jack reflected. 'He had no reason to volunteer for that job back in '42. Now Karl is off God knows where.'

'Karl has always had two fathers,' Karin said sadly, and Jack knew that she was referring to the fact that he had personally intervened to ensure that Karl was commissioned into the Australian Army, despite his place of birth. Jack had done so because he knew how important it was to Karl to prove his loyalty to his adopted country. As he had once said to Jack, 'A man cannot choose where he is born, but he can decide where he will die.'

The two sat enjoying the serenity of the day until Jack decided to finish a few more chores before he departed the following morning to report back to the army. His leave had been all too short but had taken an unexpected twist. He had not anticipated his feelings for Karin manifesting in the way they had, nor that she would reciprocate those feelings. Jack knew his life had taken a different direction and he was glad of it; he had felt bereft after Lukas's death, full of hopelessness about the future, but now he had something

261

to live for, something to return to. He had already made his decision and he only hoped that Karin would agree.

He rose very early the next morning, leaving her in a deep sleep. He shaved, changed into his uniform of shorts, shirt, boots and gaiters, slipped on his slouch hat and moved quietly around the cottage, gathering together his belongings.

Before leaving the house he removed the little leather pouch from his dog tags and placed Lukas's engagement ring on the kitchen table beside a note. Then he closed the screen door behind him and stepped into the early morning sunshine, making his way into the town along the dry, dusty track.

★

Karin awoke some time after Jack's departure and sleepily stretched out her arm to touch him, finding only an empty space instead. Annoyed, she rose and stumbled to the kitchen, where she saw the note and ring on the table. She picked up the note and read it. Then she burst into tears and slumped down in a chair at the table.

'Oh, Jack, yes I will,' she whispered softly. 'Just please come home to me, and bring my son back safely with you.'

★

When Jack reported for duty, he was informed that he would be flying out that evening on a Dakota scheduled for Port Moresby. In the meantime he occupied himself in a hotel with a wide shady verandah that was already crowded with men from America and Australia who were drinking as much beer as they could before returning to their units scattered across the Pacific.

Jack elbowed his way to the bar, ordered a beer and looked around to see if he recognised anyone. He was pleasantly surprised to see a quartermaster sergeant he knew from Port Moresby. Jack took his beer and sidled over to the beefy QM talking to a fellow sergeant. He saw Jack and greeted him warmly.

'You AWOL, Jack?' the QM asked with a grin. His expression turned sombre. 'Sorry to hear about your boy.'

Jack nodded and was introduced to the QM's drinking companion, who had a wiry build and stood around five foot five. Jack could see by the ugly purple scar on the sergeant's face that he had been severely wounded, and recently, by the look of it.

'Jimmy got that one up north,' the QM said. 'Decided wisely that a better place to be was counting blankets in my section. Jack, meet Jimmy Cotter. Jimmy, this is Jack Kelly.'

The two men shook hands.

'Where are you posted now?' Jack asked the QM.

'Jimmy and I are back on the mainland,' the QM answered. 'How about you?'

'I fly back to Moresby tonight,' Jack answered, taking a long sip from his beer. 'I'm stuck in PIB HQ.'

'I heard you got yourself a Jap bullet on some op up north,' the QM said conversationally and that pricked Jack's interest. The operation to save Ilsa was not known to many outside his own unit.

'Whereabouts are you counting blankets?' Jack asked.

'Cairns,' the QM replied without elaborating.

PETER WATT

'You blokes with the hush–hush boys?' Jack said. 'That's about the only way you would have heard of the PIB op I was on.'

The QM squirmed and glanced around the crowded bar. 'Not supposed to talk about what we do,' he said and Jack could see from the expression on Sergeant Cotter's face that they were both uncomfortable with Jack's line of questioning.

'Cobber, I'm not any kind of security risk and I would consider it a great favour if you could tell me one thing. I promise to shout you blokes beers all afternoon if you can tell me if you know – or have heard of – a pommy naval officer by the name of Featherstone. That's all.'

The sergeant and QM glanced at each other.

'Featherstone drops in from time to time at our camp,' Sergeant Cotter said. 'He's a queer coot but seems to be able to throw a lot of weight around. I last heard he was up in Moresby – I can't see any harm in telling you that, as you'll probably bump into him.'

'Thanks, Jimmy,' Jack said, raising his glass in salute. 'A promise is a promise, and it's my shout for the next couple of hours.'

Jack continued drinking with the two men until late afternoon, when he knew he must make his way to the airfield to catch his flight. He could feel the effects of the beer and hoped that the flight would not be too bumpy.

★

Lightning flashed and thunder rolled over Saigon. Karl could feel sweat rolling down his body under his clothing, as shadowy figures emerged to join him and Pham at the prearranged rendezvous site on the street. Karl was surprised to see Dr Nuyen appear with three tough-looking men, standing by bicycles, bags slung over the centre bars.

'These are my men,' the doctor said, accepting Karl's extended hand. 'Today we will strike a blow against our occupiers.'

'Striking the blow will be easy,' Karl replied. 'It will be getting away with it that's the hard part.'

'Pham has told me the outline of what you propose to do and I can help,' Nuyen replied. 'When you kill the Japanese escorts, I will drive you and the woman away to a village east of here called Vung Tau. There I have a place for you to hide until a fishing boat is able to take you out of the country to meet with an American submarine.'

'You are in contact with the Americans?' Karl asked, stunned.

'We have established contact with the Americans with one of our radios,' the doctor answered. 'The Americans have an organisation called the Office of Strategic Services, who have an interest in our great leader, Ho Chi Minh.'

'I know of it,' Karl replied. 'Why did you not tell us about your communications with the Yanks before?'

'I could not,' Nuyen said quietly. 'There is something else you must know if I am to provide you with help.'

'What is that?' Karl responded.

'The Americans have sent a message to say that they want you to dispose of Pham,' he replied quietly. 'Or they will withdraw their help getting you out of Indochina.'

'Jesus Christ!' Karl exclaimed and the Vietnamese doctor gestured for him to keep his voice down, as Pham was only a few yards away, briefing the men sent to assist in the rescue mission.

'Pham is a traitor to my country,' Nuyen said. 'He intends to collect intelligence on the Viet Minh leadership here, so that when his French imperialist comrades return, our leaders can be arrested and executed.'

'The politics in this bloody country are driving me mad,' Karl said, shaking his head. 'Why have Pham killed when it has been he who has worked with you?'

'Pham is double-faced,' Hung answered. 'He only pretends to work with us, when his real mission is to betray us as soon as the French return. He uses your mission as a cover for his own ends.'

Karl had to accept that what Nuyen was saying was true. He had never truly trusted the French officer, but he had come to accept that without Pham's help he would not have got this far in an alien land of rice paddies and rubber plantations. And Pham had saved his life, which was not easily forgotten.

'If you believe he is a traitor to your cause, why don't you execute him?' Karl asked, leading the doctor a little way into the dark shadows of the back alley as the first heavy drops of rain fell.

'Because you need him until the last moment of your operation to save the American woman,' Nuyen answered. 'But the Americans are sensitive and want you to ensure that he does not leave these shores alive. They see Pham as a dangerous troublemaker. Their OSS have established good relations with Ho Chi Minh. They don't want anything to jeopardise that.'

'The Yanks can keep their hands clean – if I kill Pham,'

Karl said. Despite Pham's aloof and sometimes arrogant manner, Karl had come to respect him, for his ability to keep them both out of the clutches of the enemy. In fact, it could be said that the man had become a friend of sorts.

'You will do it?' Nuyen queried, seeing the expression of doubt on Karl's face.

'I will do it,' he said reluctantly. What choice did he have? If the Americans did not help him exit Saigon, he and the German woman stood very little chance of surviving.

'Good,' Nuyen nodded.

When the briefing was over, Karl and Pham retreated to their safe house for the rest of the day. Both men had armed themselves with a Sten gun, and spent the day stripping, cleaning and otherwise ensuring their weapons were in perfect working order.

Karl attempted to doze. The storms that had cleared around midmorning threatened to return, bringing with them an oppressive humidity.

'It is time to go,' Pham said eventually and Karl dragged himself off the low bed to follow him.

The men left the safe house and made their way to the ambush site. Overhead the sky was ominous. Karl was pleased to see that there were not many Japanese patrols on the street and guessed that they were wisely choosing to remain close to shelter. He sent up a quick thanks to whatever Vietnamese gods controlled the weather.

An hour before the small convoy was due through the narrow intersection designated as the ambush site, Karl met up with his party of guerrilla fighters, the same three tough-looking Viet Minh whose demeanour spoke of seasoned soldiers. They carried their weapons concealed in the bags slung over their bicycles and easily blended in with the few local people on the streets going about their business amongst the street stalls.

Karl kept out of public view, behind an oxen wagon brought to the scene earlier that day by the three Viet Minh men. To all appearances it was simply a means of transporting the goods sold in the market stalls.

The storm finally broke with a violent downpour and the streets ran with riverlets. The merchants quickly battened down their tiny stalls as their customers scuttled for shelter.

Karl glanced at his watch and gave the signal. The ox cart was dragged into the street, blocking vehicular traffic from the direction they expected the Japanese convoy to come, and each man took out his weapon.

The Japanese were on time. The convoy, which consisted of a sedan and a covered lorry, ground to a halt behind the ox cart.

Two of the Viet Minh stepped from the kerb and rushed the escort car, pouring automatic gunfire through the windows, smashing glass and peppering the bodies of the three soldiers inside, who barely had time to realise the danger they were in before they died.

Karl ran to the passenger side of the truck, ripping open the door to stare briefly into the startled face of a uniformed Japanese soldier. The man was desperately attempting to bring the muzzle of his rifle around to fire on Karl, but died almost instantly as bullets from Karl's submachine gun ripped through his body.

The driver had already exited on the other side of the truck and was sprinting back up the road, where he would run into the sentry Karl had placed to warn them of any further Japanese vehicles.

Pham had already made his way to the back of the truck and dispatched another Japanese soldier, who had been foolish enough to poke his head around the canvas to see what was happening. The Japanese soldier pitched from the truck and smashed into the hard earth of the roadway. Pham clambered up into the back of the truck, his commando knife at the ready. He could not risk firing into the truck, lest he hit the prisoner they had been assigned to rescue. He was vaguely aware of a blast from a rifle and the bullet ripped through his stomach, forcing him against the back board of the truck. Pham realised too late that he had not seen the second guard in the dark recess at the back. The second guard, who had shot him at point blank range, was already chambering another round to finish him off.

Karl heard the shot and ran to the rear of the truck, where he saw the upper half of a Japanese soldier standing over someone he presumed was Pham. Karl made a split-second decision to use his Sten, as his target was clearly displayed. Any shots he fired from below would go up and not back into the truck. Karl flung the short metal butt to his shoulder and squeezed the trigger, sending a shower of projectiles into the exposed chest and head of the enemy soldier, who died almost immediately.

'Pham!' Karl yelled. 'Are you okay?' There was no answer other than a low groan. Karl scrambled up the back of the truck to pitch himself inside, falling on Pham's body. He could smell a mix of blood and cordite.

'Who are you?' a frightened female voice asked. 'You speak English.'

'Major, Australian Army,' Karl responded.

The woman took tentative steps towards Karl from the far corner of the truck, as if waking from a long sleep, then fell to her knees beside Pham, who lay on his back gripping his stomach, blood oozing between his fingers.

'Gut shot,' Pham hissed through gritted teeth to Karl. 'You have to leave me. Just pass up my Sten.'

Karl was forced to make a decision. If he left Pham he would surely die, and Karl would be able to satisfy the request of the American OSS. Already Karl could hear rifle shots from up the road, which either meant the sentry posted had shot the fleeing Japanese driver or that enemy reinforcements were on the way.

Karl dropped the back board of the truck, ordered the woman to jump down and slung his SMG over his shoulder, reaching for Pham's arms and dragging him from the rear of the truck. The French officer screamed in pain but the sound was muffled by the roar of the rain. Lifting Pham over his shoulders, Karl carried him as though he were a sack of grain.

'Follow me,' he called to the woman needlessly – she was sticking close to her rescuers. Already the street was empty of people, all of whom knew that if they were found in the street, they would be shot by the vengeful Japanese. The Viet Minh resistance fighters had already melted into the backstreets of the city.

Karl half-ran, half-walked, with Pham clinging to him and moaning in pain. He reached the alleyway that led to the parked getaway car, the Vietnamese doctor behind the wheel.

Nuyen looked alarmed when he saw Karl emerge from

the rain with Pham over his shoulders and the woman following. Karl thrust Pham into the back seat and sat him upright, snapping an order for the woman to join Pham in the back whilst he sat in the front beside Nuyen.

'Go!' Karl yelled, clutching the dashboard, and the doctor rammed the gear shift into action. The car pulled away from the kerb and slowly picked up speed.

Karl turned round and looked at Pham. Quickly he took off his shirt and passed it to the woman in the back seat. 'Here, take this. It's wet but it's better than nothing. Press it to the wound. Keep pressing until we tell you. Our driver is a doctor, but he can't stop here, it's too dangerous.' He didn't mention that the good doctor actually wanted Pham dead.

He saw that the woman was doing as he instructed. Already her thin sarong-like dress was covered in blood. Her hair was dripping wet from the rain.

'You said that you are from the Australian Army,' the woman said after a moment. 'How is it that you have risked your life to rescue me?'

Karl wiped water from his face and slid the Sten gun down beside him, out of sight. 'That is a bloody good question,' he replied. 'I don't even know who you are. You can't be Herlinde Kroth – you look nothing like her.'

'I am Ilsa Stahl,' the woman replied. 'I am an American correspondent for a New York paper.'

'You're not the woman I was originally sent to get out of Jap hands,' Karl answered. 'But, for some reason, your Yank mates want you back pretty badly.'

'You haven't told me your name,' the woman said.

'Mann. Major Karl Mann,' Karl replied.

'Mann,' she said softly. 'I have German relatives by the name of Mann who live in Papua. Are you related to them?'

Karl felt the hair on the back of his neck stand up. It could not be possible . . .

He could hear scattered gunfire somewhere behind them and guessed that the Japanese had already arrived at the scene of the ambush, taking out their fury on anyone foolish enough to have loitered in the street.

NINETEEN

Karl Mann turned his head to take a long look at the woman behind him. 'Was your father Gerhard Stahl and your mother Erika Mann?'

'My adopted father, yes,' Ilsa answered, her eyes widening. 'My mother was Erika Mann.'

'God in heaven!' Karl exclaimed in German. 'Your mother was my father's sister – my aunt – which makes you my cousin. I remember Uncle Jack telling me about you. You met him back in '42, didn't you, but you didn't keep in contact.'

'I regret that,' Ilsa said. 'I was intending to search him out when I flew to meet with my fiancé in Port Moresby. My plane crashed in the sea and a Japanese submarine found us. It's a long story, and one I don't fully understand, but somehow I ended up in Saigon.'

Karl did not know how to react to the news that he had inadvertently rescued his cousin, the daughter of a man he considered as close to him as his own father.

'You have been speaking in German,' the Vietnamese doctor said as he wound his way between deep puddles of water on the dirt road. The rain was easing off and visibility improving. 'What have you learned of this woman we were sent to rescue?'

Karl returned his attention to the driver. 'Doctor van Nuyen, you would not believe me if I told you.' Then he said to Ilsa, 'Why are the Americans so keen to have you rescued?'

Ilsa frowned. 'I truly don't know,' she replied. 'I was hoping you could tell me.'

She looked away, back to Pham. The shirt was already soaked with blood and she pressed harder onto the wound. 'Surely there must be something else we can do for this man.'

'We cannot stop until we reach safety,' Karl said. No doubt the Japanese would already have begun their search for the perpetrators of such a brazen attack on them. In time their attention would extend to outlying areas of the fishing village like Vung Tau. Pham's groans of pain each time the cramped little sedan hit a pothole reminded Karl that he had a job to do before he could expect any assistance from the Americans.

He stared out at the road in front of them; it was lined with many shanties, indicating they were approaching a large village or town. The rain had stopped now, but water was still running down the sides of the road.

'We go straight to beach,' the doctor said. 'A fishing boat is waiting to take you to sea.'

They drove through the town, narrowly avoiding a foot patrol of armed Japanese soldiers, and turned off a tree-lined street onto a road that ran alongside a wide sandy beach, where Chinese fishing junks lined up at anchor. The sun was setting behind a dark sky, and Karl was pleased to see that the enemy had not set up sentry posts along the beach.

The car came to a stop and Karl jumped out. With Ilsa's help he gently removed Pham from the back seat and laid him on the ground beside the car. He could see that his injury was very bad indeed and that his comrade had little time to live. The high-velocity bullet had been fired at close range and ripped through the top part of Pham's abdomen. Karl did not know how long they would have to wait for the extraction and could see the pleading in Pham's eyes. Maybe if they left Pham the Japanese, who were bound to be at the beach before too long, would give him medical treatment but Karl knew that he was fooling himself. The Japanese would only torture Pham, in light of the loss of their prisoner. Given the brutality of the times, Karl knew that he had only one option. Taking Pham with them was not a choice he could make.

Pham reached up and gripped Karl's arm. 'You have to leave me,' he gasped. 'Just give me a gun . . . or do it yourself. There is not much time . . . I am –' He slumped into unconsciousness.

Karl turned to the doctor. 'Do you have a pistol?' he asked but the doctor shook his head.

Karl retrieved his Sten gun from the passenger seat and clicked a full magazine on the weapon.

'What are you doing?' Ilsa gasped when she saw Karl place the short barrel of the weapon against Pham's head.

'There is no hope for him. If we take him with us, he will die. If we leave him behind, the Japanese will kill him – if he is not already dead. I have no choice.'

She took a step in his direction.

'Look away!' Karl barked.

He fired a burst of three bullets into Pham's head, and Ilsa raised her hands to her face in horror.

Karl stood up, glancing at the Vietnamese doctor, who nodded.

'You must hurry to the boat on the end,' Nuyen said. 'The captain is ready to leave now. There is no time to waste.'

'What about Pham?' Karl asked.

'You will have to take him with you,' Nuyen said. 'When you are far enough out, dump his body in the sea. We cannot afford to have him found by the enemy here or they will suspect that a fishing boat is involved in your escape.'

Karl kneeled down, lifted the body of his comrade and walked towards the boat the doctor had indicated. Ilsa followed him; he could hear her shocked sobs. When they reached the fishing boat, one of the Vietnamese crew jumped down and helped Karl push the body aboard. Karl and Ilsa were helped over the side, a sail was raised and within minutes the boat slowly picked up speed to chop its way through the water.

Karl glanced over at the beach and noticed that the doctor's car was already gone. He sat down on the deck, his back against the cabin of the fishing boat; his mind was reeling from all that had happened in the last twenty-four hours.

The boat rose and fell on the gentle waters as they sailed south. The night had cleared to reveal a sky of brilliant, sparkling stars. Already the captain of the boat had raised his signal lights, despite the danger of being spotted by any Japanese naval patrols. He did not speak English but he knew his job.

Eventually Ilsa came over and sat down beside Karl.

'I am sorry for what you had to do back there on the beach,' she said. 'I guess he was a friend of yours.'

Karl did not reply. He was too weary and his soul felt too empty.

Ilsa fell silent. She had suffered in this war herself; she understood that there were some things you could never forgive yourself for.

*

Keela was in the canoe with him, and Fuji attempted to cry but no tears would come, as his dehydrated body had nothing else to give. Days earlier, the currents had caught hold of his little craft and swept him out to sea. Then a large wave had rolled the canoe, dumping his supplies into the water and leaving him without food, water or even his clothes. He had been able to scramble back into the boat, but now he wished he had drowned because he was going to die a slow, agonising death from dehydration. The coastline was no longer visible and he was going to die alone on this flat, featureless sea.

But when the night came and stars burned in the moonless sky, Keela came to him as a wispy spectre, whispering sad words of regret for what they had lost in this lifetime. She was just as beautiful as the day he had last seen her.

He drifted in and out of consciousness, and was hardly aware that the blazing sun was already rising from the sea, He wanted only to remain with Keela and he tried to call out to her, but it seemed even she had deserted him in the last moments of his life.

'He's not a kanaka,' a voice drifted to him, and Fuji suddenly felt his body being jolted. He tried to open his eyes but was confused by what he saw, and his lips were so swollen and cracked that he could utter no words.

'Drag him aboard,' the voice said. 'He might be Chinee.'

Fuji was beyond caring and did not even feel the pain of his severely sunburned body being dragged over the wooden deck of a boat. Then came the almost-forgotten sensation of liquid trickling into his mouth. It was warm and brackish but that did not matter. Fuji opened his eyes and squinted at the burning haze of blue sky. More water trickled into his mouth and he could see a ring of black faces peering down at him. Amongst the black faces was a white one: beefy, ruddy, with a cigar stuck between the lips.

'You all right, boy?' the white man asked.

Fuji could now work out that the man was not dressed in any uniform but wore a pair of shorts over which his big belly extended. The man was almost as brown as the Melanesians staring down at him.

'Goddamned stupid question,' the man muttered. 'The son of a bitch probably don't understand American.'

'Thank you,' Fuji croaked. 'I am Japanese – not Chinese.'

His statement almost caused the man to swallow his cigar. 'You speak pretty good American – like an Aussie. Who the hell are you?'

'Chief Petty Officer Fuji Komine of the Imperial Japanese Navy and I surrender to you,' Fuji said.

'If I hadda known you were a goddamned Jap, I would have left you to burn in hell out there,' the man said, gesturing to the sea. 'I got a good mind to throw your little yellow carcass right back into the sea.'

Fuji struggled to sit up and was allowed to, although now he was aware that he was being covered by one of the Melanesian crew members holding a rifle. 'I am your prisoner of war and expect to be treated accordingly.'

'You speak pretty fancy for a Jap,' the big man said but with a touch of respect. 'My name's Melvin Jones and I'm the skipper of the boat, the *Riverside*, that has rescued you. You will be handed over to the Aussies down the coast. In the meantime, you will be fed and treated well, but I am going to have you chained to avoid you making any attempt to disrupt my boat.'

Fuji was taken forward and shackled under a tarpaulin sheet out of the sun. He was given a meal of bully beef and rice, along with a mug of strong, sweetened black tea, and near sunset he noted that the boat had steamed within sight of the coast. Already the food and drink had helped him to recover his strength, and it felt as if his life force were flowing back into his body. The black crew had mostly ignored him but Mel Jones sat down beside him and lit up a cigar.

'I'm a tad curious to know where you came from before we found you,' Mel said, blowing a great cloud of smoke into the gentle tropical breeze. 'Not that the Aussies won't find out for themselves, when they interrogate you.'

Fuji knew he did not have to volunteer any information but he was beyond caring about his loyalties to Japan. 'I was with my unit west of here, up the coast. But they are all dead now. The green ghosts attacked us and I was the only one to survive.'

'How long ago was that?' Mel asked suspiciously, and Fuji cast his mind back, telling the *Riverside* skipper when the small battle had been.

Mel puffed on his cigar in silence for a long time before saying, 'I lost a good buddy that day. He was the skipper of this boat.'

Fuji did not know that the *Riverside* had been involved in the skirmish in the village. 'I am sorry,' he replied. 'I also lost a good friend that day.'

Mel stood and stretched, passing half the cigar to Fuji. 'I hope this goddamned war finishes soon, so we can all go home.'

'Home,' Fuji said. 'Before the war my home was Port Moresby, but even if this war is finished I will not be able to go home.'

'You're from Moresby?' Mel asked. 'My buddy was from Moresby. Maybe you knew him – Lukas Kelly.'

Fuji froze. 'His father is Jack Kelly?'

'Yeah, that's right. Jack was shot in the leg by some Jap he said he –' Mel did not finish the sentence but stared down at Fuji. 'You were the one who shot Jack!'

'I wounded him,' Fuji replied. 'He did not deserve to die. He had been very kind to my father and mother.'

'Well, I'll be damned!' Fred exclaimed. 'Son of a bitch!

If your pals had succeeded in sinking the old *Riverside*, you would not be here today – and still alive. Maybe some of that Oriental stuff about karma is true. Jack told me that you shot a Jap officer and saved his life. Why would you do that?'

'It was a matter of honour,' Fuji replied but did not elaborate. 'My war is over. There is only the future now.'

The American's observations on the strange twist of fate made Fuji think about his own life. He had fought as honourably as he could for the Imperial Japanese Navy but was forced to accept that his time amongst the Europeans had rubbed off on his attitudes. He and many other comrades knew the war was unwinnable but, unlike most of them, Fuji could see no sense in throwing his life away for an ancient belief in death before dishonour. What honour was there in dying in an unwinnable war?

That night Fuji lay on the deck in his shackles and found some peace in the knowledge that his war was over. All he had to do now was satisfy his oath to his dead friend from Okinawa. That, too, was a matter of honour.

★

Although Jack Kelly was at his desk in Port Moresby, his mind was not. He pushed himself out of his chair and went in search of Major Bill Travers.

Jack found him at his desk, poring over reports.

He knocked on the open door. 'Permission to speak with you, boss,' he said from the doorway, and Bill groaned inwardly. His old friend only called him boss or sir when trouble lay ahead or he wanted something difficult.

Now he groaned aloud. 'Come in, Sergeant Kelly. Have a seat. You only call me boss when you want something, or you're in trouble.'

Jack grinned and made himself comfortable. 'Bill, have you heard of a pommy naval officer by the name of Captain Featherstone?'

'I hope you're having a good day,' Bill Travers said sarcastically, 'because your question just gave me indigestion. Yes, I've heard of Featherstone. An interfering bugger at the best of times.'

'I heard that he was up this way,' Jack said, leaning forward. 'I was hoping to have a word with him – about young Karl Mann.'

Bill Travers sighed, put down his pencil and leaned back in his chair. 'I don't know a lot about this Featherstone, but he seems to swan around wherever he wants and our own lot bows to his requests. There's a rumour he's a close mate of Churchill's, doing his bidding out here.'

'Do you know where I can find him?' Jack asked.

Bill rested his arms on the desk top. 'The last I heard was that he was out at the airfield. That was yesterday. Now, I am not condoning you going to see him, as you know full well about the chain of command, but I think you should head over to the airfield to pick up the latest batch of aerial photos. Might be something sensitive we need a senior NCO to escort back here.'

Jack saw the slight smile on his superior's face. 'Thanks, Bill,' he said. 'I'll make sure the photos get back here safely.'

As Jack was leaving the office, Bill Travers called after him, 'And if you get yourself into any trouble, it's your neck on the line. I don't know anything about this.'

'I was never here,' Jack grinned, and headed for the vehicle pool to pick up a driver and an American-supplied jeep.

It was near midday when he made the half-hour trip to the busy airfield. Men stripped to the waist and wearing only their boots and shorts laboured refuelling planes or stacking supplies onto transport aircraft. Others rearmed the weapons systems on fighters, or moved to and from gun pits at the airfield's outer perimeters, where anti-aircraft guns sat poking their long barrels at the sky.

Jack dismounted and sent the driver off to pick up the aerial photographs whilst he made enquiries as to the whereabouts of one Captain Featherstone. None of the ground crew could help him, so Jack singled out a RAAF officer he spotted talking to a group of men working on a Kittyhawk fighter.

Jack marched over and threw them his best salute.

'What can I do for you, Sergeant?' the officer asked, stepping away from the ground crew.

'Sir, I have been told to report to Captain Featherstone,' Jack lied. 'I believe he is an officer in the Royal Navy, currently stationed here.'

'Featherstone,' the RAAF officer frowned. 'He is not stationed here . . .' Jack felt his hopes be dashed. 'But he is over there,' the officer said, pointing to a man standing outside an office, a small, expensive suitcase by his feet. He was dressed in the uniform of the Royal Navy.

'Thank you, sir,' Jack said, snapping off another smart salute before marching across the dusty earth at the edge of the hardened runway. As he approached the British officer he was struck by how pale he was; everyone around him was burned almost black from working under the hot sun.

'Captain Featherstone, sir,' Jack said and snapped off yet another smart salute.

Featherstone turned his head and returned the salute. 'Yes, Sergeant, what can I do for you?'

Jack stood facing the British officer. 'Sir, you do not know me, but my name is Jack Kelly.'

Jack was surprised at the officer's reaction. 'Sergeant Kelly, I had always hoped to meet you in person one day and, as for not knowing about you, old chap; well, you are seriously misled. Your colourful military and civil record is well known to me, as is your service to King and Empire in two wars. I also know of your relationship to an extraordinary officer who, I suspect you already know, works for me, and I would like to offer my condolences for the recent loss of your brave son, Lukas.'

Jack stood speechless for a moment. It seemed that there was little Featherstone did not know about him. 'Sir,' he said finally, 'if you know so much about me, then you must know why I have taken it upon myself to meet you and ask you a question. The answer is critical to a woman who has suffered enough for her adopted country.'

'I presume that you have located me to ask on behalf of Major Mann's mother, Frau Karin Mann,' Featherstone said. 'And possibly you're interested in the fate of your daughter too.'

Jack didn't know what to say.

'You must realise, Sergeant Kelly, that such information is classified at the highest levels – only to be given out on a need-to-know basis. However, I feel you are one of the people who needs to know.'

284

'It was you who sent me that note,' Jack said.

'Now, that would have contravened all principles of intelligence,' Featherstone smiled. 'I am waiting for a crate to fly me to a debriefing, Sergeant Kelly, and when I get to my destination I will be speaking to Major Mann. He was responsible for rescuing your daughter, who is probably now sitting on a beach in Honolulu. Sadly, where Karl has been and what he has done for us – and the Yanks – will never be revealed to the world; not even to you, I'm afraid.'

'Sir, you have put my mind at rest and that of Karl's mother. That is all we need to know,' Jack said, noticing that a pilot wearing his full flying kit was walking towards them.

'Ah, I am afraid my lift appears to be ready, Sergeant Kelly, so I must bid you good day,' the British officer said, glancing at his watch. 'Goodbye, Sergeant Kelly, and may we meet again in better times.'

Instead of saluting, the British officer reached out and shook Jack's hand. Thrown off guard, Jack accepted the gesture, then stepped back and saluted Featherstone just as the young pilot reached them.

Jack's thoughts were racing as he watched the British officer walk to the small plane waiting to ferry him to only God and the highest security clearance knew where.

*

Two weeks of medical attention, on board the American submarine that had picked them up off the coast of Vung Tau and here in Pearl Harbor, had helped Ilsa's recovery. She had put on weight, to cover those bones made prominent through malnutrition, and the scars of ulcers and infected insect bites were less noticeable.

She was sitting on a palm-fringed beach, taking in the sun and surf, and gazing at the young servicemen and women enjoying the serenity of the beautiful tropical island. Although word of her rescue had been conveyed to America, there had been little detail of where and how. Clark knew she was alive and recovering in Hawaii, and had written to her, pouring out his love for her and promising that he would be with her as soon as he could get a flight from the States.

Ilsa had not replied. She still loved her pilot but so much had happened to her since she had last seen him. She was confused and was almost afraid of meeting him again. She needed time to sort out her feelings, to come to grips with the experiences war had made a permanent part of her soul. She had changed so much and she didn't know whether he would like those changes.

A shadow fell over her then and a familiar voice said, 'Ilsa.'

She turned to see Clark standing over her, wearing the uniform of his rank.

'Clark,' she replied and felt her heart skip a beat.

He sank to his knees in the sand and embraced her with all the power in his lean body. Ilsa could feel his tears on her bare shoulders and hear his sobbing words. 'I never gave up hope.'

Ilsa felt her own eyes brim with tears. 'You were always with me, even in the worst of times.'

They held each other as if they would never let go again. In that embrace, Ilsa knew Clark was the man she wanted to spend the rest of her life with. Like her, he had seen terrible things during the war; he would understand her, let her work things out in her own way. They had both survived and now they could get on with living again.

When they finally broke the embrace, Clark wiped at the tears flowing down his face with the back of his hand.

'I'll take you back to the States and we'll arrange the biggest wedding the state of Montana has ever seen,' he laughed.

Ilsa gently pushed him away from her. 'Clark,' she said softly. 'It is not that simple.'

'I love you,' he said. 'I don't care what has come between us during this goddamned war. All I know is that I love you – have loved you from the very first time I set eyes on you. Nothing has changed for me and it never will.'

Ilsa gazed into his eyes. 'But I've changed. I'm not the same woman you fell in love with. I've been to hell and back, and lost the old me along the way. I need you to understand that, to fall in love with the person I am now. Then, if you still want to marry me, I'll help you organise that big old wedding of yours.'

Clark was half-laughing, half-crying at her response. 'You've changed, and I have too. Maybe we both need time to get to know one another again. But I can promise you this – I intend to spend the rest of my life with you.'

'How about we start with the next few hours? I'm willing to bet that my hotel is better than the accommodation the army has supplied you with.' She gave him a wicked grin.

For a very brief moment, Clark looked blank, then

understanding slowly dawned. 'Lady, you can bet your ass you're right on that point,' he replied with a smile as broad as the plains of his home state. 'I better do the right thing and give up my billet to some other unfortunate flyer seeking a place to lay his head.'

They rose from the sandy beach hand in hand and slowly walked across the sand towards the town.

TWENTY

General Douglas MacArthur could not be at the medal ceremony, but he did have one of his high-ranking staff attend the investiture of service and bravery awards.

Major Karl Mann stood in a short rank of foreign recipients inside the grand plantation house's spacious marble and teak ballroom. The large double-storeyed house had been used by the occupying Japanese and was now functioning as offices for the administration of the liberated regions of the Philippine Islands. Cold drinks and alcohol were to be served after the ceremony, by hastily uniformed Filipino waiters carrying any silver tray they could scrounge to give the moment some sense of importance.

A full colonel pinned the American award on Karl's immaculately pressed dress uniform. Captain Featherstone stood to one side, watching as the awards were read out and the medals presented. Beside him was Colonel Basham of the OSS, who was also dressed in his best uniform, displaying on his chest numerous colourful ribbons for services to the US.

'Your man deserved his award for what he did for us,' Basham said quietly to Featherstone as the last medal was pinned and the recipients joined the invited guests.

'Glad that we in the diminishing British Empire could be of some assistance, old chap,' Featherstone replied.

'Congratulations, Major Mann,' Basham said, extending his hand as Karl walked towards him. 'I hope we have the opportunity of working with you in the future – if Captain Featherstone ever lets you go.'

'Well, sir,' Karl replied with a smile as a waiter offered him a crystal flute of chilled champagne. 'When the war ends I am returning to New Guinea to my old job as a government patrol officer. This has been my first and last war. So here's to the declaration of peace very soon.'

Karl raised his glass.

'The King,' Featherstone said.

'To Uncle Sam,' Basham added.

'Peace,' Karl concluded. 'And Australia.'

One of the correspondents covering the ceremony was Ilsa. She had recovered from the physical privations of her captivity and, at her insistence, returned to work. She was wearing her customary long trousers and tan-coloured shirt, and felt better than she had in a very long time.

'Is this an unofficial gathering of our newly established United Nations?' she said with a warm smile as she approached the trio.

'Miss Stahl,' Featherstone greeted her. 'I hope that you mention in your American newspapers that we British were of some help in winning the war,' he said with a smile. 'Even the colonials were some help in defeating our enemies.'

Ilsa laughed and Karl extended his hand to her. 'Hello, cousin. Good to see the rosy flush in your cheeks.'

'Hello, Karl,' she said, taking his hand between her own. 'How's the big brother I always dreamed of having?'

Ilsa and Karl had grown close during the journey back on the sub, and had swapped many stories of their families. Ilsa had wanted to know as much as she could about her father and half-brother, and Karl had spent hours recalling their childhood and schooldays together. It was only when he had met with Featherstone in the Philippines that he had learned of Lukas's death.

'If you will excuse us,' Karl said, turning to the two senior officers. 'I haven't seen my cousin for a while.'

Karl walked with Ilsa onto an open verandah overlooking a well-kept tropical garden. Ilsa took out a packet of cigarettes from the pocket of her trousers and offered Karl one. He accepted, although he rarely smoked. Ilsa lit both cigarettes and they watched the smoke curl lazily on the late afternoon breeze.

'Do you know that Jack and my mother got married a couple of weeks ago in Australia?' Karl said, and knew by Ilsa's expression that he'd surprised her.

'How do you feel about that?' she asked. 'Your mother and . . . my father!'

Karl broke into a deep, low laugh. 'I think it's good,' he replied. 'But I suppose it does rather complicate family relationships.' .

Ilsa thought for a moment and burst into laughter. 'Well, I did say I always wanted a big brother . . . now I've got one.'

'I know that Jack would like to see you again,' Karl said, suddenly serious. 'Have you tried to contact him?'

Ilsa drew on her cigarette and looked away. 'So much has happened,' she said. 'When I got sent home, back to my old job with the paper, I found out about an operation that was intended to rescue me in New Guinea. It was planned and carried out by my father. But, of course, you probably know all about that. I cannot understand why, if God is meant to be merciful, my father saved the man I was to marry, then lost his son in an attempt to rescue me. It seems like some kind of cruel trick.' Ilsa turned to look Karl directly in the eyes. 'How can I face my father knowing that I have cost him so much?'

'Ilsa, you were not responsible for Lukas's death,' Karl said gently. 'Knowing Jack as well as I do, I know he would never blame you. Besides, you know from your own experiences during the war that death is all a matter of luck. There's nothing fair about who gets to live and who dies. Lukas's death was never your fault. It could have happened to him many times over before he even went on that mission.'

Ilsa could see that Karl was trying to reassure her and she appreciated the gesture. 'I'm sorry, Karl,' she said, 'but I will always live with the guilt of my half-brother's death. I think he would still be alive today if I had never existed, or had not insisted on meeting Jack.' She gazed out at the garden in silence. Finally she turned to Karl. 'I so badly want Jack to give me away when I marry Clark,' she said softly. 'But I am still afraid of how he might react to me after everything that has happened.'

'I think you should get in touch with Jack,' Karl said, gazing across the peaceful garden of butterflies and flowers.

'Do you think the Japanese will surrender unconditionally?' Ilsa asked, changing the subject.

Karl glanced at her and was about to reply when he heard a commotion from the great hall. Someone was calling for silence for an important announcement and the words drifted through the wide French doors onto the verandah.

'Gentlemen, the news has just come through. The Japanese have surrendered. The war is over and we're all going home!'

The room erupted into shouts of joy. Karl turned to Ilsa and hugged her. 'It's over,' he said, as though he couldn't quite believe it.

Ilsa knew she should be happy – she was happy – but her thoughts were still with her father. The war was over but they would all live with the consequences for the rest of their lives.

★

Jack Kelly was on leave in Townsville when the Japanese surrender was announced. He was outside, repairing the henhouse, when Karin suddenly burst out the door.

'Jack,' she shouted down to him. 'The war is over.'

Jack straightened up, feeling the creaking of his bones from the manual labour. Sweat poured down his body. 'The Japs have thrown in the towel?' He had expected it, of course, but somehow he could hardly believe it.

'Yes, the prime minister has just made the announcement. The war is over and Karl will be coming home to us.'

Jack dropped the hammer and walked towards Karin. That the war was over was wonderful news but somehow it made things worse to know that his son had been killed in the last few months before the surrender.

'I think you should go into town and celebrate with your army mates,' Karin said from the verandah.

Jack climbed the steps and stood before his wife. He reached out and drew her to him. 'No, you and I will celebrate together, and raise a glass to those who cannot be with us.'

Together, hand in hand, they stepped through the door of their home to celebrate this happy, but sad, day together.

EPILOGUE

Townsville, Far North Queensland
June 1946

There were only three men standing by the newly dug grave, whilst a fourth, the grave digger, hung back in the shade of a gum tree some yards away.

One of the men sprinkling the dry earth onto the coffin in the grave was a Lutheran pastor uttering the timeless words, 'Ashes to ashes, dust to dust.'

The two mourners were men, one young, one old, standing side by side as if requiring each other for physical support. Although the day was warm, both men wore dark suits and ties.

'C'mon, Jack, it's time to go,' Karl said gently, taking Jack's elbow to guide him back to the car parked outside the little country cemetery.

Jack Kelly hardly knew the world was going on

around him and he let Karl guide him from the place where Karin now lay in eternal rest, far from the land of her birth. A week earlier, having complained of a severe headache all day, Karin had collapsed; a blood clot in her brain, Jack found out later. Jack had held his wife as she died. He had been helpless when she collapsed, as the nearest doctor was a long drive into town and he had been forced to make a decision. He had sensed that she was near death and had chosen to be with her in her last minutes, whispering words of love as the life ebbed from her body.

Karl had come as soon as he'd heard the news. The two men had spent the evening before the funeral sitting on the verandah of the house Karin had loved. Few words had passed between them; they had sat mostly in silence into the early hours of the morning, sharing a bottle of gin. Karl knew that Jack was a man who kept his grief to himself, but when they finally retired he could hear Jack sobbing inconsolably from the bedroom he had shared with Karin.

Karl had lain awake staring at the ceiling, guessing that not all Jack's tears were for Karin alone. In his lifetime Jack had buried three wives and one son – along with many friends. It was a lot for one man to bear.

After the Japanese surrender Karl had returned to a world where civilians talked about how tough it had been on the home front because of rationing. Karl had kept his mouth shut, but he'd wanted to explode at their petty complaints when his memories were of men who had gone without sleep, food and medical attention in the stinking hell of the tropical battlegrounds. Many of them hadn't survived; those that had were still haunted by the horrors they had seen. Karl couldn't stand the complaints that there had not been enough sugar or tea during the war, so he found himself avoiding company, unless it was that of other soldiers, who understood without a word needing to be said.

When he arrived back in Sydney he considered contacting Sarah again, but he was unsure of himself. What if she had forgotten him? What if she had met another man, as Marie had? He had made no attempt to contact Sarah since he'd left her flat that morning – perhaps she would be angry with him for that. But after a few days he forced himself to hail a taxi to her flat. He was still in uniform and the ribbons on his chest reflected his courage in the face of war but not in that of love.

He knocked on her front door and held his breath. A voice asked who was there and Karl answered, although he wanted to walk away. Better just to have kept the memory of their wonderful encounter that New Year's Eve than to spoil it like this. The door opened and Sarah was there, just as he had remembered her. Then she was in his arms and Karl was surprised to see the tears of happiness in her eyes. They had barely been apart from then on. At night, when Karl would invariably relive the horrors of combat, Sarah would hold him as if he were a child, whispering soothing words until he was able to stop trembling. Her gentle ways impressed Karl as much as her extraordinary beauty.

He had been about to ask her to marry him and go with him back to New Guinea when he had received the news of his mother's death.

'Uncle Jack, is there is anything I can do?' Karl asked now, as the two men drove from the cemetery.

'No,' Jack replied. 'Just having you beside me today is enough. I'll be all right.'

Karl frowned. He was worried about Jack. 'What do you plan to do now?' he asked. 'Will you go back to the plantation?'

'I can't see any reason to,' Jack answered in a distant voice. 'Without your mother beside me the place would be haunted by too many ghosts . . .'

'You're not thinking about doing anything stupid, are you?' Karl asked, glancing sideways at him. 'The bloody war's already taken enough from me.'

Jack reached over and gripped Karl's arm. 'Promise I won't do myself in, but right now I'm lost for any real purpose in life. It seems that God has singled me out for a cruel joke. I get to live, but I have to bury my son and three women I loved very much.'

Karl could see the bitter tears welling in Jack's eyes. 'How about we get you home and have a beer,' he said gently as Jack released his grip on his arm. 'I'll cook us something.'

They reached the little house, and Karl escorted Jack inside. He stayed with Jack for another night before catching the train back down south. As the train puffed away from the station, Karl could see Jack standing alone on the platform. Even at a distance he could see how beaten Jack looked. Karl would have shifted the very foundations of the earth itself if it meant giving Jack his old life back.

★

The Island of Okinawa

No one took much notice of the solitary Japanese man wearing a battered naval cap and trudging along a winding dirt road towards a village set amongst fields of rice. He was just another wretched and beaten man returning from some front of the war.

Fuji had travelled to Okinawa after he had been released from the prisoner of war camp in Australia. This island still bore the scars of a bitterly fought and bloody war, and its people were still raw from the American invasion twelve months earlier.

A jeep containing two smartly dressed American officers bounced past Fuji, but he barely noticed. He was exhausted after the endless journey from Australia. He had been proved to be a model prisoner and had been given the opportunity to be repatriated to a place of his choosing in the Japanese islands. At least now he could honour his promise to a dead comrade.

When Fuji finally stumbled into the village he walked to the square, where he found a well from which he drew water to slake his thirst. The day was hot and he had walked a long way. Fuji had noticed the lack of fit young men in the village, and a cluster of old women, old men and children seemed to dominate the square. A couple of old women stared at Fuji with expressions of curiosity as he sat on the edge of the well.

'You are not from here,' one of the old women broached boldly. 'You do not look like one of us.'

Fuji had trouble understanding her, as the Japanese she spoke was heavily accented. 'No, old mother,' he replied politely. 'I am from a country to the south and was a dear friend of Petty Officer Oshiro, who died for the Emperor in a faraway land.'

'Oshiro!' the old woman gasped. 'He was my son!'

Tears began to flow down the old woman's wizened cheeks. Fuji had not expected to meet Oshiro's family so soon and was at a loss for words as he attempted to comfort the old lady stooped over in age and grief. Her friend uttered soothing words to her and put an arm around her shoulders, speaking into her ear before turning to look at Fuji.

'You are Japanese but speak with an accent that is not Japanese,' she said. 'Oshiro's mother thanks you for coming all this way to relate the death of her son. Until now she did not know of his fate, but she suspected that he had been killed.'

'I promised her son that I would go to his wife and children to tell them that he had died bravely, honouring the Emperor with his death,' Fuji said. 'Could you tell me where I might find them?'

'Oshiro's wife was killed in the fighting when the bombs landed on our village,' the woman answered. 'Only her sons and daughters survived. They live with Oshiro's mother. She can barely feed them on her own and will need help now that we know Oshiro will not be returning to us. Can you help?'

Fuji had promised his friend that he would do all he could for his wife and children.

Oshiro's mother wiped away her tears and took a step towards Fuji. 'You come with me and stay at my house,' she said. 'My family needs a man to plant the rice, and all the men from the village are gone.'

Fuji allowed himself to be led to a hut that was badly in need of repair, having obviously suffered the effects of an explosion. Oshiro's mother took him inside and Fuji met the children of his dead comrade: two boys and three girls, ranging from three years of age to twelve. They stared at him with a mix of curiosity and animosity. The little girl was the only one who smiled at him.

'This man has come to help us,' Oshiro's mother said. 'He will be your new father and I will find him a wife to be your new mother.'

Stunned, Fuji listened to the old woman's declaration. This was going beyond anything Oshiro would have expected from him, but when he looked into the trusting eyes of the little girl he knew that he would never leave this place. His mother and father had died in internment, supposedly from natural causes, but Fuji suspected they had died from broken hearts at being taken from the land they called home. Fuji had had no home or family, then suddenly this old woman had given him both.

Fuji bent down and scooped up the little girl.

'What is your name?' he asked her.

'What is your name?' Oshiro's mother countered and Fuji turned to her, holding the little girl in his arms. 'My name is Fuji Komine and I was born in the Australian territory of Papua, but this will be my home and I will look after your family.'

★

Sydney, New South Wales

'Sir Rupert Featherstone,' Karl chuckled. 'Do you know, all that time I worked for you, I didn't know your first name.'

'Well, old boy,' Featherstone smiled self-consciously, 'at the time it did not seem to have much importance.'

'So the King recognised your services during the war,' Karl continued as the two men sat at a table in one of Sydney's finest restaurants, sipping Scotch from iced-filled glasses.

'I am pleased that my recommendation for your DSO was approved,' Featherstone countered as a waiter hovered nearby, waiting to take their lunch order.

'How long will you be staying in Australia?' Karl asked, signalling the waiter to approach.

'I will be returning to London as soon as I finish some business in Malaya,' Featherstone replied, scanning the menu. 'You colonials are fortunate that you do not have the severe rationing we have in England. What I see here is fit for any of the best tables back home.'

When they had ordered and the waiter had departed, Featherstone leaned forward to speak. 'Have you considered my suggestion of resigning from the territorial administration and taking a position with us? I have reason to believe that the young lady you have been courting in Sydney is not very eager to live with you in Papua.'

'I never fail to be surprised by just how much you know about my private affairs,' Karl growled. 'I am not even going to ask how you knew that.'

Featherstone leaned back slightly and picked up his glass. 'You were the best agent I have had the pleasure of working with,' he said, raising his glass in a toast. 'Your considerable talents in intelligence are wasted on those headhunters and cannibals. The world is moving into an undeclared war between the free world and the communist bloc. Working for us would promise a better future for your young lady.'

Karl groaned. Featherstone had identified his Achilles heel – Sarah Kensington. Karl was in love with this enigmatic and beautiful young woman, and she had agreed to marry him – on the condition that they remain in Sydney. Karl had considered resigning his career as a patrol officer to go into the world of finance, but the thought did not appeal to him. He was restless and had grown too used to living off adventure and adrenaline.

'What are you offering?' he asked.

A broad smile spread across Featherstone's face. 'Dear chap, do you remember your short time with those Chinese guerrillas in Malaya? Well, we need a hand to sort out a few problems they're causing us. If you accept my offer I will have you put on the payroll with a salary commensurate with that of an army colonel. I promise that it will be more than you are getting now, and it will solve your delicate problem of Miss Kensington not wanting to live in Papua.'

Karl sighed. One life was over and another about to commence. 'There is just one thing I need you to do for me before I sign up,' he said. 'I know that you can call upon your considerable contacts in the United States to do me a favour.'

'Within reason,' Featherstone replied cautiously. 'Just what can I do for you?'

Karl explained and the matter was settled. When lunch was over, both men went their respective ways knowing that they would meet again as comrades in this new war between democracy and communism.

Karl picked up an afternoon newspaper on his way to the cinema to meet Sarah. He was early, though, and had time to sit in the foyer with his feet up, perusing the latest news of the world. As he flipped through the paper a photograph in the social pages caught his eye. He recognised Megan's face immediately. She was wearing a stylish hat and was standing beside a rather handsome but gaunt man. Karl read that Dr and Mrs Charles Crawford had returned from their honeymoon. Dr Crawford was a well-known Sydney specialist with a practice in Macquarie Street; he had a distinguished service record with the RAAF, serving in the Pacific Islands towards the end of the war. Dr Charles Crawford had met his bride during his time overseas and they had married six weeks earlier.

'Well, I'll be damned,' Karl muttered, closing the paper.

It was pleasing to see that Megan had found someone after Lukas's death – she deserved all the happiness in the world, Karl thought. When he looked up, Sarah was standing only feet away. His breath caught in this throat at the sight of her and he stood up to kiss her.

Townsville, Far North Queensland

Jack waved to the stock and station agent as he drove away from the little house on the outskirts of Townsville. The papers had been signed and the house was on the market. So, too, the plantations in Papua. All told, the sales would fetch a moderate amount for him to retire on.

Jack had already paid for a fare on a ship steaming to Europe. Now that his life was empty he wanted to return to all those old places from his past. He would visit France and Belgium, and walk the old battlefields of his youth. He would visit the cafes and bars in Paris, and remember a time when the Great War was drawing to a close and he drank with his mates to the permanent peace that surely had to follow such a terrible conflict. The war to end all wars, so they had said.

On his last visit to the doctor in town he had been warned that the sheer physical demands of being a soldier had taken a toll on his body. The doctor had put down his stethoscope and said with a grim expression, 'Jack, you need a lot of rest to let your heart recover from the strain it has been under.'

It had not only been the physical but also the emotional strain that had affected Jack's heart, he knew. But he wanted to make that pilgrimage. After that, he did not care what happened to him.

Jack walked up the steps to the verandah, and was surprised to hear the stock and station agent's car returning. He turned and raised his hand over his eyes to gaze up the road where the car had gone, only to see that the approaching vehicle was in fact a taxi.

Jack stood on the verandah as the car pulled up in front of the rickety fence overgrown with a choko vine. The door opened and a young woman stepped out, a young man following her. She was dressed in an expensive skirt and blouse, and a large, stylish hat hid her face; the man wore an expensive dark suit and tie.

Jack frowned. Maybe buyers for the house, he thought. The taxi driver removed a leather suitcase from the boot and placed it beside the woman, who now lifted her head to gaze up at the verandah. Jack thought then that his heart would stop beating, just as his doctor had warned.

'Ilsa!' he heard himself gasp. He glanced at the tall young man. 'Clark!'

Jack gripped the railing and then slowly made his way down the wooden steps until he was standing a few feet from the couple. No one said a word for a few moments.

Finally Ilsa broke the silence. 'It has been a long time,' she said. 'I don't even know what to call you.'

Clark stepped forward and extended his hand. Jack gripped it firmly.

'Hello, Jack,' Clark said. 'It's good to see that you made it through.'

'It is good to see you both,' Jack replied, still gripping the young American's hand. He turned to Ilsa, who hung back slightly, as though afraid of how he might react. 'It's too late to call me Dad, so I'll settle for you calling me Jack,' he said. 'Now, let's get out of the sun and I'll make us a cup of tea.'

'Jack . . .' Ilsa said and ceased speaking as the tears began to flow. 'I don't really know what to say to you.'

'Maybe you could tell me that this larrikin Yank has made an honest woman of you,' Jack replied gently.

'No,' Ilsa said, sniffing back tears. 'I need a father to give me away first. His parents are a bit old-fashioned like that. I need you in my life but so many terrible things have happened . . . I wouldn't blame you for holding me responsible for Lukas's death.'

'Lukas volunteered,' Jack said. 'If it's anyone's fault, it's mine, but there's no changing that now. You're my daughter; apart from Karl, you're all I have in the world. Let's not waste any more time. You're too precious to me for that.'

'Oh, Jack,' Ilsa said, the tears flowing uncontrollably as she flung herself into his arms. 'You don't know how much this means to me. You are the only family I have left.'

'What about me?' Clark protested in good humour.

'And you will be,' Ilsa said with a light laugh between sobs. 'As soon as my father gives me away.'

Jack held the beautiful young woman in his arms. Maybe there was a God after all. His son had been taken from him but he'd been given a daughter, even if he barely knew her. He sensed, though, that they would like each other, that they shared something deep, something that would help them get through the weeks and months and years ahead. Jack smiled. For both of them the war was finally over.

AUTHOR'S NOTE

As the years pass since the end of World War II, many of our fascinating stories of courage, endurance and initiative are being forgotten.

I wrote this book to remind Australian readers of the forgotten people who helped change the course of our history. Not in the well-known campaigns such as Tobruk or Kokoda, but behind enemy lines in places like Timor, where the tiny 2/2 Independent Company held down a Japanese army with their guerrilla activities. Or the coast-watchers, who monitored Japanese movements in the Pacific and helped rescue stranded Allied personnel, often working alone with only a handful of loyal Pacific Island-ers. Such men as Lieutenant Arthur Evans in the Solomons, who rescued a young American naval officer by the name of John Fitzgerald Kennedy when his torpedo boat was cut in two by a Japanese destroyer. How different would history be if JFK had not been rescued?

There were other men, such as Captain Jock McLaren, Major Rex Blow and Frank Holland, to mention only three of many who did similar work to our north. Some operations could have come straight from an action novel, such as the rescue of the Sultan of Ternate from Japanese confinement by Aussie soldiers WO Perry and Lieutenant Bosworth, or the experiences of the two hundred and fifty men sent to China to train members of the nationalist army there.

In the tradition of remembering the little-known heroes of World War II, I have placed the fictional character of Lukas Kelly in the employ of the United States Army Transportation Corps. They braved the same dangerous conditions as the military forces but received little credit when the war ended. In the same light, I placed Jack Kelly with the Papua Infantry Battalion, who fought alongside our own forces in the territories of Papua and New Guinea. They were greatly feared by the Japanese, who gave them the title of the green shadows out of respect for their deadly ability to strike hard and fast in the tropical rainforests. Many people are familiar with the work of the Fuzzy Wuzzy Angels, but not so many know about the men of the PIB. For information on the operations of the PIB, I was able to refer to James Sinclair's book, *To Find a Path: The Life and Times of the Royal Pacific Islands Regiment: Vol One*, Boolarong Publications, 1990.

Ilsa Stahl is in the novel as a reminder of the courageous American women who worked as war correspondents on the front lines, witnessing and sharing much of the horror the combat troops endured. And let's not forget our own women in the armed forces who served in Australia and overseas. Without their support in a wide variety of areas, from the Land Army to the Red Cross, from those labouring in factories to those keeping the home fires burning, the war in the Pacific could not have been won.

ACKNOWLEDGEMENTS

The production of a novel always has a team behind it. In this case I would like to acknowledge publishing director Cate Paterson, my publisher Alexandra Nahlous, and her team of Samantha Bok and Julia Stiles. Their input was invaluable in the final outcome of this project. Thanks is extended to Louise Cornegé for her ongoing work in the publicity department.

Others in my life have influenced my writing year and, at a local level, I would like to continue my thanks to Kevin Jones OAM and his family. Also, thanks to Mick Prowse and Andrea, Jan Dean, Dr Louis Trichard and his wife, Christine, and to Kate Evans and Phil Scoope. Also thanks to Bill and Tatiana Moroney, along with my local librarian, Fran McGuire, and also Tyrone and Kerry

McKee, John and Isabel Millington, and my family in Tweed Heads and Hazelbrook. Not to forget my Kiwi double, Bruce Forsyth, who was born the same day as I was, on the other side of the Tasman.

A special thanks to Kristie Hildebrand for her ongoing administration of my Facebook site and to the one hundred and fifty-four members who have joined at time of press. Ongoing thanks to Peter and Kay Lowe for my website administration. Thanks to Jaroslav Zeravek in the Czech Republic, who has done such a great job on his translation of my books in his part of the world. It is rare for an author to actually know the person in another country who is responsible for translating all the books into another language.

A special thanks to my neighbour John Riggall, who, despite being a former federal member of parliament, proved he has a lot of other life skills, and who helped me construct my new office. And thanks to June, his wife, who gave him permission to work through the blazing summer, and torrential rains of autumn, to help me finish the project.

I would like to extend my thanks across the Pacific, to a few Yanks who do not believe, as American publishers state, that my books are 'too Aussie' for release there. The following people promote me as much as possible to their countrymen and women. They are Karen Bessey Pease in Maine; the members of the American Legion Post no. 87 in Manhattan, Montana; Jodie Harp Luneau, former Aussie girl who served with the US armed forces in Iraq; and Maureen Oblachiniski.

Ongoing thanks to Rod and Brett Hardy, who work towards the *Frontier* project appearing on screen.

Since the release of my last novel, the following wonderful people have passed from our ranks and I miss them.

My uncle, John Payne, who served Australia through the darkest days of World War II with the Royal Australian Navy, aboard such famous ships as the *Vampire* and *Hobart*. He was aboard the *Vampire* when it was sunk by Japanese aircraft in the Bay of Bengal, and on the *Hobart* during the Battle of the Coral Sea and when it was later torpedoed. Also, Irvin Rockman CBE, John Blackler APM and Mrs Charlotte Trichard in Africa. The world has lost some of its best with their passing.

I'd also like to give a reminder that my old mate Tony Park is out there somewhere between Africa and Australia, turning out great books. His latest release, *African Dawn*, is now in the bookshops, along with his many others. Also, Steve Horne's novel *The Devil's Tears* has my endorsement as a great read.

Continuing thanks to another author, my mate Simon Higgins, and his wonderful wife, Annie; his friendship is valued for his ideas and special humour.

But, above all, I would like to express my special thanks and love to Naomi, who keeps me on track with my writing.

Peter Watt
Cry of the Curlew

*I will tell you a story about two whitefella families who believed
in the ancestor spirits. One family was called Macintosh and
the other family was called Duffy . . .*

Squatter Donald Macintosh little realises what chain of events
he is setting in motion when he orders the violent dispersal
of the Nerambura tribe on his property, Glen View. Unwitting
witnesses to the barbaric exercise are bullock teamsters
Patrick Duffy and his son Tom.

Meanwhile, in thriving Sydney Town, Michael Duffy and
Fiona Macintosh are completely unaware of the cataclysmic
events overtaking their fathers in the colony of Queensland.
They have caught each other's eye during an outing to Manly
Village. A storm during the ferry trip home is but a small
portent of what is to follow . . . From this day forward, the
Duffys and the Macintoshes are inextricably linked. Their
paths cross in love, death and revenge as both families fight to
tame the wild frontier of Australia's north country.

Spanning the middle years of the nineteenth century, *Cry of
the Curlew* is a groundbreaking novel of Australian history.
Confronting, erotic, graphic, but above
all, a compelling adventure, Peter Watt
is an exceptional new talent.

Peter Watt
Shadow of the Osprey

On a Yankee clipper bound for Sydney Harbour the
mysterious Michael O'Flynn is watched closely by a man
working undercover for Her Majesty's government. O'Flynn
has a dangerous mission to undertake . . . and old scores to
settle.

Twelve years have passed since the murderous event
which inextricably linked the destinies of two families, the
Macintoshes and the Duffys. The curse which lingers after
the violent 1862 dispersal of the Nerambura tribe has created
passions which divide them in hate and join them in forbidden
love.

Shadow of the Osprey, the sequel to the best-selling Cry of
the Curlew, is a riveting tale that reaches from the boardrooms
and backstreets of Sydney to beyond the rugged Queensland
frontier and the dangerous waters of the Coral Sea. Powerful
and brilliantly told, Shadow of the Osprey confirms the
exceptional talent of master storyteller Peter Watt.

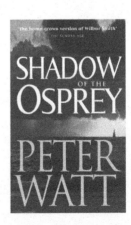

Peter Watt
Flight of the Eagle

No-one is left untouched by the dreadful curse which haunts two families, inextricably linking them together in love, death and revenge.

Captain Patrick Duffy is a man whose loyalties are divided between the family of his father, Irish Catholic soldier of fortune Michael Duffy, and his adoring, scheming maternal grandmother, Lady Enid Macintosh. Visiting the village of his Irish forebears on a quest to uncover the secrets of the past, Patrick is bewitched by the mysterious Catherine Fitzgerald.

On the rugged Queensland frontier Native Mounted Police trooper Peter Duffy is torn between his duty, the blood of his mother's people – the Nerambura tribe – and a predestined deadly duel with Gordon James, the love of his sister Sarah.

From the battlefields of the Sudan to colonial Sydney and the Queensland outback, a dreadful curse still inextricably links the lives of the Macintoshes and Duffys. In *Flight of the Eagle*, the stunning conclusion to the trilogy featuring the bestselling *Cry of the Curlew* and *Shadow of the Osprey*, master storyteller Peter Watt is at the height of his powers.

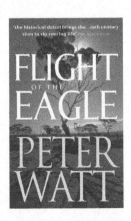

Peter Watt
To Chase the Storm

When Major Patrick Duffy's beautiful wife Catherine leaves
him for another, returning to her native Ireland, Patrick's
broken heart propels him out of the Sydney Macintosh home
and into yet another bloody war. However the battlefields of
Africa hold more than nightmarish terrors and unspeakable
conditions for Patrick – they bring him in contact with one he
thought long dead and lost to him.

Back in Australia, the mysterious Michael O'Flynn mentors
Patrick's youngest son, Alex, and at his grandmother's request
takes him on a journey to their Queensland property, Glen
View. But will the terrible curse that has inextricably linked
the Duffys and Macintoshes for generations ensure that no
true happiness can ever come to them? So much seems to
depend on Wallarie, the last warrior of the Nerambura tribe,
whose mere name evokes a legend approaching myth.

Through the dawn of a new century in a now federated nation,
To Chase the Storm charts an explosive tale of love and loss,
from South Africa to Palestine, from Townsville to the green
hills of Ireland, and to the more sinister politics that lurk behind
them. By public demand, master storyteller Peter Watt returns
to this much-loved series following on
from the bestselling *Cry of the Curlew,*
Shadow of the Osprey and *Flight of
the Eagle.*

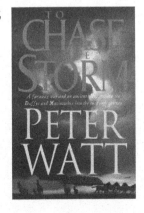

Peter Watt
To Touch the Clouds

*They had all forgotten the curse . . . except one . . . until it
touched them. I will tell you of those times when the whitefella
touched the clouds and lightning came down on the earth for
many years.*

In 1914, the storm clouds of war are gathering. Matthew
Duffy and his cousin Alexander Macintosh are sent by
Colonel Patrick Duffy to conduct reconnaissance on German-
controlled New Guinea. At the same time, Alexander's sister,
Fenella, is making a name for herself in the burgeoning
Australian film industry.

But someone close to them has an agenda of his own –
someone who would betray not only his country to satisfy his
greed and lust for power. As the world teeters on the brink
of conflict, one family is plunged into a nightmare of murder,
drugs, treachery and treason.

Peter Watt
To Ride the Wind

It is 1916, and war rages across Europe and the Middle East.
Patrick and Matthew Duffy are both fighting the enemy, Patrick
in the fields of France and Matthew in the skies above Egypt.

But there is another, secret foe. George Macintosh is passing
information to the Germans, seeking to consolidate his power
within the family company. And half a world away from the
trenches, one of their own will meet a shocking death.

Meanwhile, a young man is haunted by dreams of a sacred
cave, and seeks fiery stars that will help him take back his
people's land.

To Ride the Wind continues the story of the Duffys and
Macintoshes, following Peter Watt's much-loved characters as
they fight to survive one of the most devastating conflicts in
history – and each other.

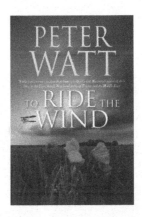

PHOTO: DEAN MARTIN